THE WARD BROTHERS

Meet the Travellers
BOOK ONE

CAROL HELLIER

The Ward Brothers – Meet the Travellers
Text copyright © Carol Hellier 2025

All Rights Reserved

The Ward Brothers – Meet the Travellers is a work of fiction. All characters, places, and events are from the author's imagination. Any resemblance to persons, living or dead, events or places is purely coincidental.

The author respectfully recognises the use of any and all trademarks.

With the exception of quotes used in reviews, this book may not be reproduced or used in whole or in part by any means existing without written permission from the author.

Warning: The unauthorised reproduction or distribution of this copyrighted work is illegal. No part of this book may be scanned, uploaded, or distributed via the Internet or any other means, electronic or print, without the author's written permission.

DEDICATION

A big thank you to my family for the support you have shown. It is greatly appreciated, and I love you all.

Also thank you to Darren, the owner of Rumours hair salon in Chelmsford for stocking my books and Donna for your help getting the word out.

And most amazingly, thank you to everyone who has bought or downloaded and read my books, you are all fabulous. Without you, this writing journey would be a lonely one.

Lastly, thank you to Emmy Ellis, a bloody brilliant editor, and Francessca Wingfield for the amazing book cover. Both amazing women.

Family is the most important thing in the world.

~ Princess Diana

The family is one of nature's masterpieces.

~ George Santayana

PROLOGUE

Maeve and Paddy Ward married young. He was seventeen, she just sixteen. Paddy always claimed it was love at first sight. Her long black hair and sparkling blue eyes had drawn him in like a magnet. She, in turn, had been captivated by his cheeky smile. They made a striking couple.

Their wedding took place in a small Catholic church. There was never any question of them running off like some Gypsies did; everything in their lives was centred around the good Lord.

Once married, they took to the road, travelling across Ireland in a traditional wagon, called a Vardo, alongside their family. They lived a hard but happy life, finding work where they could. The open road was their home, and though they faced prejudice from some of the gorjas, they embraced their way of life with pride.

Paddy's true passion was horses, not just gambling on them, but breeding them, too. He had a special love for the Irish Cob, also known as the Gypsy Cob or Gypsy Vanner. These sturdy, strong-willed horses had been developed by the travelling community and were not only valuable but essential, pulling their wagons and serving as a source of income.

Then, in 1949, Paddy struck gold with a winning bet on the horses. He never revealed exactly how much he had won, but it was enough to change their lives. With his dream finally within reach, he packed up and moved his young wife to England, settling in the Essex countryside near Basildon. The town was newly established, one of eight built around London to ease the post-war housing crisis. But Paddy, never one for built-up areas, chose land far enough from the town to feel the freedom of the countryside while still being close to everything he needed.

By 1951, their family began to grow. Their first son, Tommy Lee, was born. Two years later came John Jo, followed by Sean Paul eighteen months later, and finally, fourteen months after that, Paddy Junior, better known as PJ.

With their family complete, Paddy poured his energy into building a successful business breeding Cobs, while Maeve dedicated herself to raising their four boys, a task that proved anything but easy.

Tommy Lee was the wild one, always testing boundaries. At seventeen, much to Maeve's dismay, he enlisted in the British Army. When he was stationed in Northern Ireland in August 1969, her heart nearly broke. The conflict in Belfast dominated the news, and every Sunday, she clung to her rosary beads at Mass, praying for his safety. Six years later, he left the forces, but her worries didn't end. He disappeared for months at a time, travelling overseas, returning with plenty of money but few explanations. She longed for him to settle down, take a wife, and build a family. But Tommy Lee was a quiet man, one whose temper, when roused, was unmatched.

John Jo followed in his father's footsteps, becoming a bare-knuckle fighter, a tradition deeply ingrained in the Traveller way of life. Paddy had fought before him, so it was no surprise. Still, Maeve worried for him. He needed to marry, but she knew better than to tell her boys what to do.

Sean Paul married at eighteen, giving Maeve two grandchildren, so far. He shared his father's love for horses and worked hard breeding them.

PJ, the youngest, was the easiest of the four. He never answered back, never gave trouble. He did as he was told, unlike his brothers. Maeve sometimes wished they were all more like him. It would've made her life a lot easier. Or so she thought.

CHAPTER 1

May 1976

The pub was dimly lit. Old Albert sat at the table and studied his cards, the air thick with the smell of smoke and beer hops, along with anticipation from the spectators. He raised an eyebrow as if thinking. He didn't want to appear too eager, but damn it, he was. He pushed the last of his money into the kitty. He grinned. This was the best hand he'd had all night. Lady Luck was with him, he couldn't lose. Taking a large gulp of his beer, he sat back and stared at the youngster.

John Jo showed no reaction. At only twenty-four years of age, he had become a shrewd poker player. He had heard the stories of Old

Albert, betting everything on a card game, no matter the cost. Gambling his life away. Glancing around the crowd that had gathered to watch them, John Jo leant forward. Everyone had fallen silent, waiting for the grand finale. Well, he was ready to give it to them. He placed his money on top of the pile.

"Raise you a hundred," he said in his Irish Traveller accent.

Albert felt his pockets, panic written across his face.

"You can 'ave me trailer." Desperation dripped from his voice.

"I 'ave me own vardo, Albert, why would I want yours?" John Jo rubbed his chin. "You're gonna have to do better than that." He had him right where he wanted him.

Albert new the rules they played by. He would get three chances to offer something for the kitty. If the youngster declined the third, then Albert would win by default.

"I've got a fine filly, three-year-old." Although that wasn't strictly true. It belonged to his son, Henry, who was likely to blow his top if he found out, but Albert reasoned he wasn't going to lose, so no harm would be done.

"I don't keep horses, old man. Now offer something valuable." John Jo knew each bet had to be better than the last, and this would be the third, so he would have to accept.

Albert grabbed a beer mat and scribbled on it. "Gypsy, me granddaughter. She's the most valuable thing I have. She'll make a good wife."

Gasps and murmurs rose around the pub from the Irish Travellers and Romanies watching.

"So valuable you'd bet her life on a game of cards." John Jo spat in disgust.

This man was a disgrace to his family and the Romani people.

"I don't plan on losing," Albert said with an air of smugness that not only riled John Jo, it also challenged him.

He glared at him. The man's bulbous nose caught the light, casting a shadow over half of his face. His smile showed decaying brown teeth. What if his granddaughter looked like him? The thought made John Jo uneasy. If he accepted this bet he'd be a laughingstock. He didn't need a wife, least of all an ugly one. And besides, there were always gorjas throwing themselves at him. All he had to do was give them a smile and a wink and they'd drop their drawers quick as a flash. No, he didn't need the embarrassment of a woman like that.

"What are you scared of, boy?" Albert jibed.

He narrowed his eyes. The old man was goading him. Trying to make him look a fecking eejit.

Shite.

"Are you sure you want to do this?" John Jo eventually replied.

"I wouldn't have said so if I wasn't, boy."

John Jo gave a short, sharp nod, although this didn't sit right with him, gambling with a life, even if it was an ugly one.

Albert threw the beer mat on the table and revealed his cards. "What did I tell ya?" He grinned, laying two aces down and reaching for the money.

"Not so fast, old man." In the middle of the table lay an ace of hearts and King of hearts. John Jo flipped his cards over one at a time. "Queen of hearts, jack of hearts. That's a royal flush." He pulled the kitty towards him. Grabbing the beer mat, he placed it in the pocket of his shirt. "I'll expect her in the morning."

Albert sat, his heart thumping. He had lost a lot in his time, but this, he knew, had gone too far. "I'll get you the money in the morning."

"You'll bring me Gypsy, that was the bet," John Jo snapped. "But I won't be marrying her. Instead, she'll pay the price for your stupidity." He stood and stared down at the old man. "I would say this will teach you a lesson, but we both know it won't." He turned and left the pub.

"I'll buy you a beer, Albert, you look like you need a drink," Reuben said, placing his hand on his shoulder.

"He won't really take her, will he?" Albert asked. "What type of man would take away another man's family?"

"You can't blame this on the lad, you did this. Not him. You should've quit when you were winning. Dordi, dordi, dordi, what about Henry? He's gonna 'ave a fit when he finds out." Reuben placed the pint down next to Albert and shook his head. "Poor Gypsy."

Albert put his head in his hands. He now had to tell her she was the property of John Jo Ward. Romanies and Irish Travellers did not mix well.

***

John Jo pulled up outside his trailer. The handbrake was sticking again. "Fecking piece of shite." He glanced at his brother, Sean Paul. He hadn't spoken a word since they had left the pub. "Okay, spit it out."

Sean Paul turned in his seat. "What goes through your head, John Jo, when you have these stupid ideas? Jaysus, a gypsy. You gambled for a fecking gypsy."

"Calm down, boy. I'll keep her for a while and then take her back." John Jo sighed. "What was I supposed to do? He tried to make me look stupid, I had no choice."

"Maybe you should have took the filly... Good luck telling Mother." Sean Paul yawned. "Right, I've got a wife keeping me bed warm. I'll see you in the morning." He jumped from the truck and disappeared from sight.

John Jo sat back and closed his eyes. He had a good life. No one to worry about but himself. He could pack up at the drop of a hat and hit the open road without a care in the world. Now he would have someone's life he'd have to consider.

He glanced towards the bins. Something with a long tail was scavenging through the rubbish. Rubbish that gorjas had left, but no doubt his kind would get the blame. They had only been camped here for two days. Two days, and already the local police had tried to move them on.

"Fecking gavers," he mumbled.

They were heading to Appleby. Always left early and spent a bit of time travelling up there. It was all well and good having their father's land to live on, but nothing beat this freedom.

He climbed down from the truck. He needed his bed. The door creaked as he opened it. He closed it behind him and slipped his boots off. He lay back on his bed and stared at the ceiling of the trailer. The memory of Old Albert's face replayed in his head. The smug look when he'd thrown the beer mat into the kitty. John Jo smiled. He had soon wiped that off his mush.

He moved onto his side, content. He'd had his fun, made the old man suffer. When they arrived in the morning, he would let them buy her back. He didn't need the responsibility of a woman, an ugly one at that, despite his mother nagging him to take a wife. No, he was enjoying life, and he would continue to do so.

CHAPTER 2

Tommy Lee left the airport and sauntered over to PJ. He climbed into the motor and grinned. "Well, ain't you a sight for sore eyes," he said while ruffling his brother's hair.

"Jaysus, will you leave off, I'm not a little boy anymore," PJ said indignantly.

Tommy Lee held his hands up in surrender. His smile broadened. "Duly noted. So, what have you been up to?"

"Not much…actually, I need to talk to you about something."

Tommy Lee glanced at him. He looked worried. "Go on."

"Promise me this stays between us," PJ pleaded.

"Of course, now spit it out, boy." Tommy Lee kept his eye on him. A film of perspiration had gathered on his forehead. "You're starting to worry me."

A short silence followed.

"I've been seeing this gorja girl, it was just a bit of fun… She reckons I've got her pregnant."

"I thought you were marrying Violet Conners?" Tommy Lee was no fool, he knew most of the Travellers messed around, especially before they tied the knot, some even after. However, this was a big feck-up by PJ. The Conners were proud people, and although most of the men cheated, he couldn't see Violet's father taking this as anything but an insult to his daughter.

"I am…or was. What if they find out? There'll be murders."

"I'd worry more about what Mother has to say. And what about the baby? You're gonna be a father." Tommy Lee rubbed his chin while thinking. "It's early hours of the morning, let's get home and have a think. All problems can be solved, PJ." He settled back into his seat and closed his eyes. He had just left one war zone and now he was entering another.

***

Gypsy woke early. The sun shone through a gap in the blind, illuminating the inside of the trailer. It matched her mood, which was bright.

She had woken in the night at the sound of her grandfather crashing through his trailer door. Thank God she didn't have to pick him up. It was becoming par for the course. He would go to the pub, get drunk, and then one of her cousins would drop him off and wake her to see to him.

She stretched her arms above her head and yawned before throwing the covers off. Today she was going shopping with her aunt, Prissy. They would be off to the Epsom Derby in a day or so. She loved it there. Show Out Sunday was her favourite day. The market seemed to stretch for miles. The china, lace, and gold stalls were her favourite. The Derby was one of the biggest Romany and Traveller meets of the year. There was always lots to do and see. Many of her family would be there.

She washed and dressed quickly, opening the door and taking a deep lungful of air. She loved this time of year, the beginning of the summer months when she could sit outside chatting with family, putting the world to rights.

Gypsy glanced at her grandfather's trailer. He was already up and sitting on the step. Her uncle, Henry, was standing over him. She couldn't hear what he was saying, but his face was contorted with rage. Her grandfather sat looking at the ground.

"Gypsy," Aunt Prissy called, walking towards her. Her arms enveloped her in a warm hug.

"What's going on, Aunt Prissy?" she mumbled into her shoulder.

"Your grandfather can explain." When Prissy pulled away, her eyes were watery.

Was he ill? Gypsy's pulse quickened.

Please God, no more death.

It had been three years since her grandmother had died, and nine years before that she had lost her family in a trailer fire. She was expecting it. Heartache was never far away.

She glanced at the lane. A group of women stood gossiping. One woman pointed towards Gypsy, then turned back to the others. Were they talking about her?

She approached Old Albert. "What's going on, Grandfather?"

"I'm sorry, girl." He didn't look at her; instead, his eyes remained downwards.

She swallowed her fear, sauntered to the end of the yard, and hopped over the fence. She ignored the horses and trudged past, following the worn path to the little stream that ran along the bottom of the field. She sat on the bank, took off her shoes, and dangled her feet in the cool water. Although it was only the end of May, it was already warm. One of the elders had told her it would be a warm summer. Warmer than normal. Gypsy had taken it with a pinch of salt, but maybe they were right.

The birds chirped in the lush green treetops. A squirrel ran down a trunk, soon joined by another. They frolicked in the long grass. A smile spread across her face. Nature had the ability to lift her mood.

"Gypsy!" Henry's voice bellowed across the field.

Her mood immediately dipped. Were they going to tell her now? The knot in her stomach grew while she pulled her shoes on. She began the walk back, her feet squelching in her now sodden footwear. She wiped her brow. Was that the heat or the sick feeling that was devouring her? She was tired. At eighteen years of age she had suffered more than she should have. Losing her family, and then her grandmother, and being left to look after Old Albert, the drunk. She understood that he found it hard without his wife—after all, she wasn't selfish—but shouldn't he have looked after her? She had been just a child.

***

John Jo stood at the entrance of the car park, his temper hotter than the tarmac he stood on.

"Where the feck is he?" he roared. "Fecking Romanis can't be trusted, not the none of 'em." He marched back and forth with his fists balled. "I told him morning."

"Calm down, John Jo," Sean Paul replied. "Getting angry won't do no good."

"This is calm. Go get the truck." John Jo glanced at a passing motor, his temper building when it wasn't Albert. The truck drew up, and he yanked open the driver's door. "Move over, I'll drive."

The journey was short. He continued up the lane and into Henry's yard, stopping in the centre. He climbed out and marched towards Henry and another man. "Where's Old Albert?"

Henry stepped forward. "I want to pay his debt. However much it is, name your price."

John Jo balled his fists again. "I've come to collect what's mine. Now where is she?"

Old Albert appeared from his trailer. "She hasn't taken the news well." He appeared to have aged overnight.

"Shouldn't you have thought about that before you gambled with her life? Now where is she?"

John Jo caught a glimpse of a young woman over Henry's shoulder. He stepped aside to get a better look. She walked towards him. Her long black hair hung in waves down her back. Her blue eyes were red from crying and her skin blotchy. Swept away by her beauty, he was momentarily stunned. Composing himself, he glanced down to the large bag she carried.

"I'll not let you take her." Henry stepped in front of her, blocking his view.

John Jo glared at him. Did this man think he could stop him? It was both foolish and honourable at the same time, but anyone who knew him, knew he wouldn't be told what he could or couldn't do.

"No!" Gypsy said. "I'll not have bloodshed on my account."

Henry stepped aside and grabbed her shoulders. "You don't need to go."

"But I do. All debts must be paid." She stood at John Jo's side. Her shoulders slumped.

"Get in the truck," he ordered after taking the bag. "Next time, old man, bet with your own life, not someone else's." He placed the bag in the back of the truck then climbed in next to her.

Gypsy sat between the two men. It was suffocating. She kept her head down. There was no way she would let the Irish pig see her tears. When the truck roared to life, she spun around and stared out of the back window. Her grandfather had disappeared. Henry stood with his arm around Prissy. When the truck inched out onto the lane, she turned back with her head down and her hands clasped tightly in her lap.

The car park where John Jo was camped soon came into view. There were wagons and carts as well as trailers dotted around. Horses were tethered in the field next to them, and a bloody great big horse box was parked at the front.

John Jo yanked the handbrake up. "Stay there."

That was her told. Glancing up, she spotted a woman marching towards the truck, her face as hard as nails.

"What the feck are you thinking, boy, taking her away from her family?"

Gypsy almost smiled. Was she on her side?

"Don't you mean what was the old fecker thinking?" he asked.

"Where's she gonna stay? You can't sleep in the same trailer, you'll have to get married." She threw her arms in the air.

Gypsy gasped. She wouldn't be marrying him. She knew what men were like. From the age of six she'd heard her grandfather come in from the pub at night, then grapple her grandmother. The trailer had rocked, and he'd let out a moan. No. There would be none of that, and he couldn't force her.

"I'll not be marrying anyone, least of all Gypsy. I'll sleep in the truck, she can have the bed."

Gypsy stiffened. Of all the cheek she'd heard in her life, this had to be the biggest insult. It was her who wouldn't marry an Irish Traveller. She knew they were a different breed. "Can't trust 'em," her grandfather had said, but then she couldn't trust him either.

CHAPTER 3

PJ sat on the sofa in the mobile home that his parents owned, with a bottle of beer in his hand. Tommy Lee walked into the front room. He dried his hair and flung the towel on the chair.

"Bit early for that, isn't it?" He wasn't a big drinker like his brothers. Guns and alcohol didn't mix well, and along with his temper, it was best for all concerned that he remained sober.

"I need it," PJ said.

"You'll not find answers in the bottom of a bottle, boy, and you need to stop feeling sorry for yourself. Have you spoken to this girl?" Tommy Lee swooped down and grabbed the bottle.

"What are you doing? Give it back," Paddy complained, reaching for it.

"No." Tommy Lee took it and tipped the contents down the sink. "I'll make us a tea." He busied himself filling the kettle. "I'll ask once more: have you spoken to the girl?"

"Only when she told me… I turned and ran, like a coward."

"And you're sure she's pregnant and that the baby is yours?" Tommy Lee filled the teapot with the freshly boiled water. He was looking forward to this. No matter where he worked in the world, he could never get a decent cup of tea.

"She's a nice girl, don't see why she'd lie," PJ replied flatly.

"You've got three choices. One, you call off the wedding with Violet and marry this girl. Two, you tell this girl you're not interested, marry Violet, and move away so you don't see her again. Three, pay her off, send money for the child, and call an end to it, but two and three mean you never get to see your baby if you can live with that."

"The kid means nothing to me, I wants to marry Violet. All the plans are made for this wedding, I can't let her down."

"You should've thought about that before messing with another woman," Tommy Lee snapped. He took a deep breath to calm his temper. "Here, drink this." He handed PJ his tea. "Just remember you did this, you need to take responsibility."

He sighed. They called *him* the reckless one. If only his parents knew what his brothers got up to.

"Anyway, enough of this, I've got a bit of land to go and look at up the road. You can drive me." While he was home he would make the most of his time and money. Investing in land was the way forward.

***

Gypsy glanced around the small trailer. It was clean and tidy, no doubt thanks to his mother. The bed was already made; well, she wouldn't be sleeping in that. She'd rather sleep on the floor.

"Come on, girl, there's clean bedding for you. Strip the bed while I fetch it." The woman disappeared, leaving Gypsy alone.

She hurriedly stripped the bed, folding the blankets as she went. She could smell his scent on the covers. Anger replaced her sadness. What type of man was he?

Standing stock-still when his mother stepped in, Gypsy stared at the floor. "What should I call you?"

"You can call me Maeve. Don't be so sad, girl, no harm will come to you here."

"But I don't belong here, do I?" Gypsy hoped the woman would agree, but all she got in return was a tut.

"Maybe you should talk to your grandfather about that. Now make the bed." Maeve's voice hardened. Of course she would side with her son. Family is blood.

Gypsy waited for the woman to leave and then set to work. Her life here was no different from home. She may not have been ordered to do stuff, but it was expected. She was her grandfather's cook and cleaner.

It was common in Romani and Traveller communities that the girls took care of the home while the men worked, often marrying at sixteen. Gypsy was never allowed, her grandfather had put his foot down. She was needed to take care of him, and any boy who took a liking to her got sent on their way.

"Here, girl, sweep the floor after." Maeve propped a broom up in the doorway.

John Jo's voice drifted through the open door. "I'll go chippy later. Can you make me a sandwich for now, I'm starving."

"You're always hungry." Maeve tutted. "Don't forget the floor, girl," she said to Gypsy.

"You eat fish and chips?" he asked her.

Gypsy continued making the bed; she didn't turn to him.

Ignore him and he will go away.

The trailer moved. He was behind her. He grabbed her arm, yanking her around to face him. "I asked you a question."

Still she remained silent, offering nothing but a hate-filled glare.

"If that's the way you want it, starve." He stormed out.

The sting of tears filled Gypsy's eyes. Could her life get any worse?

John Jo slammed the trailer door behind him. What was he thinking, accepting her instead of something he could sell? He should have accepted Henry's offer, but thanks to his own stubbornness, he'd had no choice but to say no. It would have been a different story if they had brought her to him like they'd agreed. Then he would gladly have said okay. It was only about showing them who's boss.

Glancing around the car park, he sighed. They would be packing up in a couple of days' time to make their way to Appleby. Out of all the horse fairs they travelled to, he enjoyed this meet the most. Would he this year? He doubted that, thanks to the headache he'd won.

He yanked his top over his head, wiping his brow with it. He loved the sun, but it was already warm for the time of year. Marching over to his father's prize mare, he cursed again. "Here, girl."

The horse obliged and walked towards him. His father intended to sell her. She had produced a foal three years running, and now she would fetch a better-than-expected price.

Although he was great with the horses, he wasn't interested like his father and brothers. He was a fighter. Fighting and betting were his chosen means of making money. Poker being his favourite.

Not anymore.

"Boy, why's the trailer door shut?" his mother bellowed, storming towards him. "She'll fecking cook in there."

He cursed again. Gypsy had been in his life for thirty minutes, and already everything had changed.

"Here." Maeve stopped in front of him, handing him two plates. "Give the girl hers," she ordered. "I've enough to do. You accepted her, you look after her."

Gypsy stood back and studied the trailer. The bed was made and the floor clean. The temperature was stifling inside, her clothes sticking to her. How she wished she were sitting in the shade next to the stream. She spun around when the door opened.

"Here, girl. Eat this." John Jo placed the plate on the side and then disappeared.

She glanced at the sandwich. Her stomach rumbled. She wouldn't eat their food. That was the one thing she had control over. What went into her mouth. She sat on the edge of the bed, and her mind turned to Aunt Prissy. Would she go shopping without her? Of course she would. They would be off to the Derby. Without her. Gypsy grabbed her bag of belongings and tipped them out onto the bed. Was this all she had to show for her life? A toothbrush, washcloth, hairbrush, and a few items of clothing. A loud sigh escaped her mouth when John Jo reappeared. She began to shove it all back into the bag when he spoke.

"You can put your stuff in here." He opened a door and pushed his own clothes to one side.

Was he expecting her to share a cupboard?

"Why haven't you eaten your sandwich? Jaysus, it's as hard as a brick." He stared down at her. "This is your life, girl, until I say otherwise. Get used to it."

"You've taken me from my family, I will never get used it... You're a monster," she said.

"Who's the real monster? Me or your grandfather who bet you on a game of cards?" John Jo turned and stormed out of the trailer.

Gypsy closed her eyes in a feeble attempt to stop the tears. He was right, who was the real monster?

CHAPTER 4

Tommy Lee stared at the land. It was a good few acres and no doubt would be wanted for building at some point. After heckling, he managed to get the price down. Shaking the man's hand, he nodded, then made his way back to the motor with his brother on his tail.

"What is it you do to earn so much money?" PJ asked.

"I told you, it's security work." Tommy Lee never discussed work. Work and money were private matters best kept to yourself, and besides, if it ever got back to his mother, she would have a fit. Mercenary work wasn't your normal run-of-the-mill day job, after all.

"It sure pays well, this security job… Why is it always in other countries?"

"Because the pay's better abroad." Tommy Lee climbed in the motor. "I'm more interested in knowing what you're gonna do about your situation."

"I think I should tell Violet. It was a mistake, after all."

Tommy Lee blew out slowly to stop the laugh that was building in his throat. As far as he was concerned, sticking your cock in another woman wasn't what he would class as a mistake. "Before you do anything, do me a favour and tell Mother. She will know the best way forward, PJ. It's not like you're the only man this has happened to." That was the best advice he could offer. Whether PJ took him up on it was down to him. "Let's get back, I'm fecking starving."

He already had his next job lined up, so while he was here, he wanted to eat well and sleep well.

***

Gypsy stared out of the window. John Jo was laughing with a couple of men. He'd been parading around all afternoon, half-naked. She glanced at his arms. The sun highlighted his biceps as they moved. He turned and looked straight at her with his piercing blue eyes. His hair was short at the sides and had a slight curl on the top. He had greased that back to keep it out of his eyes. She couldn't deny he was handsome, but his heart was ugly.

"Irish pig," she muttered while turning away.

"Gypsy. Come outside and get some fresh air," Maeve called through the open door.

She stepped outside. It was cooler now. The sun was lower. Maeve motioned to her to follow. She walked behind her; people were watching the weird Romani girl. It was like putting a baby rabbit into the middle of a snake pit. She swallowed as she passed John Jo. His eyes bore into her, and she glared back at him.

"Sit on the step, girl, and I'll make us a drink."

Gypsy did as she was told. She sat there on show to the rest of the Irish Traveller camp. She wrapped her arms around her knees and hugged them. From the corner of her eye, she spotted him. He was coming towards her. The knot that had formed in the pit of her stomach tightened when he leant in above her, his torso only inches from her face.

"I'll go chippy now, Mother." He pulled back, his gaze resting on Gypsy. "You do want fish and chips or are you still sulking?"

Sulking? Had he no idea what it felt like to lose everything?

Her stomach rumbled, and she glanced up. He was grinning. Of course he'd heard it. It sounded like an earthquake. She shook her head, her focus returned to the ground.

John Jo climbed into his truck, a loud sigh leaving his mouth. He was frustrated. He looked towards Gypsy. She remained on the step, her head down. He classed himself as a simple travelling man. Didn't like drama but would always confront it if it came for him. Well, here he was, with one big fecking drama in the form of Gypsy. The best and easiest thing to do would be to take her back, get the cash, and sail off into the sunset.

So what was stopping him? The answer was simple. What had started out as teaching Albert a lesson had now turned into a game of cat and mouse. It had nothing to do with her beauty, that he was certain of. Starting the motor, he reversed out of the car park, and with one last glimpse of Gypsy, he smiled and left for the chippy.

***

Gypsy stared at the big pile of fish, chips, meat pie, and sausage as John Jo placed them on the side.

"As you wouldn't talk to me, I didn't know what you liked, so I got you one of everything," he informed her. "I've put salt and vinegar on 'em. Enjoy." He turned and left.

She breathed in the appetising smell. Her stomach grumbled and mouth watered.

Shit. So he's playing dirty. Well, I'll show him.

She stood and stared at the food for what seemed like minutes, the smell playing with her senses. She could almost taste the fish and hear the sound as she bit into its crunchy batter.

Just one chip, he won't notice.

"He's probably counted them," she said to herself. Without another thought, she grabbed a handful of chips and sat back, stuffing them into her mouth. Before she knew it, she had eaten the fish, most of the chips, and taken a bite out of the pie. She lay back on the bed, her stomach overfull, and drifted off to sleep.

***

John Jo stepped into the trailer, his gaze landing on the half-eaten food. A slow grin spread across his face. He'd won this round. She'd eaten.

His attention drifted to Gypsy, sprawled across the bed in deep sleep, her hair fanned out across the pillow. Asleep, she was even more beautiful, maybe because, for once, she wasn't wearing that miserable scowl.

He picked up the pie, chuckling at the small bite missing before taking one himself.

"I guess we're on to round two tomorrow," he murmured. "But be warned, darling—I never lose."

CHAPTER 5

The next day, Gypsy sat in the truck, pressed as close to the passenger door as she could manage. They were on their way to Appleby. Her heart had sunk when he'd told her. In her head she'd thought she would be going to the Derby, then she could have run away. Her cousins would have hidden her. What an idiot. She should've known better.

They had barely been on the road for a few minutes when he started talking.

"I think you'll enjoy this," he said, grinning like he was doing her a favour.

"I enjoy the Derby, my family all go there," she said flatly.

"Is this the same family who gambled with your life?" John Jo asked. "Cos personally, I wouldn't..."

"Finish what you were going to say." Gypsy turned to him. "I know what everyone thinks of me, poor little Gypsy, the bringer of sorrow."

"I don't think that." He slowed at the traffic lights. "I think you're worth more than what you've been given."

"More? What, more shit to deal with, more heartache?" She rested her head back on the seat and closed her eyes.

"You know what I mean. What you've lived isn't your fault... Tell me, how come your name's Gypsy and you're a gypsy?"

The question almost made her smile, but in an instant she was reminded of what she'd lost. "My mother sent my father to register my birth, only he called in every pub on the way. Wetting the baby's head." She smiled. The made-up vision of her father stumbling through town to the registry office was one she always thought of when her mum and then nan had told her the story of how she was named. "By the time he got to register my name, he was three sheets to the wind. When the woman asked my name, he said Gypsy Girl. So the woman put Gypsy as my first name and Girl as my middle name. My nan told me my mum had hollered blue murder when he came back with the birth certificate." Gypsy laughed and then fell silent as the emptiness took hold.

"I think it's a pretty name, and you shouldn't be sad. That's a good story to tell your children and grandchildren."

"I'm not gonna get married, so there'll be no children." She sighed.

The cab fell silent. He indicated and veered into a lay-by.

"What are you doing?" she asked, blinking away her tears.

"We need snacks, it's a long drive... You coming?" he asked while opening the door.

She shook her head then watched as he ran across the road and disappeared into the newsagent's. He emerged minutes later with an armful of sweets and drinks.

"There we go, all set." John Jo threw the goodies onto the seat. "Help yourself." After climbing in, he pulled his T-shirt over his head and placed it on the back of his seat. "Jaysus, it's hot."

Gypsy's face heated, and she averted her gaze from his naked torso. She stared out of the window. This, she decided, was going to be a long day.

***

It was just after four p.m. when they parked up for the night. It was proper country here. Green fields and no houses, which meant no gorjas who would complain. Gypsy watched John Jo unhook the trailer and push it into place while she stood in the shade of the truck. He had told her they could get there in a day, but it wasn't good for the horses, being cooped up for hours. They needed to stretch their legs just like people.

"Come give me a hand, girl," Maeve called over. "We'll get the food on."

"What shall I do?" Gypsy asked from the door.

"Peel the potatoes. Here, go fill the pan with water." Maeve handed her a large cooking pot.

Gypsy took the lid off of the chrome urn and poured the water into it, careful not to spill any. It was a precious commodity when travelling. You could never be sure when you would be able to fill up again.

Gypsy sat outside with Maeve as they prepared the meal. She often stole a quick glance at John Jo who was always staring back.

***

John Jo wiped his plate clean with a lump of bread and stuffed it into his mouth. He needed that. His stomach had felt like his throat had been cut. He drank down the last of his tea then handed Gypsy his cup. "That was handsome," he told her with a wink and a smile. His smile broadened when she blushed. Was she shy? He hadn't noticed before.

An awkward silence followed, then she turned and walked away. Never in his life had he been tongue-tied. His mother said he had the gift of the gab. So why was he finding it difficult to talk to her?

Plucking up the courage, he followed her to the trailer. "We'll be leaving early in the morning," he said as he stuck his head in the doorway. "Should get there about ten a.m."

Gypsy nodded.

"I think your gonna like it. They have stalls like the Derby," he added.

"What, like Show Out Sunday?" she asked without looking up.

"Well, not as many, but there's some good stalls, china, gold, it depends on what you want."

"Well, considering I've no money, I won't be wanting anything." She sighed.

This conversation wasn't going to plan. He stepped into the trailer and plunged his hands into his pockets. "I've got money. If you want something, you tell me."

"Why would you spend your money on me?" Her eyes went wide. "Is this some kind of trap?"

"Do you always think badly of people?" He turned to the door and lingered. "Not everyone's bad, Gypsy."

"Says the man who won me in a poker game." She huffed.

Spinning around, he glared at her. "How about getting angry at the man who bet with your life?"

Immediately her face changed, like all the fight had left her.

"Get to bed, it's getting late." John Jo closed the door behind him. What the feck had just happened?

CHAPTER 6

PJ stared at Tommy Lee in disbelief. "You've only just got back."

"It's an important job, the money's good, and I need to leave. It's only six months, I'll be back before you know it."

"And what do I tell Mother?"

He shrugged. "Tell her about your own problems and leave me out of it." He threw the last of his belongings into the holdall and zipped it up. "Is that a motor outside?"

"This conversation isn't over." PJ turned to the window. "Shit, it's Violet."

"Don't tell her about the baby, speak to Mother first. Right, I've got to go. See you in a few months." Tommy Lee grabbed his bag, threw it over his shoulder, and without another word, left.

His lift was waiting for him out on the road. He gave a quick wave to PJ before climbing in. As they pulled away, doubt gnawed at him.

Was he doing the right thing leaving? He knew things were going to get tough for PJ, but then it was time he started to take accountability for his actions. Being the baby of the family, he had always had an easy life. Their mother had coddled him, defended him, made excuses for him.

Let's see what excuse she comes up with this time.

***

John Jo had been driving for three hours. He found the silence deafening. Every time he had tried to make conversation, he was met with a grunt.

"How come you don't wear any gold?" he asked in a last attempt.

"I haven't got any other than me earrings," Gypsy said sharply.

"I thought all women liked jewellery?" He glanced at her and immediately wished he hadn't. The look he'd got in return reminded him of his mother. She'd looked at him that same way when he'd played up as a teenager. The look was normally followed by a clout around the head. "Sorry."

"Why are you sorry, it's not your fault." She let out a sigh before continuing. "I had a thick gold chain. It was my mother's."

"Had. What happened, did you lose it?" He peeked at her quickly.

Unshed tears glistened in her eyes.

"I didn't lose it, my grandfather did. In a card game."

"Jaysus, and this is the man you want to go back to?" It was John Jo's turn to sigh. "You deserve better, Gypsy."

"Maybe I do, but it still doesn't change the fact that he is my family and that's where I belong."

There was nothing to be added to that statement. He knew Travellers and Romanis had the same family morals. Family was everything, and indeed, that's where you belonged, but couldn't she see what he had done to her? She had nothing, owned nothing. No wonder she didn't want to marry, he had put her off men for life. He opened his mouth to speak but then thought better of it. This was something she would have to realise herself. If she already hadn't.

***

It was just past eleven-thirty a.m. when they rolled onto the field. The place was still quiet, but by lunchtime, John Jo knew it would be packed. His father and brother made their usual grand entrance atop the wagons, their horses prancing beneath them. Showing off the animals was the main reason they'd come — there was always a deal to be struck.

John Jo kept one eye on Gypsy. She stood apart from the others, looking lost, alone. The sight of her stirred something in him, though he'd never admit it.

Once the trailers were set up, they gathered outside with mugs of tea and bacon sandwiches. More trailers and wagons were pulling in. The sound of horses neighing, laughter, and excited chatter filled the air. Everyone seemed happy and content.

Everyone except Gypsy.

She watched the banter between the group. It made her miss her family more. This was what it was like at the Derby. Everyone chatting, seeing old friends and family. Catching up on all the gossip. She collected the cups ready to wash up, away from the group. With her mind on her family, she went into autopilot, tipping the washing-up liquid and bleach into the bowel. She began washing and drying. She glimpsed John Jo approaching and swallowed down the knot in her chest. Why couldn't he leave her alone?

Because you're his property.

"You don't have to do that," he called. "You're not to wait hand and foot on everyone."

"Then why I am here?" she asked, spinning around to face him.

"I don't know, let me think... Maybe it's because of your grandfather, or maybe it's because you could have a better life away from him."

"What, a better life with you, being kept prisoner?" she snapped.

"You're not a prisoner, and what's so wrong being with me? I'd look after you…"

John Jo stormed away. His heart was thumping through his chest. Where the feck had that all come from? He'd said things he didn't realise he felt. Five minutes, just five fecking minutes she had been in his life and already it had been turned upside down.

"You all right, boy?" his father asked, falling in step beside him.

"Yep." He continued walking. What was he supposed to say? I've fallen for Gypsy? He had not seen this one coming. She hated him, that much was clear.

"Women are funny things, boy."

John Jo stopped dead and looked at his father. "What's that supposed to mean?"

"I could see it, your mother could see it—"

"See what?" John Jo rubbed the back of his neck. Did he really want to know?

"Every time that girl's about, you can't take your eyes off her." Before John Jo could protest, his father held his hands up to him. "Hear me out, son. You can't help who you fall in love with, and if you choose to marry a Romani, that's fine with us. Now I'm gonna take the cart for a spin later, I needs to show off Storm, so I get a good price for him, too… Why don't you come, it'll give you chance to clear your head."

***

Gypsy followed Maeve towards the horses tethered behind the trailers, the scent of hay and damp earth filling the air. The evening sky burned with streaks of orange and pink, casting long shadows across the camp. The rhythmic clatter of hooves and the low murmur of voices created a gentle hum of life around her.

She couldn't help but steal glances at John Jo. He moved with an easy confidence, his hands sure and steady when he helped his father harness a powerful black horse to a cart. The stallion, Storm, was magnificent. His coat gleamed like polished obsidian, his muscles rippling beneath the setting sun. The horse tossed his head, nostrils flaring, as if aware of his own beauty. He knew his name. He knew his power.

Gypsy took a step back. The cart lurched forward, its wheels crunching over the dirt. John Jo sat beside his father, his posture relaxed yet commanding. They passed her, and his eyes caught hers, steady, deep, unreadable. Her heart stumbled, a warmth spreading through her, unfamiliar and unexplainable. What was this feeling? She didn't have the words for it.

Maeve's knowing smile unsettled her more than she cared to admit.

"Okay, girl, let's get the dinner going." Maeve slipped an arm around Gypsy's shoulders, gently steering her back towards the vardo.

Gypsy's thoughts still lingered on John Jo, but Maeve's next words made her stop in her tracks.

"My son likes you."

The statement hung in the air between them, heavy and unexpected. Heat rose to Gypsy's cheeks. What was she supposed to say to that?

Maeve's expression softened. "I know you met under...strange circumstances. I don't know if that's the right way to put it. But sometimes, things happen for a reason."

The night air seemed to press in around Gypsy, filled with unspoken truths and possibilities she wasn't sure she was ready to face.

She looked down to the floor before answering. "I don't know your son, not properly, and what I do know I don't like."

"Really?" Maeve asked.

"Yes. Really." Annoyed, Gypsy picked up the large pot ready to get the water.

John Jo's mother caught her arm, stopping her. "I've seen the look in your eyes. You can deny it to yourself, but don't take me for a fool, girl."

CHAPTER 7

The riverside teemed with horses, their glossy coats catching the golden light of dawn. The water glistened under the rising sun, until the surface was broken by the splash of hooves. Standing by the river, Gypsy watched the Romanis and Travellers ride into the cooling water. Some were completely immersed up to their chests while others choose not to go in so deep. The horses neighed and pranced around like showmen. Gypsy had never seen such an amazing sight. The world felt alive, pulsing with energy, and for a moment, she was utterly spellbound.

"Gypsy," John Jo said.

She turned to see him sitting on Storm, his hand held out to her.

Without thinking, she took hold, and with him helping her up, she mounted the horse behind him.

"Ready?" he asked. "Hold on tight."

She slipped her arms around his waist, her heart racing. Was that from the closeness or from what they were about to do?

The water was low at the river's edge, but as they walked through farther it was soon up to their waists. Storm carried them around and out the other side. She smiled. John Jo slid off and held his hands out to help her down. Her body brushed against him as her feet touched the ground. Their eyes locked. Was he going to kiss her?

"John Jo," Sean Paul called. "Get Storm back, Father's having a fit. You shouldn't have took him."

"You take him. I'm busy." He grabbed Gypsy's hand and walked off through the bustling crowd.

"Are you going to get into trouble?" she asked.

"No, and besides, if I do, it was worth it." He grinned.

Leading her behind a tree, she stood motionless, unblinking. What was he going to do?

"Now, where were we?"

He brushed his lips against hers.

A tiny flutter started in her tummy, building with each second that passed. When he eased back, she opened her eyes, breathless.

John Jo stared down at her, momentarily stunned. He wasn't expecting to feel like this.

"I want to marry you, Gypsy," he finally spluttered out.

Silence.

"I will give you a good life, we could be happy together," he continued.

Silence.

"Say something, even if it's no." His heart sank with each passing second.

"I don't know what to say… Is it right you marry someone you own?" she asked.

"I don't own you, I never have." He took the beer mat from his pocket. It was soggy from the dip in the river. He tore it into pieces and placed it into her hand before getting down on one knee. "Will you marry me, Gypsy?"

"But what about my fam—"

"I will go and see your uncle and ask permission. We will do it all properly... Say yes, Gypsy." He studied her face. What was she thinking? Had he read the signs wrong?

She kissed him back, and he was certain she enjoyed it as much as he did.

"There'll be no funny business beforehand, John Jo Ward. You'll keep those hands to yourself."

He could feel the smile spreading across his face. "So is that a yes?"

"Yes," she replied, her own smile broadening. "But we can't tell anyone until my family know."

"Agreed... So how's about a little kiss to seal the deal." He stood and drew her to him, readying himself to plant his lips on hers.

***

Gypsy lay on the bed, her mind spinning. Was this really happening? *Of course it's happening, you said yes.*

But what would Uncle Henry say? Would he be pleased for her? What if he said no? That was unlikely. Either way, that was one conversation she was glad she wouldn't witness.

"Gypsy, come on, let's take a walk." John Jo popped his head through the doorway.

She rolled onto her side. "A walk where?" she asked suspiciously. There would be no more hiding behind trees, that was for sure.

"A walk around the stalls, see if there's any bargains."

She stood, smoothing her dress down. "And no funny business?" She glanced at him.

"Depends on what you class as funny business?" He winked.

Folding her arms, she glared. "You know exactly what I mean, John Jo."

"Fine. No funny business. Now come on." He held his hand out. "And don't say I can't hold your hand in public. We're to be married, Gypsy. It's part of the courting."

She knew she couldn't argue with that, and it seemed his parents knew before she herself had. "I wouldn't dream of it."

John Jo headed lazily towards the stalls with Gypsy by his side. He wrapped his hand around hers, squeezing gently. The place was a hive of activity, the bustling crowd laughing and chatting as they wandered through. Catching sight of the gold stall, he tugged her towards it, pushing through the crowd to the front. His gaze roamed over the jewellery until he spotted what he wanted.

"What's your best price for that, mister?"

"I'll take seventy-five, not a penny less," the man said.

John Jo rubbed his chin. "Seems a bit expensive, I'll give you fifty."

"Seventy," the man said.

This was always the best part of the sale for him, you'd see what you wanted and then barter them down. John Jo loved this bit. "Fifty-five."

"Sixty-five," came the reply.

"Sixty, final offer." John Jo spat in his hand and held it out to the man.

"Deal." The man did the same, and they shook.

John Jo took the chain and placed it over Gypsy's head. "No one will ever take that from you, and if they try, I'll kill them."

CHAPTER 8

Maeve smiled when they drove onto their ground. The tree-lined land was nestled away from the main road and made it difficult to spot. The paddock was to the side with stables at the back. Paddy had fenced this area off, keeping the Cobs safe from any would-be thieves.

The mobile came into view, and it was a welcome sight. Two weeks they had been away, and it was now the middle of June. She didn't know where the year had gone, time just seemed to speed up as you got older. She wiped her hanky on the back of her neck; the heat was already stifling.

"Home sweet home, Paddy. I love going away, but it's good to get back. I'll put the kettle on and empty the trailer later."

"Do us something to eat, darling, I'm starved." He pulled the horsebox to standstill.

She climbed down from the motor and glanced at John Jo. He was helping Gypsy down. It warmed her heart, another of her boys settling. Only Tommy Lee to go, but she wouldn't hold her breath with that one. He was a law unto himself.

"Mum, can I have a word?" PJ asked whilst walking towards her.

"Jaysus, boy, can I get in first?" she muttered, reaching the step. "What's wrong?"

He closed his eyes.

This was going to be bad, she decided. "Get inside… Right, let's have it."

"I've got a girl preg—"

"You fecking eejit." Throwing her hands in the air, she turned away, the overwhelming feeling to strangle him too much to take. "And what about young Violet?"

"She doesn't know…yet."

"You make sure it stays that way." She sighed.

"Tommy Lee said I should tell you before I do anything," he added.

"And where is that brother of yours?" She spun around. The little hope she had of seeing her eldest son soon faded when she looked into PJ's eyes.

"He's gone, he was only here a couple of days. Said he'll be back in six months. Mother, what am I going to do?"

Being the baby of the family, her youngest had been spoilt, by her. She had mothered him far more than the others. He could still fight, but there was a gentler side of him that she had never seen in the elder boys.

"You don't do anything. We never speak of this again, because if this comes out it will cause murders."

She watched him leave, then her thoughts turned to Tommy Lee. Just what did he do to earn his money? She suspected he killed for it, but with no hard proof she would never share her thoughts, not even with her husband.

***

Gypsy stared around the land. It was more spacious than her uncle's. John Jo's father was leading the two new horses into the paddock. They joined the other four and trotted around, enjoying the freedom. She climbed into the trailer as soon as he had set it up. Things were different now. She belonged with him, but as they weren't married, she would still sleep on her own.

Whilst they were at Appleby he had bought her pots and pans, a set of china, and a milk churn for water. She had picked out tea towels and cutlery. They were now set for married life.

"Tea's ready," Maeve announced.

John Jo popped his head in the doorway. "Coming?" He grinned.

She loved his smile, it was cheeky and made his whole face light up. She nodded then, taking his hand, they walked together.

"Tommy Lee came back while we were gone." Maeve moaned. "He's gone again and won't be here for yours or Paddy's weddings. It's a disgrace."

Gypsy glanced at John Jo; he didn't seem bothered. She had never met him, so it didn't bother her either.

"You know he works away, Mother, we'll just have to celebrate again when he's back," he said. "Anyway, I wants the wedding as soon as possible, I can't keep sleeping in me motor."

"And what about Gypsy's family?" Maeve asked, her face more concerned.

"I'll go and see her uncle tomorrow and ask permission." He rubbed the back of his neck. "Now can we drink up in peace."

Gypsy had an uneasy feeling. Her uncle wasn't the most understanding man going, and after the way they had last parted, would he give them his blessing?

CHAPTER 9

The next day, Gypsy and John Jo pulled into Henry's yard. It was as if she had never left. The mobile stood proudly at the front of the ground, with the smaller trailers behind. There were two brick sheds, one for washing and the other contained a toilet.

She felt sick. She would see Prissy while he spoke to Henry. She swallowed down her nerves and peeked at him.

"Stop worrying. Everything's gonna be okay," he reassured her. "You sure you want to stay here until we're married?" His voice was full of disappointment.

"It's the right thing to do, and besides, you'll have your bed back," she answered.

"I'd willingly sleep in the truck for the next ten years if it meant I'd get to lay with you at the end of it."

"Why, Mr Ward, I do believe you're being romantic." She laughed.

"Not romantic, just the truth. Come on, let's get this over with."

Gypsy climbed down with the help of John Jo. Henry marched towards them.

"Look out," she warned.

"Go see your aunt, I'll deal with this."

John Jo stared at Henry, hard-faced. "I want a word."

"Go on then, you've got my attention," Henry said, equally hard-faced.

"I've come to let you know I asked Gypsy to marry me, and she said yes."

"No," was all he got back.

"No?" John Jo laughed. "I'm not here to ask permission, I'm telling you what's going to happen. Now you can give your niece your blessing and for once do right by her, or you can tell her you don't want her to be happy. The choice is yours."

"You think she'd be happy with you, cos I don't. Our people don't mix for a reason. Now I shouldn't have let you take her last time, so this time I'll definitely be stopping you."

Gypsy watched the goings-on from the window. Both men looked angry.

"Gypsy, come away, this is men's business," Prissy ordered.

"No, this is my future, it concerns me," she snapped back. "I think they're gonna fight."

Her aunt grabbed her arm and pulled her away. "Why would you want to marry an Irish Traveller anyway? I think he's brainwashed you."

"Brainwashed?" Gypsy let out a loud sigh. "The truth is, he's treated me better than any of yous. Do you know he's slept in his motor, so I had a bed to sleep in... And look, he bought me this chain because I was sad about my mum's chain, you know, the one

Grandfather bet with and lost." She walked towards the door, stopping briefly. "Not only do I love him, but I also belong with him, and God help anyone who tries to stop me."

Bursting out of the doorway, she marched towards the two men. "Can we go now?" she asked John Jo.

"You'll not be going anywhere, Gypsy. Get inside," Henry ordered.

She glanced around the yard. "Where's my trailer?"

"I'll buy you another trailer, go inside now," her uncle bellowed.

"Do not talk to her like she's a dog." John Jo balled his fists. The first punch knocked Henry off his feet.

Not wanting to witness any more, she walked to John Jo's truck and climbed in. Minutes later, he joined her.

"That went well." He laughed while starting the engine, then reversed out.

Gypsy turned her attention to her uncle who was being helped up by Prissy. His face was bloodied. The glare he gave her when he stared back was one of disgust. This bridge had well and truly been burned.

***

John Jo searched under the bunk. He had been stashing his money there after every poker game or fight. Laying it out, he counted it. Although there was a fair amount, now he had a wedding to pay for he would also need a bigger trailer, and there simply wasn't enough.

Gypsy sat on the bunk opposite. "I could get a job. It's not fair you should have to pay for everything."

He spun around and studied her for a moment. Her face was sad. He blamed that shit-cunt Henry. Why would he treat her like that?

"It's not your job to provide, Gypsy, it's mine, and no wife of mine will be working." He returned his attention to the pound notes laid out in bundles of a hundred. "We can arrange the wedding, and in the meantime, I'll earn what we need."

"We could get married in a registry office, it would be cheaper," she offered.

"No, that's not an option." Being an Irish Traveller, religion was important to them all. Brought up as devout Catholics, they had always gone to church and so would only be married in one. Not that he held much faith in religion. He had seen too much suffering, especially in the travelling community. "I don't want you to worry… We'll move on to East Ham, I've got cousins there, and work will be easier to find. Now, are you going to give your man a kiss?"

Gypsy placed her hands on his chest, pushing him back. "Isn't East Ham London?" Her mind raced. All concrete, smoke, thousands of people. She shuddered. Had she made the right choice?

CHAPTER 10

Gypsy stared around the Traveller site. Everything appeared grey. There were no trees or grass, just concrete. Even the air was different. How did people live in these places?

"I'll set up, then you can sort the trailer." John Jo walked around the truck. "It's not that bad here, and remember, it's not forever."

She smiled in return. Did it matter where she was, as long as she was with him? No, of course it didn't. She planted a kiss on his cheek then stood back. "It's fine."

They were going to see the priest at the local church later. John Jo wanted the wedding booked in as soon as possible. He had given her money to buy a dress and reminded her not to worry. She would go with Maeve and Sean Paul's wife, Shirley Ann. Her mind turned to Prissy, and a sadness filled her.

***

John Jo sat in the pub. The wedding was booked for three weeks' time. Three weeks until he got to take Gypsy as his wife. He smiled at the thought. He wasn't sure how much longer he could keep his hands off her.

Sean Paul took a seat at the table and placed the drinks down. "I've found a nice trailer, you can go see tomorrow, and that bloke over there?" He flicked his head in his direction.

John Jo glanced over towards a table of suited men and nodded.

"The bloke sitting at the end, the fat one, needs some muscle. I said we'd both be interested." Sean Paul continued. "Things are on the up, brother."

"Muscle for what?" John Jo eyed the man suspiciously. "He's surrounded by muscle."

"Collecting payments from businesses," Sean Paul whispered.

"Sounds like an extortion racket." Did he really want to get involved in illegal activity right before his wedding?

"It's all kushti, and the pay's good. It'll be a short-term thing. You get the money for the trailer, and then we can get out of this dump. Never liked London and don't like the fact we've left the horses behind," Sean Paul moaned.

John Jo stood and picked up his pint. "They're safer where they are with Father and PJ watching them. Now let's go and 'ave a chat with Mr Big."

***

Gypsy sat in bed staring out of the window. It was long past midnight. Where was John Jo? Had something happened? She spotted the headlights and jumped out of bed. Opening the door as the truck came to a standstill, she folded her arms and glared when he walked towards her.

"Have you any idea how worried I've been? Where were you?" she whispered in temper. Without giving him the chance to reply, she continued her rant. "I've had this all my life with my grandfather, I'll not have it with you, too."

"Calm down, Gypsy." He stepped in, closing the door behind him. "I was working."

"Working?" she spat. "Jesus, I've heard some excuses in my time, but working? You must think I'm a right dinlow."

John Jo took a wedge of notes from his pocket and threw them on the side. "I was working, and I will be doing the same next Wednesday." Drawing her towards him, he wrapped his arms around her waist. "Sean Paul's also found us a nice vardo. Buccaneer. It's got an end bedroom, so no more putting the bed away in the daytime. We'll go and look at it tomorrow. Now give us a kiss."

She glanced at the money; there must have been at least a hundred pounds. He was telling the truth, but what line of work paid so well? "One kiss, then out. I've got to be up early."

"There'll be no getting up early when we're married, woman." John Jo grinned.

He kissed her, annoyed when she pushed him away. He felt his cock harden. At this rate, he would have to have a wank. Turning and heading to the motor, he heard the click of the lock when Gypsy closed the door. She was safe. Safe and sleeping in his bed. He only wished he were in there next to her.

Not long now, boy.

His mind wandered back to the night's proceedings. Demanding money with menace. It wasn't the career he had dreamed of, but it was easy money. The men had handed the money over straight away when they'd seen him and Sean Paul.

He closed the truck door and lay back on the seat with a pillow behind his head. Jaysus, he needed a bed so he could stretch out. At least with the summer weather he didn't need a cover. The vision of Gypsy slipped into his mind, the kiss, her body tight against his. He dipped his hand inside his pants. There was no way this would go down tonight without a little help.

CHAPTER 11

The trailer was pushed into place, a 1974 Buccaneer that appeared brand-new. Gypsy knew it would; Romanies and Travellers took good care of their homes. She stood back while John Jo and his brother hooked it up to the electric and then unlocked it, ready for her to clean and swap everything over. The outside would need a wash and polish, it was dusty just from the journey. These chrome trailers were beautiful, but they were a handful to keep clean, and with the weather as dry as it was, Gypsy suspected it would need washing and polishing up every few days.

She stepped inside with the bucket of soapy water and glanced around. To the right of the door was the end bedroom. She peeked inside. There were wardrobes and a drawer set. Turning towards the living area, display cabinets ran around the top of the trailer; she would start there first. That would be for the Crown Derby and cut crystal. Next to the bedroom was a kitchen area with full-size gas cooker. The middle had the fire one side and a seating area with a table on the other. Everywhere she looked there were cut-glass mirrors. She smiled. Their new home was perfect.

With only a week until the wedding, everything was coming together nicely, although they couldn't find a venue for the reception. Everywhere they went they got rejected as soon as they opened their mouths. No one wanted to host a Traveller wedding for fear of the place being trashed. Whilst there often were fights and things got broken, they always paid for the damages.

John Jo was working Wednesday nights collecting money for some man, and he had started working Friday and Saturday nights on the door of a nightclub. She wasn't sure how she felt about him working so late, but the cash was rolling in. Would he still want to leave after the wedding? Maybe not. Not now he was earning so much. He had come home a couple of times with black eyes and a split lip, but he had assured her it was nothing to worry about.

She busied herself cleaning out their new home, ready to move into. John Jo would now sleep in the small trailer until their wedding and then sell it.

She felt his arms slip around her waist, and his breath tickled her ear. "No shenanigans, Mr Ward. I'm busy."

"Not even a kiss?" he asked before kissing her neck. "And shenanigans is what us Irish men are good at with our women."

"Save it for a week's time. Then you can have all the shenanigans you like." She spun around. "Now out. Let me get finished. I need to change the bedding in the other one."

"No. Leave the bedding as it is. I'll feel closer to you then." He grinned. "Right, I'm off, got a bit of business to sort. I'll see you in a couple of hours." John Jo kissed her then left.

***

He entered the club, a small dingy place down a backstreet, with Sean Paul beside him. They had been called in for a delicate job. John Jo suspected the boss wanted someone bumped off. Although he had never killed before, it was something he would consider if the money was right.

"Gentleman, please take a seat." Mr Shitbag didn't even have the decency to look up.

This got John Jo's back up straight away, but nonetheless, he took a seat and motioned to Sean Paul to do the same. "You wanted to see us?"

"Yes... I've noticed you have a flair for this kind of work. I've got a job that needs a little discretion."

"And that is?" John Jo asked. He didn't like this man, he was smarmy. Made money from other people's sweat.

"I need someone taken care of. I can't give you details until I know you're prepared to do what it takes." He picked a glass up and swilled it around before taking a sniff of the contents. "You know, this cognac is the most expensive in the world."

John Jo glanced at Sean Paul. He looked as confused as he was himself.

"Your point is?"

"My point is, Mr Ward, wouldn't you like to have the finer things in life?"

John Jo thought of Gypsy. As far as he was concerned, he had already hit the jackpot. "Man puts too much value on possessions and not enough on their loved ones."

"But what if you could have both? After all, don't we strive to better ourselves so our loved ones also prosper?"

"What's the bottom line?" Sean Paul asked; he sounded annoyed.

"You will get five thousand pounds each. Half now and the other half when the job is done."

"That's a lot of money to bump off a nobody, which means the target is high-profile." John Jo sighed. "When would you want the job done?"

"Sooner the better." The man took a long sip of his cognac then added, "I know you'll want to discuss this between yourselves, so why don't you come back here tomorrow, same time."

"No. You obviously know the target, so we will meet somewhere neutral. We won't be able to be seen with you again after this." John

Jo stood. "One o'clock. The White Heart in Whitechapel high street." Turning, he opened the door and left, without waiting for a reply.

***

Gypsy had just finished putting the last of her clothes into the wardrobe when John Jo pulled up. She lit the gas and placed the new kettle on the stove.

When he walked in, he stood staring at her. She couldn't decide if he was angry or sad.

"Have I done something wrong?" she asked to break the silence.

He shook his head. "No. You do everything right… Tell me, Gypsy, if you had money, enough to do whatever you wanted, what would you do?"

She frowned. What a weird question. "I guess if money were no option I would buy my own bit of land, somewhere no one could take away from me. I'd feel safe." She glanced up him. What was he thinking? "Why do you ask?"

"I've got a chance of making some big money. If I do the job, we will leave immediately afterwards, go Kent or Essex. Maybe even buy a bit of ground."

"This job, is it dangerous?" Did she really want to know? She had a bad feeling she wouldn't like the answer.

"No. It's not dangerous." He turned to leave without looking at her.

She knew he was lying. "Before you go, just remember, money would mean nothing without you."

CHAPTER 12

John Jo and Sean Paul were parked up in Stepney. They sat in the car across the road from the Old Artichoke public house.

"Jaysus, it's fecking hot," Sean Paul moaned, wiping the sweat from his brow. "Could do with a pint to quench me thirst."

"You know we can't go in there, now shut up and keep focused," John Jo replied, his attention fixed on the pub.

The target would be coming out soon. Their plan was simple: follow him, and when the moment was right, they would strike.

Gypsy's words kept playing over in John Jo's mind. 'Money would mean nothing without you.' He felt the same. What good would money be without her? It wouldn't.

And then there was the other problem, Shitbag. Or Mr James, as he liked to be called. If this job was so important, why wasn't he using his own men? The answer was clear: he didn't want this coming back on him. He was afraid. And if he was afraid, then the man they were about to cross was higher up the food chain.

"I don't trust Shitbag," Sean Paul mumbled.

"Neither do I," John Jo admitted. "He's using us to do the dirty work. Then I reckon he'll have his own men take us out." His grip tightened on the wheel. "And let's be honest, the police ain't gonna break their backs looking for the killers of two Irish Travellers."

"So what do we do?"

John Jo's eyes flicked to the pub door. The target had stepped out.

"We play both sides." He turned the key, the engine growling to life.

Across the street, their mark moved.

"Ready?" John Jo asked.

Sean Paul exhaled slowly. "Ready."

They followed the car to the outskirts of town. Neither men knew this area well. Stepney wasn't somewhere they had reason to visit. The road ended at a patch of waste ground. A few run-down buildings dotted the area. It was secluded and away from prying eyes. The perfect place to conclude business.

John Jo slid his gun under the seat. "Hide your gun, but make sure you can reach it if I give the nod. He knows we are here." He stepped out of the car.

The man they had been tailing turned to face him, gun in hand.

"D'ya think I'm fucking stupid?" He sneered. "I clocked you miles back."

"It's not what you think. We ain't armed." John Jo put his hands up.

"That supposed to make me feel better?"

"We just need a word, mister."

"Mr Kelly to you."

"Fine. Mr Kelly." John Jo moved closer. "We've been paid to kill you."

"And you're telling me that because?" Paul Kelly raised the gun higher.

"Because the man who's hired us to do it will probably kill us after," Sean Paul said from the car.

"We figured if we didn't do it he'd send someone else. This way you get to sort him out and we walk away with the money he's already given us. Think that's called a win-win." John Jo looked at the gun. "You don't need that. If we wanted you dead, you wouldn't have seen us coming."

Paul Kelly lowered the gun. "So you gonna tell me who it is?"

John Jo smiled. "He calls himself Mr James. Not sure if that's his real name. He likes everyone to call him Boss."

"He runs a club in West Ha—"

"I know who he is," Paul Kelly cut in. "So what do you want?"

"Nothing. I'm getting married tomorrow, then we will be leaving. He thinks we are going after you on Monday, but by then we will be long gone."

"How can I get hold of you?"

"You've no need to get hold of us, Mr Kelly. That's us done. Come on." John Jo motioned to Sean Paul.

"Wait. Would you be interested if any jobs came up?" Paul asked. "You said you're not leaving for a couple of days."

Both men shook their heads. "No."

"Wouldn't you like to get revenge on the fat prick? I'll make it worth your while," Paul pressed.

"What did you have in mind?" John Jo asked. "And how much?"

"I wanna make him pay, I want him to know that he's fucked up, and what better way to do that than to have you two by my side?" Paul grinned. "Come on, fellas, when he sees your faces he's gonna right royally shit himself. That's called payback on your behalf."

"How much?" Sean Paul added.

"Hundred quid each. I'll have my own men there to clean up, it's literally to show your faces."

The Ward brothers remained silent.

"Okay, a hundred and fifty each, that's good money for doing nothing."

"Okay." John Jo looked at Sean Paul. "Write down Eddie's number, you can reach us on that. Don't give any details, just a time. If you wanna meet, we'll meet back here."

Paul held out his hand. "Deal."

After shaking, John Jo turned and began to walk back to the motor. "One more thing, you owe us now, so if ever we need anything, we'll be in touch," he said over his shoulder.

CHAPTER 13

The wedding day went off without a hitch. The church had been packed, mostly with Irish Travellers. Gypsy's side had fewer Romani guests, which saddened her, but the sight of John Jo waiting at the altar quickly lifted her spirits. She had never seen him in a suit before. He looked handsome, but if she was honest, she much preferred him in his work clothes, preferably without a shirt.

The ceremony flew by in a blur, and soon, everyone was heading back to the reception, held on the Traveller site. They had tried to book a venue, but no one was willing to take them in. Too many gorjas feared their place would be wrecked. But that didn't matter now. Music blared into the night, laughter and song filling the air while people celebrated with the newly married couple.

"I'm feeling pretty tired." John Jo mock yawned while stretching his arms over his head.

Gypsy arched a brow. "That's a shame. And to think it's our wedding night. But don't worry, I'll let you sleep," she teased.

He grinned. "Come on, it's bedtime, Mrs Ward." Without warning, he scooped her into his arms. "I need to carry me bride over the threshold."

She wriggled in protest. "We can't go to bed yet, everyone will know what we're doing."

A voice shouted out from the crowd, "There's gonna be some loving tonight!"

Gypsy's face burned. "See? I told you," she whispered.

John Jo laughed. "I couldn't care less what they know. Tonight is all about us." He reached for the vardo door and tugged the handle. "Why's the fecking door locked?"

"Because you locked it," she said.

"Where's the fecking key? Have a look in your bag."

"John Jo, I haven't got a bag."

"Check your pockets then," he urged.

"Have you seen this dress? Where exactly do you think the pockets are?" She sighed. "Have you checked your pockets?"

"If I don't get this door open now, I'm gonna take you around the back and…" Placing Gypsy down, he reached into his pocket and found the key.

"And what?" She laughed.

Plunging the key into the lock, he yanked the door open, then with renewed determination and a dramatic swoop, he lifted her into his arms again. "Never mind." He grunted. He was going to do this properly. Romantic, just like the movies.

He adjusted his grip, her weight shifting. He placed his foot on the step then threw himself forward.

"Jaysus, breathe in," he murmured, while turning sideways to get them both through the vardo door.

His shoulder smacked into the frame, and her foot caught on the door handle. He stood for a moment, thinking.

"Are we stuck?" she whispered, trying not to laugh.

"No," he lied.

So much for fecking romance.

Finally, in a last-ditch attempt, he lunged forward, and they both ended up in a heap on the floor.

Gypsy laughed. "Well, you did it."

He responded with a grunt.

Lifting her back up, he then placed her on the bed and closed the door and locked it. He felt like he'd just done ten rounds in the ring.

Ten rounds would have been easier.

He slid his jacket off and threw it on the floor, then took his tie off. Lying on the bed next to her, he could barely contain his excitement. "It feels like I've waited for this my whole life."

He kissed her while grappling with the tiny buttons at the back of her dress.

"Jaysus, Gypsy, how the feck does this thing come off?" Without waiting for an answer, he ripped the back in half, drawing the dress down.

"Me dress, you've ruined it." She shrieked.

"Feck the dress, I'll buy you another one."

He stopped and looked at her body. It was better than he'd imagined. Reaching for her lacy briefs, he peeled them off. He knelt, staring. She was blushing, her hands moving to cover herself.

"Don't." He grabbed her hands and placed them over her head. "I want to see you, all of you."

Unbuttoning his shirt, he took it off and threw it to the floor, his gaze still roaming her body. Next he slid his trousers and pants down. He was now naked and lying on top of her.

"This is going to be a night to remember."

***

John Jo rolled off of Gypsy, and a sigh of contentment left his mouth. Two days they had spent in bed. Two whole days of heaven. He had explored her body and knew every inch. She had a freckle on the inside of her thigh which he had noticed as he'd kissed his way up to her soft, sweet parts. Every inch of his new wife he had tasted. He felt himself starting to harden at the thought.

"John Jo!" Eddie said through the locked door.

"Stay there," he told her while putting on his trousers. He opened the door and stared down at the man. "This had better be fecking important."

"Well, if you're gonna give my phone number out, you're gonna get disturbed. Some bloke wants to meet at six p.m. He said you'd know where." With that, Eddie turned and walked away.

***

John Jo and Sean Paul leant against the side of the truck. It was almost six p.m. They had both brought a gun, which they had tucked into their waistbands.

"Here he comes." John Jo nodded. "Looks like he's got company."

Paul Kelly jumped out of his motor, and another man joined him.

"This is Tony, my right-hand man." He motioned with a flick of his head.

"What's this about, Mr Kelly?" Sean Paul asked.

"It's about finishing the job. Tonight. You up for it still?"

John Jo nodded. "What's the plan?"

"We'll find a phone box, you ring him, tell him the job's done and you want to come and get your money. He will no doubt arrange to meet you somewhere. If, as you say, he's planning on killing you then he'll send his men. I've got a few of my boys watching his club. We go in, do the deed, and then yous sail off into the sunset." Paul grinned. "Think this is gonna be a good night's work, lads. Ready?"

***

Gypsy sat outside with Shirley Ann and John Jo's cousin. The two women were chatting away. They did try to include her, but she didn't know the people they spoke about. The best she could offer was a smile or nod in the right places.

She glanced around the area. It appeared better at night. With the glow of lights it softened the harsh concrete view. Even the flats in the distance seemed more appealing. She fanned herself with the newspaper that had been left on her seat by Sean Paul earlier.

"Seems to be getting hotter every day," she remarked while breathing in the hot, dry air.

"Going to get hotter according to the man on the radio," Shirley Ann said. "Could you imagine being pregnant in this heat? Jaysus, the baby would cook." She peered at Gypsy. "You'll be next, the way he keeps dragging you off to that trailer."

Gypsy blushed. Things like that should never be talked of. Pleased when the sound of John Jo's Transit caught her attention, she stood. "I best get in in case he wants something to eat. I'll see you both tomorrow."

She walked towards the Transit. John Jo jumped out and grabbed her and swung her around.

"We're moving on tomorrow, my darling." He grinned.

Those were the words she had longed to hear. They had only been here a month, but it felt a lot longer.

"Where will we go?" She giggled.

"I think it's time we bought ourselves a bit of land." His eyes twinkled as the light from the window caught them. "How does Essex sound?"

***

John Jo snored gently next to Gypsy. She liked watching him sleep. It was the only time he was ever still.

Her thoughts turned to the move. Would she see her family again?

But they're not your family anymore, they disowned you.

Gypsy sighed. She had a little empty space inside her that couldn't be filled. Would it, in time?

Would you rather be with your family or your husband? John Jo didn't make you choose, they did.

"I know."

"What?" John Jo asked lazily, his eyes half open.

"Nothing, go back to sleep." Gypsy ran a finger down the side of his face in a soothing motion.

"You've been fidgeting for the last thirty minutes." He pulled himself up in to a sitting position. "What's wrong?"

"Nothing's wrong, I was just thinking about my family."

"I'm your family… I told you once they didn't deserve you and I've been proven right. Now we are leaving tomorrow to follow our dreams. It's something to smile about, Gypsy, our own piece of land. That's what you said you wanted and that's what I've worked for."

"How did you get that much money in so little time?" she pressed. This wouldn't have come from being security on a door.

"It's men's business and nothing to worry about. It's my job to look after you. Now you can look after me by giving me a kiss."

John Jo was on her in a second, his mouth pressed against hers. There was a lot to be said for this marrying malarky. It was the best thing he'd done in his life. That and getting into the crime game. He would be making a lot more money soon, thanks to Paul Kelly, but he wouldn't share that bit of information with his wife.

CHAPTER 14

August 1976

The church was packed tighter than a can of sardines, the pews creaking under the weight of every aunt, uncle, cousin, and distant relative from both sides of the families. Maeve suspected there were a few hangers-on also. Saint Cuthbert's, with its high vaulted ceilings and a smell that could only be described as incense and sweat, was buzzing with the excited murmur of the congregation. The stained-glass windows shone a holy light across the altar that was draped in white cloth and gold. The choir, in their matching cassocks, had just finished their out-of-tune version of 'May the Road Rise to Meet You'.

Maeve adjusted her hat. It was a gaudy affair with bright-peach feathers in it. They matched her outfit perfectly. They had been given a dress code from Violet. As if they couldn't decide what to wear themselves. She rolled her eyes at the thought.

She sat in the first row, on the right side of the aisle, with her son, PJ, the groom, John Jo, who was best man, and her husband, Paddy. She felt blessed that her baby was finally tying the knot—not necessarily with Violet, she had never warmed to her. She had worried, though, when PJ had told her about the pregnant gorja, the fecking eejit. But in her mind, boys will be boys, and it was better to have red-blooded men in the family rather than these gays she'd heard of. Not that she had anything against them personally, but the good Lord didn't condone that sort of behaviour so neither would she. Her thoughts turned to Tommy Lee, another wedding missed. What would he be doing now, murdering someone?

She glanced up at the large statue of the Virgin Mary and made the sign of the cross by touching her forehead, chest, left shoulder, then right shoulder. It wouldn't do any good to be having bad thoughts in front of the blessed mother.

She felt her husband's hand grip hers, as if he knew what she was thinking. In her mind that was God giving her comfort.

"I've got a bad feeling, Paddy," she whispered.

"Shh, everything will be as it should, girl," he replied soothingly.

She glanced at her watch. The bride was late. Of course she was. If Violet Conners wasn't making a grand entrance, it wasn't worth her time. There were her family, all at the front, her mother and sisters, whispering and clucking away like a bunch of hens.

Taking a peek at PJ, Maeve noticed he was sweating. Was that from the scorching summer sun, or was he nervous? Probably both, she decided. One thing was for sure, though, he seemed miserable, like he was heading to the gallows. She felt her heart drop. He looked so smart in his suit, it fitted him perfectly, although his tie was crooked. She made a mental note to clout him later for not letting her fix it.

Suddenly the doors opened, and the organ music started. Violet approached on the arm of old man Conners. Her hair was piled up so high, it could probably be spotted from space.

Jaysus, that must have taken some backcombing, and is that a crown perched on top?

Maeve laughed inwardly.

The Conners always did think they were royalty.

She looked ridiculous in the oversized meringue she was wearing. Her poor father was bent sideways, three feet away from her, for fear of stepping on her dress. Maeve's smile broadened.

I bet his back's gonna play up after this.

Behind Violet there were six bridesmaids. The music stopped, and just as Violet handed the bouquet to her mother and stood next to PJ, the priest raised his hand.

And that's when it happened.

From out of nowhere, a bloody great crow swooped into the church and flew straight to the giant crucifix above Father O'Rielly's head. He froze, mid-blessing, his hand hovering awkwardly in the air. Half the congregation erupted into chaos while the other half sat open-mouthed.

"It's a sign," someone screeched.

"Bad luck," shouted another.

Violet had stopped dead in her tracks, her mouth opening and closing like a fish out of water. PJ had gone as white as a ghost.

"Oh, for the love of…" old man Conners muttered, standing up. "It's just a fecking bird, not the angel of death, now sit down, the lot of you," he roared.

When everyone had taken their seats, the crow then decided to fly over Violet's head and shit. Not just a little. It seemed like it had been saving that lot up for some time. It splattered on to her shoulder, splashed up onto her face, and slid down, marking her dress.

Maeve could hear the gasps and mumbling of prayers. People were crossing themselves in the hopes that the bad luck would pass them by.

John Jo burst out laughing.

Violet screamed and took off running back down the aisle with her mother, father, and sisters all chasing after her.

The crow, satisfied with its work, took off out of the church, squawking loudly. Maeve thought it sounded more like the bird was laughing.

Father O'Rielly cleared his throat, his face ashen. "Well…perhaps we should reschedule?"

Maeve glanced at PJ who was still standing there like a statue and sighed.

"Go after her, you eejit," she snapped.

He turned towards her, and for the first time that day, he smiled. "Maybe it's for the best, Mother."

"The best. You mean to tell me I've spent a fecking fortune on this hat? For nothing?" She pointed.

He shrugged. "Well, at least Violet's father paid for the food."

John Jo patted him on the back. "I think you've had a lucky escape." He started laughing. "That bird was definitely full of blackberries. Did you see the colour that came out of its arse?"

"You're not helping, son. Where's your father?" Maeve asked, peering around.

"He's outside talking to the Conners. They're agreed the wedding is off," Sean Paul answered. "Come on, Mother, let's get you home."

CHAPTER 15

October 1976

Gypsy stared out of the window, the rain making it difficult to see, the storm clouds giving the illusion of nightfall. On the one hand she had been pleased that the drought was over, on the other she was sad to be cooped up in the trailer. They had been living here for just over a month and half. The land they had bought with Sean Paul was in Wickford, Essex. Close enough to the town, far enough away from prying eyes. They had two shower blocks with toilets built. The land was surrounded by trees. John Jo and Sean Paul had put a driveway in and hard standing for the trailers.

Gypsy missed Maeve. She had been kind, in a rough, no-nonsense way, and although she didn't live far away, it wasn't the same.

It was nearly four p.m. The dinner had been bubbling away on the stove for the last hour. Bacon pudding was John Jo's favourite. She was expecting him home around five. He was out a lot working; he never told her what he did, but he always had wads of cash. Did it worry her? A little, if she was honest, although he gave her whatever she wanted. The display cabinets were full of Crown Derby and lead crystal, and she had a jewellery box full of gold.

She placed another handful of coal on the fire and watched the flames dance. It was toasty inside, so much so that she would open a window just to let some of the heat out.

The sound of John Jo's truck caught her attention. He was early. She opened the door as he jumped out of the motor, and his face broke into a huge smile when he saw her, her face doing the same. She stood back while he entered. Kicking his boots off, he grabbed her waist and pulled her close.

"We're going away for a couple of weeks, on business."

"What kind of business and where?" Her stomach dropped. She was still getting used to living here.

"Not far, a little site in Halstead. It's protection for Paul Kelly." John Jo kissed her before she could speak.

Pushing back, she studied his face. "Why would you need to protect him?"

"It's not him, it's his wife, Millie. Do you remember Duke Lee? Well, this Millie is his daughter."

Gypsy nodded. "I heard the rumours. So what will you have to do?"

"Nothing, just stay on the site until he catches the culprit who's after her or him or both… It's money for old rope."

"Sean Paul coming, too?"

"Yes, we're all going."

"When do we leave?" she finally asked.

"Tomorrow. Now how long's that bacon pudding gonna be?" He swooped her up in his arms and marched to the bed.

"Long enough." She giggled.

***

A loud noise erupted. John Jo leapt from his bed, but with his foot tangled in the sheet, he crashed to the floor with a thud.

"What was that?" Gypsy whispered, her hair sticking up in all directions.

"Somebody's outside," he muttered while fumbling to put on his trousers. He grabbed his gun, torch, and remaining dignity, then motioned for her to stay put.

He shifted with speed to the end of the trailer and yanked the curtain back, squinting into the darkness. His van was out there, sitting pretty, but something had moved. He was sure of it. His eyes darted to Sean Paul's trailer just as its curtain twitched. Great. He wasn't the only one hearing things.

He grabbed his boots and pulled them on, readying himself to face the intruder. Opening the door a fraction, he flicked on the light and spied out. The Transit lit up.

"You better fecking run before I get my hands on you," he bellowed.

Sean Paul stepped out of his door and marched towards where the noise had come from. John Jo met him, and they both scoured the area.

Nothing.

"There's no one here," he said while shining the torch around.

"Then what was the noise?" Sean Paul asked. "Because we both heard it."

From the corner of his eye, John Jo caught movement. "Look over there." He flashed the torch, and in the beam a family of deer were grazing.

"For the love of all things holy, don't tell anyone about this. We'll be a fecking laughingstock," Sean Paul mumbled.

"True, but maybe you should stay here. We need better security, in case anyone thinks of robbing us. I'll go and do the job for Kelly, and we can split the money," John Jo said, still eyeing the deer.

"Yeah, we could do with some proper outside lighting. I'll get that sorted. I'll give Cousin Billy a shout, he can help while you're away."

John Jo nodded then headed back inside to a panicking Gypsy. "It's okay, darling, we scared them off," he reassured her without letting on it was the local wildlife.

CHAPTER 16

John Jo drove into the site and reversed the trailer into place. "Wait here while I get set up, no point us both getting wet." He pecked Gypsy on the lips then jumped out.

His boots squelched in the mud as he made his way to unhook the trailer. A couple of men joined him and pushed it into place. After thanking them, he took a quick gander around. The place was tidy enough, but the dreary day made it appear dirty. There was an old painted wagon nestled amongst the trees, smoke wafting out of the tiny tin chimney. He smiled. Thoughts of Ireland, visiting his grandmother, flashed through his mind. Her painted vardo with the pot hanging outside on the fire. He could almost smell her rabbit stew when he closed his eyes. The laughter and chatter of the family all sitting around speaking of times gone by.

"Can I get out now?" Gypsy called, breaking into his thoughts.

Glancing over, he smiled. Every time he saw her it was like the first time all over again. The way his breath caught in his throat, the way he struggled to string a sentence together. She had that effect on him.

"Let me unlock the door." He walked towards her and reached across for his keys.

Gypsy wrapped her arm around his back when he leant in.

"You're soaked," she exclaimed. "You'll need to get out of those wet clothes before you catch a chill."

"Then I think you should get out of yours, too." He grinned.

"But I'm not wet...what are you doing?" She squeaked.

John Jo took her from the cab and held her against him in the rain. "You were saying?"

"I thought you were going to be busy meeting Duke?"

"This is more important." Slamming the truck door shut with his foot, he lifted her over his shoulder and carried her to the vardo.

"Put me down, people will be watching," she whispered.

"Good," he bellowed. "Now hold still while I unlock this door."

***

John Jo greeted Duke with a nod then helped push his trailer into place. He glanced at the two blonde women standing watching. He recognised Connie, Duke's wife. He had seen her at a few of the bare-knuckle fights that had been held around the country. The woman next to her had a face that would turn sugar to salt. This must be Duke's daughter, Millie. Thank God he didn't have to spend time with the miserable malt.

Turning his attention back to Duke, he motioned him to the back of trailer. "Everything in place?"

"No one knows she's here, so I'm not expecting trouble. You spoke to Paul?" Duke asked.

"Yeah, he's filled me in. I'm opposite if there is any trouble, but to be honest, anyone would have to be mad to try anything here," John Jo said.

"Agreed." Duke nodded. "Right, I'll see you later round the fire for a chat."

John Jo frowned. "A chat?"

"Don't know how long we're gonna be here, so I thought I'd arrange a couple of fights." Duke grinned.

"I'll be up for that." John Jo headed back to his trailer.

Gypsy was busy preparing dinner. She spun around when he entered, her face illuminated with a smile.

"Everything okay?" She turned back to the stove and lit the gas.

He slipped his arms around her. "Everything is perfect. What's for dinner?"

"Beef stew, and I can't cook while you're holding me."

He tightened his grip. "It's a man's right to hold his wife whenever he wants." He felt her tense.

"John Jo Ward," she began. Spinning around in his arms, she glared. "If you want your dinner, you," she stabbed at his chest with her finger, "will leave me in peace while I make it."

"Okay, but give me a kiss first." He didn't wait for a reply. His mouth smashed into hers, and she relaxed into his body. He reared back. "That's more like it."

He made his way to the end of the trailer and sat on the bunk, moving the giant lace cushion out of the way. He glanced at Gypsy who now appeared to be in a good mood. "Duke's arranging some fights while we're here."

Her face changed; he knew it would. She didn't like him fighting, but as a Traveller's wife he knew she wouldn't say anything. It was part and parcel of everyday life in their community.

"It'll only be one fight," he then added.

"But you said you were making good money here, why the need to fight?" she asked, staring at him.

"You know I'm splitting the money with Sean Paul now, as he's guarding the ground. Also I've been asked. I can't say no, Gypsy, you know that," he explained.

"Who will you be fighting?" She sighed. It was no good arguing with a Traveller or Romani, the men did what they wanted regardless of the woman's feelings.

CHAPTER 17

Gypsy stood back and glanced around the trailer. It was spotless. Pleased with herself, she watched, speechless, when John Jo marched in with muddy boots. Jumping up, she stormed towards him. "Out." She pointed.

"Jaysus, woman, it's raining outside," he argued.

"John Jo Ward, I've spent all morning cleaning, and look what you've done!" she exclaimed. "Now out."

He stepped outside with Gypsy standing on the step.

With her arms animated, she continued her rant. "You take them off before you come inside."

"But I was desperate to see the love of my life." He held his arms out to her, pleading. "Sorry."

Well, that was a first, she had never heard him apologise before.

"Do you forgive me, or will I die of a broken heart?" He grabbed his chest.

She couldn't help but laugh. Talk about over the top. "You'll not be dying of anything. Take them off and come inside." She turned to Duke's trailer. Was she being watched? Her eyes met the woman's called Millie. She was staring at her from the window. "Come inside, John Jo, seems we have an audience."

He glanced over then followed Gypsy in, taking his boots off at the door. "She's a miserable one, that woman, don't know how Paul puts up with that."

"Maybe she's like that because she's away from him. I'd feel the same." She turned and placed her arms around his neck. "I would hate to be away from you, and don't forget someone's after her. That can't be fun, knowing you're that hated."

"Well, one things for sure, you'll never be in that position. Can't see anyone hating you." His lips met hers as his hands slid down to her bum.

***

PJ stood at the door of the house and knocked. His palms were sweating, and while he had come up with a speech earlier, he now couldn't remember a word of it.

"Can I help you?" the woman asked.

"I'm here to see Tracy," he said.

"It's you, the monster who got my girl up the duff. Well, no, you can't bleeding well see her. Now fuck off."

The door slammed in his face before he could respond.

He climbed back into his motor and drove to a quiet pub on the outskirts of Basildon. He had never been to this one, John Jo had told him to steer clear. Why, he had never said.

He opened the door. There were only five people in there, and one of them was the barman.

"Pint of Guinness, please," he mumbled while rummaging through his pocket for change. He took his drink and perched on a stool at the end of the bar.

"Haven't seen you in here before," the man who'd served him said. "You here drowning your sorrows or do you always look like that?"

PJ raised his head and studied the man. He must have been late thirties. "You were right the first time."

"Nothing's ever that bad. Maybe you need a new perspective... My name's Sam." The man held out his hand.

"PJ." He gave the man's hand a firm shake.

"Lovely to meet you, PJ. Now why don't you tell me what's wrong."

***

"I'm going over to the fire, I'll only be an hour or two," John Jo called from the door.

"Okay, I'm going over to see Patience for a bit," Gypsy said back.

He stepped back in. He had never met Patience, but obviously the men on the site had warned him. "Do not ask for a reading, Gypsy. I'm not asking, I'm telling."

"I'm not going for a reading, I promise." She walked towards him. "She's my aunt, I need to say hello."

"How can she be your aunt, she's at least two hundred years old?" he snapped.

She laughed. How rude was that comment. "Great aunt, I don't know, we're related somehow, and she's one of the few Romanies who still talks to me. Now get yourself off, I'll only be with her a short while."

He paused in the doorway before heading out. She grabbed her cardigan and did the same. Her mood had dipped. Why were people so against Patience? She had the gift, although many thought it a curse. Gypsy was sure if she could rid herself of it she would.

As she approached the wagon the door opened, and the old woman's smiling face appeared. Her toothless grin brought a smile to Gypsy's face.

"I wondered when you'd pay me a visit," Patience said, stepping back to allow her in.

The wagon was just as she'd remembered, although the paintwork looked tired. The bed was neatly made with brightly coloured blankets, and two pots hung above the stove on hooks.

"Kushti divvus, Aunt Patience." She'd greeted the old woman as a Romani would.

"Kushti divvus, Gypsy, take a seat… So I hear you've caused quite a stir with your family."

"Are you going to tell me I did the wrong thing?" she asked. Out of everyone she knew, she didn't expect a lecture from her.

"Are you happy, girl?" Patience opened the fire. She stoked it, the logs crackling.

"Yes, I am." Gypsy eyed the old woman carefully. She hadn't come for a reading, and she didn't want one. "Whatever happens in my life, happens, and I don't want to know."

"Calm yourself. I think you done the right thing, too. Old Albert didn't deserve you." Patience hoisted her skirt up and sat beside her. "What's troubling you?"

"Nothing," Gypsy said quickly.

"Come now, girl, you can't fool me, something is on your mind."

Gypsy placed her hands in her lap and stared at them. She had promised John Jo she wouldn't ask for a reading. "I told you, I wanted to say hello."

"Very well… Now tell me what's been going on with you apart from being won in a poker game?"

***

John Jo stood with his back to the fire, half listening to the conversation with Duke and another man. His attention held firmly on the wagon. Gypsy had been in there forty minutes. He wasn't happy.

"I'm heading in, fellas, this fecking weather is pissing me off." Without waiting for a reply, he stormed towards the wagon. Grabbing the handle, he threw open the door and stared at Gypsy and the old woman.

"John Jo!" Gypsy gasped.

"Come on, we need to go." He grabbed her arm roughly.

"What are you doing?" she asked.

"What are *you* doing, more to the point." He glanced at Gypsy's hands; she was holding old photos.

"Aunt Patience was showing me these, pictures of my mother and father." Gypsy gazed up with tears in her eyes.

That knocked the wind right out of him. Letting go of her arm, he took the photo and studied it. "You look like your mother."

She smiled up at him, but he could see the pain behind her eyes.

"I'm going in. Don't be long."

"I'm coming now. Aunt Patience, I'll come see you tomorrow." She kissed the old woman on the cheek and handed her the photo.

"You keep that, girl. Think of it as a wedding gift."

Gypsy smiled. She had no photos of her parents. This was the best present she had been given. "Thank you."

Joining John Jo outside, she fell into step with him. "What was that all about?"

"I was worried." He stuffed his hands into his pockets. "I don't want us being cursed, Gypsy."

She stopped. "Cursed? I told you I wouldn't have a reading. Don't you trust me?"

He sighed. "Of course I trust you, it's the witch I don't trust."

"She's not a witch... I'm sick of people being nasty to her. They ask for readings, and when they don't like what they hear, they blame her. She's never cursed anyone. If anything, she's the one who's been cursed. She's lived a life of loneliness because of it." She ignored him and stormed towards the trailer.

"Wait." He gripped her arm, pulling her around to face him. "Okay, I'm sorry, I only know what I've been told. If you promise not to get a reading then I'll promise to keep my mouth shut. Deal?"

CHAPTER 18

PJ woke to the sound of rain battering the window. Still partly drowsy, he peered around, not knowing where he was. He felt an arm across his chest and stiffened. Turning his head, he glanced at Sam.

Shit.

His pulse quickened. What the feck had he done? He gently moved the man's arm and found his clothes. He rushed downstairs quietly, then dressed and left the pub. He felt sick as the night's antics slowly came back to him. Did he really do that?

***

Gypsy had spent the day ignoring John Jo. She had almost thrown his lunch at him. There were only so many times he could say sorry. Pulling his boots on, he glanced at her.

"I'm going to see Duke, I won't be long."

Silence.

"What time will dinner be ready?" He was met with a loud sigh. "Jaysus, Gypsy, I've said I'm sorry."

"Maybe you shouldn't listen to gossip. Honestly, those men around that fire are worse than a bunch of old women gossiping. I wonder what they say about us…and I'm not cooking tonight."

Knowing when to quit, he left the trailer and headed towards the fire. There were ten or so men standing nattering. Maybe Gypsy was right, they did like a gossip.

"All right, John Jo," Duke greeted.

"Duke." He nodded in reply. "How's things?"

"Kushti. Here, fancy a beer?" Duke held out his hand.

Taking the bottle, John Jo pulled off the top and took a long swig. He wasn't much of a drinker but today he could've drunk a pub dry. He hated arguing with Gypsy, he hated the way her sad eyes lost their sparkle. It hit him right in the pit of his stomach. He stared over at one of the men who started talking to him.

"That woman of yours giving you trouble? She's caused her family more than enough. You wanna keep a close eye on—"

Before he had finished speaking, John Jo had punched him in the face, cracking his nose open and knocking him off his feet. When the man staggered back up he balled his fist and hit him in the face again. The rest of the men stood back and watched on. He could hear them taking bets on who would win. John Jo grinned. This was just what he needed to get his frustration out. Pity he couldn't place a bet on himself.

Gypsy watched in horror from the trailer window. John Jo was on top of the man, smashing his fist into his face. Duke and another man were trying to pull him off. Relieved when he finally stood, she ran to the door and, slipping her shoes on, she stepped outside just as he came marching towards her. His lip was split, and blood smudged his chin.

"What the hell was that about?" she asked.

"Nothing." He grunted.

Gypsy followed him in and placed the kettle on the stove. "Sit down and I'll clean you up."

"So you're talking to me now?" He grinned.

"Looks that way," she said, annoyed. She busied herself tipping salt into a bowl and filling it with water. Reaching for a clean cloth, she felt his arms slip around her waist.

"I'll remember that for next time," he whispered in her ear, his breath tickling her cheek.

Butterflies fluttered in her stomach. Damn this man. He could make her go weak at the knees anytime he wanted.

"R...remember what?" she stuttered.

"When you're not talking to me, I need to fight and get injured."

***

John Jo walked out of the chip shop with an armful of food. Gypsy smiled. The last time she'd had fish and chips was when she had first arrived at his camp. He had bought one of everything because she wouldn't speak to him and he didn't know what she liked, then she'd pigged out and almost ate the lot.

He climbed into the truck and handed her the food. The delicious aroma filled the cab.

Gypsy's stomach rumbled. "You sure you've bought enough?"

"I'm a growing boy." He grinned. "And besides, you haven't eaten all day. You must be starving." He started the motor and began the drive back to camp. "Duke's arranged the fight. It's in two days' time."

"Where's it going to be held?" she asked, her stomach sinking.

"In a barn up the road from camp." Stopping, he jumped out and opened the gate, then climbed back in and drove through. "I want you to place a bet on me, to win."

When they arrived at the trailer, she noticed the flash Range Rover parked outside Duke's. "Who do you reckon that is?"

"That, my darling, is Paul Kelly's. Maybe the job's over. I'll have a word with Duke later. Come on, I'm starving."

Gypsy had just finished dishing up when she jumped at a loud knock on the door.

"I'll get it," John Jo told her while marching to answer it. "Paul. What can I do for you?"

"A word, in private," Paul said.

John Jo turned to Gypsy. "I won't be long."

She stared at the closed door and then at the mountain of food that was fast becoming cold. Why didn't he say no, I'm about to eat, and more importantly, why was this gorja Kelly calling the shots?

The door reopened, and John Jo stepped in.

"What was that about?" she quizzed.

"Just a bit of business, nothing for you to worry about." He stuffed a handful of chips into his mouth. "Think we should eat then have an early night." He winked, changing the subject.

It didn't take a genius to know he was up to something, and in the time they had been married she could suss him out quite easily. Grabbing her plate, she smiled and joined him at the table. Whatever he was planning with Kelly, she would find out eventually.

CHAPTER 19

Gypsy and John Jo stared out of the window watching the comedy unfold outside. Duke was teaching his daughter, Millie, to drive. The crunching of the gears had first caught their attention. They both laughed as the pickup truck bunny-hopped into the side of Duke's Transit van, creating a loud bang. Millie then jumped out, shouted at Duke, slammed the door, and then the headlight fell to the ground. A roar of laughter came from outside as people had gathered to watch.

"Jaysus, poor man." John Jo laughed, turning towards Gypsy. "Well, that's the entertainment over… What do you fancy doing today?"

"You not working?" she asked, surprised.

Even though guarding Millie was the job, he still slipped away to do other things. What, she wasn't sure of.

"No, today I'm all yours." He grabbed her hand and guided her onto his lap. Holding her tightly so she couldn't get away, he nibbled at her neck, his cock hardening immediately.

"John Jo!" She gasped.

Pleased that he affected her the same way she did him, he continued kissing around her face and planting his lips on hers. "I love you, Gypsy Ward," he murmured against her mouth. Then carried her to the bed.

***

Gypsy glanced at John Jo; he was asleep. Gently moving his arm off her, she pushed the covers back slowly, careful not to wake him. Her feet barely touched the floor before strong arms wrapped around her waist, dragging her back down.

"Where do you think you're going?" he muttered.

"I was going to put the kettle on," she said softly.

"Wait, I want to talk to you." He propped himself up, shifting to sit beside her. "Paul's arranging a fight, it's—"

"So that was the business last night." A knot built in the pit of her stomach. Although she knew he was a good fighter, she didn't think she would ever get used to seeing John Jo in the ring. He had won all the fights she had been to, but that didn't mean he had never been injured. Black eyes, split lips, a ripped shoulder, the list went on. "So he wants you to fight?"

"It's good money, Gypsy—"

"Money isn't everything," she snapped before she could stop herself.

"Money is what gives us this lifestyle. You have whatever you want, remember that." Annoyance tinged his voice.

She knew when to back down, the edge in his voice a warning. Instead of staying for a full-blown argument, she slipped on her clothes and left him there, going to put the kettle on.

She busied herself getting the cups out. John Jo was moving around the bed. He was obviously getting dressed.

"I'm going out," he told her as he tugged on his boots.

"I thought we were spending the day together?" she asked, glancing in his direction.

"I've got things to do." With that, he left, slamming the door behind him.

A loud sigh left her mouth. With slumped shoulders, she watched the truck reverse out and drive away. She had never been a lonely person, but in that instant she felt lonelier than ever. She placed the teacups back in the cupboard and grabbed her coat. After slipping her shoes on, she headed over to see Patience.

"Come in, Gypsy, before you let all the heat out," the old woman called before she had opened the door.

"How did you know it was me?" Gypsy asked, surprised. "I hadn't even knocked."

"It's the gift. Now I'm more interested to know what's wrong with you?"

Patience stared deep into her eyes, and Gypsy's face heated up.

"I've come to see how you are," Gypsy said.

"Rubbish, something's on your mind, girl, now what is it?"

"Is this what my life is going to be? Isolated and lonely...? I thought my life was bad enough before, but now if I say the wrong thing, John Jo gets the nark with me. When is it going to get better?" Gypsy plonked herself down onto the bunk and clasped her hands in her lap.

"Do you love him?" Patience asked.

"What. Of course I love him, he's my husband." Gypsy stood. "I shouldn't have come here."

"Sit down, Gypsy, you came here for a reason. Now tell me what's happened."

"Paul Kelly has arranged a fight for John Jo. It's going to make us a lot of money, but I don't care about money. I care about my husband, and I don't trust that Paul Kelly. There's something off about him," Gypsy added.

"You're right not to trust him, he loves the money and power too much, but—"

"But. There is no but," Gypsy snapped.

"Let me finish, girl… John Jo is a proud man, like all Irish Travelling men. It's not good for his wife to doubt him. You need to support him. He will know when something is wrong. Have a little faith."

"And in the meantime, I sit on my own and worry. This is no life for a woman." She swiped at her eyes as the tears started to fall.

Patience's hand rested on her shoulder.

"Your life is just beginning. Before you know it, you will have a family and there'll be no time to worry. Now get yourself home. He'll be back soon with his tail between his legs."

***

It had been an hour and half since John Jo had stormed out. So much for being back soon. Gypsy switched the portable TV off and knelt in front of the fire. Opening the door, she poked at the half-burnt log and placed another on top. It was cold outside, but the trailer was toasty. A loud crash made her jump. Darting towards the door, she threw it open and stared at the huge pile of logs John Jo had tipped off the back of his truck.

"This should see us okay for a couple of weeks." He grinned, as though they hadn't rowed. "I've got four bags of coal for night-time, too."

Gypsy stood on the step and glared. *Typical fucking man. Acts as though nothing has happened.* She glanced at Duke's trailer. Millie was watching them from the window, spying.

"Nosy malt."

"What?" he asked, scratching his head.

"Nothing. I'll put the kettle on while you move that lot." She turned and went back in, pulling the door shut.

"Hang on." He yanked the door back open. "I got you these, too."

She glanced at the bouquet in his hand. "You didn't have to do that."

"No, I didn't, but I wanted to. Listen, Gypsy, it's my job to look after you, to make sure you have food to eat, clothes to wear, and a roof over your head. You may not like the way I do it, but it's the only way I know." He thrust the flowers towards her. "I got you these because I love you and I always will."

CHAPTER 20

It was a bright but cold day. PJ watched the horses frolicking in the field. Even in this weather they would run around. Maybe to keep warm. He stared at Thunder, his father's new Cob. He was a magnificent horse. His cock hung between his hind legs, swinging back and forth. He was surprised it didn't snap off with the cold.

PJ's thoughts turned to Sam. It was the first time a man had sucked his cock, and as ashamed as he felt, and as wrong as he knew it was, he'd still liked it. The image of Sam's mouth swallowing him whole aroused him in a way that being with a woman never had.

"I'm not gay," he mumbled.

"What, boy?" Paddy asked, joining him.

"Nothing," he replied.

The sound of a motor driving in had them both turning to the gate.

"Tommy Lee's home." Paddy grinned. "This will make your mother happy."

The motor trundled to a stop, and he jumped out. Tommy Lee was the one person PJ could talk to, but how could he tell him this? In fact, how could he tell anyone?

Maeve came rushing out of the mobile, her smile lighting up her hard weatherbeaten face. She wrapped her arms around her son.

"You're strangling me, Mother." Tommy Lee pushed her away. "How is everyone?"

"I'm more interested in knowing how you are. Come inside, I'll put the kettle on."

He followed his mother in. Paddy and PJ followed.

"So how long are you back for?" she asked. Was she hopeful he'd stay?

"I'll be here for Christmas."

His mother's face lit up.

"So what have I missed, other than the shite at the wedding?" He laughed. Sean Paul had told him all about it.

He took a peek at PJ. He looked in a world of his own. He was obviously troubled. Did he miss Violet, or was something else going on?

"I don't want to hear about that wedding, I've never known such a disaster. The embarrassment of that poor girl, getting shat on." Maeve shook her head. "She'll be lucky if she finds a husband after that."

Tommy Lee eyed PJ who showed no emotion. If anything, his head was miles away.

"PJ, come show me the horses." Tommy Lee stood and left the mobile.

PJ followed. They stomped across the muddy ground in silence. Once they reached the fence, Tommy Lee turned to him.

"Are you going to tell me what's going on?"

***

Gypsy sat with Patience, both sipping tea. "Can't believe how cold it is after the heatwave."

"Nature has to balance itself out, girl," Patience said.

"I guess so... That girl, Millie, she comes to see you a lot."

"She's troubled."

"Is troubled another word for miserable?" Gypsy laughed.

"You shouldn't laugh. The girl's got a lot to deal with." Patience placed her cup down and turned to Gypsy. "You two will be close one day. Family."

"What?"

"She's with the wrong man. The universe has a way of making everything right, just trust me." Patience motioned to the door. "You need to get back, John Jo will be waiting."

***

Tommy Lee unpacked his things into his parents' vardo. He wouldn't sleep in the mobile, he needed his own space. He was still mulling over the conversation he'd had with PJ. He knew he wasn't telling him the truth. Something else was going on, but what could be so bad that he couldn't tell him? Where John Jo and Sean Paul had always been close, he and his youngest sibling had also been.

"Mother said dinner will be twenty minutes, she's made an Irish stew," PJ called from the door.

"Come in, you can get the fire started for me while I finish unpacking. So this gorja who's had your baby, you still not seen her?"

"No."

"And you're okay with that?" Tommy Lee asked, a bit surprised. "If it was my child, I'd want to see it... Do you know what she had?"

"No." PJ placed the kindling into the log burner and stuffed some coal on top. "This should keep you nice and toasty."

Was he putting on a brave face or did he really not care?

"I know you've had a tough year, what with the wedding and all, but—"

"Look, Tommy Lee, I know you mean well, but that's all in the past and best it stays there." PJ lit the match and placed it into the screwed-up paper. The flames rose and caught the kindling. "There, all done. I'll see you inside."

Tommy Lee watched him leave. There was something different about him. He'd shut down. Whatever was going on with him, it was more serious than he had first thought.

**

Paddy stood and reached for his coat. "Come on, boys, let's go and have a pint together."

Tommy Lee joined him at the door. "You coming, PJ?"

He shook his head. "Not tonight, maybe tomorrow, I've got a few things to take care of." He put his head down, knowing they would all see he was lying. That was one thing he wasn't good at. His mother always said he was like an open book, she only had to look at him to know if he was telling the truth.

"See you in the morning then," Paddy muttered. "Maeve, we won't be late."

"How many times have I heard that?" she joked. "Just don't wake me up when you come crashing through the door."

PJ watched them leave then made his way out to his motor. As he climbed in, his mother called.

"Where are you off to, boy?"

"I told you, I've got some business to sort." He started the engine and drove away.

He kidded himself that he didn't plan on going back to see Sam, but in the back of his mind, it was the only place he wanted to be, the only place he could be himself.

Stopping, just far enough away from the pub so as not to be caught, he waited for the pub to empty, then headed for the door. What would he say after sneaking out on him? Would he want to see him again?

He pushed on the door and rattled the handle, but it was already locked. He turned to walk away when he heard the bolt draw back and the door opened. He was met with a smiling face.

"You coming in then?"

CHAPTER 21

The wind whistled through the cracks in the barn door, rattling the tin walls. Gypsy stuffed her hands deep into her pockets, trying to keep warm. She glanced at John Jo beside her, his jaw tight as he waited for his fight to begin. Sean Paul had driven over; he was always there when his brother fought. Poor Shirley was home with the two children, as usual.

In the ring, Duke was fighting. It looked like he was going to win, despite his beat-up appearance. The crowd roared, voices rising over the wind. She scanned the faces, then stopped. There, slipping towards the back, was the woman called Millie. She seemed distressed. Patience's words echoed in her mind.

You'll be close one day. Family.

Chasing through the crowd, she finally caught up. Millie stopped and leant back against the barn wall with her eyes closed.

"Are you okay?" Gypsy asked.

"I'm fine, thanks," Millie said, opening her eyes.

"My name's Gypsy. I've seen you at the camp."

"Yeah, I've seen you, too, and your husband." Millie gazed at the ground, shifting awkwardly. She appeared uncomfortable. "You're not Irish then?"

"No, but I married an Irish Traveller. I'm a Romani."

"Isn't that the same thing?" Millie glanced up.

"No, Irish Travellers are a different breed. I'm like your dad." Gypsy laughed.

"Paul, that's my husband, his family are Irish, just regular Irish, I guess… So do you live here all the time?"

"No, we're here because of you."

Millie's eyes went wide. "What… Why?"

"John Jo was hired by Duke to watch you. I thought you knew. So were a couple of the others." Had Gypsy fucked up and said the wrong thing?

Shit.

The bell sounded; it was the end of the match.

"It was nice meeting you, Gypsy, I need to find my mum, Connie." Millie sauntered away without another word.

God, she was hard work. Was Patience sure about her prediction, because Gypsy couldn't see them ever becoming friends, never mind family.

***

Paddy was on his fifth pint while Tommy Lee sipped at his second. He didn't mind going to the pub, he just didn't like getting pissed up. He had always been the sensible one, the quiet one. Noticing all the things the others missed.

The tobacco smoke hung in the air like a thick fog, and the noise of the Travellers almost deafening. It reminded him of his army days. You'd work hard and play harder, and when the men all got to let their hair down, all carnage would break loose. He smiled; he had some great memories of those days. Would he go back? No. The work he did now was much more lucrative. He could earn in a couple of hours what the army paid him for a month, plus the benefits of working for wealthy men also paid dividends. The beautiful women, fast cars, and expensive restaurants were all an added bonus. But something was missing from his life, and he wasn't sure what that was.

He glanced at his father, his hands animated as he told one of his stories to the listening crowd, while also slopping his pint all over the place. Tommy Lee waited for him to finish and the raucous laughter to die down before he grabbed his attention.

"Father, have you noticed anything different about PJ?" He wasn't going to broach the subject, but there was definitely something wrong.

"No, boy, he's probably got himself another girl, you know what he's like," he said, almost scornfully. "Talking about girls, don't you think it's time you settled down?"

"When I meet the right girl, I will. Until then, I'm going to work hard and enjoy my life, and while I do, you and Mother need to watch PJ. Something's not right with him."

"He's fine, stop worrying," Paddy said.

Knowing when to give up, Tommy Lee decided it would be the last time he'd mention it. The only course of action left would be to follow him and find out what he was up to.

***

John Jo held his hands up in triumph. That was another win and with it a nice little payout. He handed the money to Gypsy. "Put that in your bag, I'll go and get changed."

"I'm going to make tracks. I don't like Shirley and the boys being on their own at night," Sean Paul told him. "I'll see you when you're home."

John Jo nodded while pulling on his trousers. "I'll be back soon, there's no way I'll be spending Christmas here, especially if big brother has blessed us with his presence." He laughed.

"Talking about Tommy Lee, he asked me what's up with PJ. Have you noticed anything odd going on?"

"Like what?" John Jo pulled his jumper over his head. "We don't see him as much now we've moved, but Mother would have said something. You know what she's like, nothing gets past that woman."

"Maybe…"

"What did he say that's got you so worried?"

"It was more how he said it. Anyways, I'll see you when you're back." Sean Paul turned, waved to Gypsy, and walked off.

John Jo was left standing there with the sinking feeling of guilt. It was true, they didn't see much of PJ now. That would change when they got home. Maybe he'd like to stop on their ground rather than being stuck with Mother and Father. He sighed. PJ had coped with a wedding that had gone tits up and a baby he'd never see. That had to be tough. And here he was, at Paul Kelly's beck and call while, if what Tommy Lee had said was true, his little brother was struggling.

"Are you ready?" Gypsy asked, tugging him from his thoughts.

"Yeah." He grabbed her around her waist and drew her tight to his body.

"You stink, man, get off." She giggled and punched him playfully.

He stared down into her eyes and felt the stirring in his loins. He was lucky to have her. "I've decided I'm not fighting for Kelly. In fact, I won't be dealing with him again after this is done."

Her face lit up, and he knew he had made the right decision. He would just need to find another source of income that paid as well.

CHAPTER 22

Tommy Lee kept a close eye on PJ for the next few days, watching his every move. Did he know? Possibly, he was being very cagey. His mood was up and down, too, he wasn't the joyful younger brother he knew and loved. He'd also started to lose interest in the horses.

Could he be on drugs?

He mooched over to where PJ stood leaning against the fence. He was staring into the distance. Did he wish he was somewhere else?

"Penny for them?" Tommy Lee called while joining him. "You look a million miles away."

"Just thinking about life and how things might have been different."

"Do you miss Violet?"

Could that be it? He should've been married now, then his life would most certainly have been different.

"No. Think I had a lucky escape, and with the baby… I'm not fit to be a husband or a father." PJ straightened. "Take no notice of me." He smiled. "I'm just feeling sorry for myself."

"How about we go into town after dinner and get a couple of girls to pass the time with?" Tommy Lee winked.

"Not tonight, I'm not in the mood, maybe tomorrow." PJ put his head down and ambled across the grass to his trailer like he was off to a funeral.

Tommy Lee scratched his head. Every other time he had returned home, his little brother had been the happiest to see him. Now it was like he didn't exist. Was it because he'd been away so much or was it because he had grown up?

The sound of a motor made Tommy Lee spin around. Sean Paul was driving in. Shirley Ann was with him, which meant the children would be, too. Once he had pulled the motor to a stop, he jumped out and made his way towards him.

"Evening." Sean Paul glanced at PJ who was climbing into his trailer. "How's he been?" he asked with a flick of his head.

"The same… Anyways, what's happing?" Tommy Lee swiftly changed the subject. He wasn't about to let on anything until he knew what was going on in PJ's head.

"John Jo will be home soon. He's not staying much longer whether the job's done or not… He's looking forward to beating you at darts." Sean Paul sniggered.

"Well, he ain't beat me yet, boy, so I don't like his chances." Tommy Lee laughed. This was more like it, a bit of banter between siblings. It had lifted his mood after the depressing chat earlier.

"Right, I need to go and see those nephews of mine." Slapping Sean Paul on the back, he strolled next to him towards their mother and father's mobile. He still planned to follow PJ. Hopefully tonight. Once he knew what he was up to, he could then sort him out.

The evening flew by. Tommy Lee played with his nephews after dinner, and when it was time for Sean Paul and Shirley Ann to go, he carried the boys out, one on each shoulder. PJ had been more his old self, chatting away with Paddy and Maeve. There had been stories told of when the boys were young. Maeve complained that they were a handful, but she had a glint of humour in her eyes as she did so.

"I'm off to me bed," PJ told them. "Goodnight."

"I best get some sleep, too," Tommy Lee added, kissing his mother on her cheek.

She grabbed his arm and smiled. "It's good to have you back, son."

"It's good to be back. I'll see you in the morning." He headed off to the trailer, resting back on the bed. He didn't bother taking his shoes off, he needed to be ready, just in case PJ slipped out again.

It was ten-thirty p.m. when he heard the pickup start up. Peeking through the curtain, he watched PJ reverse out of the ground and turn right. Jumping in his Range Rover, Tommy Lee drove up and followed, keeping his distance. When his brother parked up fifteen minutes later, he pulled in and cut the headlights.

PJ set off on foot. Tommy Lee watched him from the motor until he disappeared from view. Starting the engine, he drove along the road slowly until he caught sight of him walking towards a pub. A soft glow came from one window downstairs. When the door opened a man appeared, he then stepped back, allowing PJ in.

Tommy Lee frowned. It didn't appear like a lock-in. The place seemed deserted. There were no other vehicles about, and why did PJ leave his truck so far away?

Tommy Lee sat forward when the light went out, the pub plunging into total darkness until a soft glow illuminated from an upstairs window. He wound down the window, for a better view, when the silhouettes of two men stood close together. One reached out to touch the other's shoulder. Were they kissing?

He froze, his breath catching in his throat. Bile filled his mouth which he swallowed down.

"What the feck have you done?" he whispered.

He sat there for a long time, the Range Rover now cold, his breath blowing out like white smoke. A hundred questions filled his head, questions he wasn't ready to face. This was bigger than he'd imagined. So big, if it ever came out, it would change the family forever.

CHAPTER 23

Tommy Lee loaded his things into his Range Rover, his heart heavy to be leaving, but he had no other choice. He needed time away to think. If he told anyone about PJ it would mean murders. He didn't want to be responsible for that, for causing heartache and pain to the family. Now he couldn't even look at him. The thought of what he'd done left a vile taste in his mouth. He knew he was still his brother, and he loved him. He just didn't like him very much at the moment.

"You sure you've got to go, boy?" Maeve asked, her face a picture of true sorrow.

"It's just for a couple of months. I'll be back January, promise." It pained him to lie, but what was the alternative?

She wrapped her arms around him and sighed. "You be good."

"I'm always good, Mother. Now go inside and keep warm. I love you." He climbed into his car and started the engine. Turning his head at the sound of a tap on the window, he sighed.

PJ stood there, like butter wouldn't melt. "You not going to say goodbye?"

Tommy Lee opened the door a fraction, and without looking at him, he spoke quietly. "You need to make better life choices." Then he pulled the door shut and drove away.

PJ stood motionless. Despite the cold, biting wind, a sweat covered him.

Better life choices?

Did he know? No. He couldn't, he would've told. Everyone would know. He'd been careful not to get caught. Was always home before anyone was up. He was worrying for nothing. But a little niggling feeling was now inside his head.

***

John Jo hitched the trailer up to the truck. He couldn't wait to get home. He'd got his money from Paul last night and now he was off. He glanced over to Patience's wagon. Despite it needing a touch-up, it was in pretty good nick.

"I'm getting myself one of them." He nodded to Gypsy. "It can stand out the front, and then the children can have it to play with, all six of them."

"Six?" she said, resting her hand on her belly. "Wait and see how much trouble this one is first before you go getting any ideas."

"He'll be an angel, just like his father." He laughed. Even he would admit he was a little sod growing up.

"Hmm." She rolled her eyes. "That's not what your mother says."

"Right, get in the truck, darling, I'm taking you home." He climbed in next to her.

She always looked pretty to him, but now she was carrying his child, he thought she was beautiful, in a way he couldn't put into words. He wanted to give her the best of everything.

"I was thinking, maybe it's time we get a mobile like Father's."

"Really?" Her face lit up like a child at Christmas.

"Yep, really. We can go and have a look at the weekend. We need to make sure we get the one we want, though, I'm not buying any old crap." He was pleased. He had made her happy. On the downside, he could do with getting more money in and fast. Having bought the bit of ground, he didn't have as much left as he wanted, so with that thought in his head, he set of back to Wickford.

The journey there was slow, and he had difficulty seeing the road because of the rain. The windscreen wipers were working overtime, causing little difference. He wondered if the damn weather would ever change.

When they reached the town, he stopped at the chippy and loaded up with piping-hot food, his stomach rumbling from the smell. He handed the food to Gypsy while glancing at the bank. It was in total darkness. The thought of all that money sitting in there made him smile. Could that be the answer to all his problems?

***

Tommy Lee slid the key into the lock, opened the door, and stepped into his sterile, impersonal hotel room. It was plush, as always, with his line of work. The men who employed him had pots of money and made sure everyone knew it. He, on the other hand, although not as wealthy, hid what he did have. He was taught to keep all of his personal information to himself. His bank balance being one of them. "Don't let your left hand know what your right hand is doing," his father always told him, and that was his number one rule. Everything work wise and money wise was kept to himself.

He would have much preferred to be in his trailer, with his family around and looking forward to Christmas. He sat heavily on the bed, running his hand over his face. His mind flicked back to PJ; it was his fault. There were lines unspoken that you never crossed, yet his younger brother had. A wave of shame, disgust, and guilt accompanied the thoughts. Tommy Lee had always prided himself on loyalty to the family, but how could he be loyal to them all? If this came out, his mother and father would disown PJ, and there was no telling what John Jo and Sean Paul would do.

Should he have stayed? Most probably. Could he have stayed? No. He was certain he had done the right thing. But what if they found out in his absence, and he wasn't there to calm things down? It was a risk he was willing, no, he had to take. He needed the distance. He needed to come to terms with the knowledge he'd learned. He loved his brother, and there was a part of him that felt ashamed for running, but the other part told him he was right.

Tommy Lee had never been big on self-reflection. The world of security work, of keeping people safe from external threats, had left him unprepared for the kind of inner vulnerability that he was fighting inside. His job for the next couple of weeks, a short contract protecting some bigwig arsehole, was a welcome distraction.

He stood and walked into the bathroom. Staring at his reflection in the mirror, he searched his face for answers, but none came.

The knock on the door startled him. He had never been jumpy in his life, always took things in his stride and faced things head-on, calmly. He shook his head, clearing the storm inside that was building, and headed to the door.

"Mr Ward. Your employer has arrived and is waiting downstairs in the bar for you."

Tommy Lee nodded and closed the door. Although his head remained heavy, this was the distraction he needed. He had a job to do, his own personal crisis would have to wait.

CHAPTER 24

John Jo kissed Gypsy then watched her leave the trailer. He had persuaded her to go and have a chat with Shirley Ann, his brother's wife. The trailer door creaked as she left. Twenty minutes later, Sean Paul appeared.

"You took your time," John Jo said while handing him a beer.

"The children were playing up, so I got them settled first. Anyway, what is it you want that's so secretive?" He pulled off the bottle cap.

"Take a seat… Now you know buying this bit of land took most of our cash, plus now we're not working for Kelly we are running low on funds." He paused, waiting for a response. Sean Paul gave him a nod but said nothing. "Well, what do you reckon to making a lot of money in one night?"

"Go on."

"A bank job." John Jo watched Sean Paul's eyes widen. "Not here, another town," he added.

"You're serious!" Sean Paul gulped at his beer. Was he lost for words?

"I've been thinking about this for the last week, this isn't some drunken idea. I have it all planned," John Jo eagerly explained.

"You've got to know this ain't easy. You're talking about a bank. They have alarms, and when the alarms go off, the police actually show up."

"That's why we need to do it right." John Jo drained his beer and reached for another. Cracking it open, he took a long swig. "I've scouted out a bank in Chelmsford. The manager's a lazy sod, and the interior looks like it needs updating."

Sean Paul shook his head, but there was a glint in his eye. "And what, you think the two of us can pull it off?"

John Jo hesitated. "I've been thinking about Tommy Lee."

Sean Paul's face darkened. He set his beer down with a loud thud. "Tommy Lee, are you mad?"

"Listen," John Jo said quickly, leaning forward. "He's the smartest of us all. You know it, I know it, and if anyone can figure this out, he can. The safe, the getaway, it's him."

"He's got his life all sorted, whatever these jobs are he does for a living. Do you really think he'd risk all that for a bank job? Pass us another beer." Sean Paul flopped back. "Anyway, what if he says no?"

"Then we'll do it without him, but I'm telling you, with Tommy Lee's help, we've got a real shot of pulling this off. Now drink up, Gypsy will be back soon." John Jo grinned, his head full of beer and easy money.

***

Gypsy stood ready to leave. "I've got a bad feeling, Shirley Ann, I think our husbands are up to no good." She wasn't going to mention it, but it had been niggling at her since John Jo had insisted she go see Shirley Ann.

"No good, like other women?" She gasped.

"No. I mean they're up to something. I can always tell when John Jo's plotting and scheming. His been different since we came back last week." She looked at Shirley Ann who now seemed worried.

Shit.

"Take no notice of me, I'm sure whatever they are up to they'll tell us eventually. Right, I'll see you tomorrow."

As she mooched back to her own trailer, her thoughts were firmly on John Jo and his actions of late. He was always deep in thought. She hoped whatever it was he was planning wouldn't affect them all.

***

It was pitch-black up the lane, no streetlamps to brighten the way to their driveway, just the headlights of the motor. It was on a tight bend; if you didn't know where it was you would miss it. PJ ground the motor to a halt, allowing his father to get out. He had taken him to the pub up the road and was now dropping him back after closing.

"Where are you off to, boy?" Paddy slurred.

"I'm off to see a girl, Father, I'll see you in morning." The lies rolled of PJ's tongue easier these days. He wasn't proud of that fact, but needs must.

"See you in the morning." Paddy waved and then staggered to his door.

PJ reversed out and continued along the road, the excitement already building inside him. He had fought many demons lately, but he wasn't going to fight anymore. He wanted to see Sam, and as long as he was careful, he could continue. He stopped down the road as normal, hiding the motor out of sight, and carried on by foot.

The pub came into view. PJ smiled. It was in darkness, but he knew Sam would be waiting. He stopped and looked around, making sure there were no prying eyes. Once content, he sneaked around the back. The gate had a latch on the other side. Instead of reaching for it, he hauled himself up onto the wall, then lowered himself down the other side. As he approached the door, he slowed. It was ajar. Was that for him?

"Sam?" he called, his voice hesitant. Something wasn't right. He pushed the door open. It creaked loudly in the dead of night. A sinking feeling settled in the pit of his stomach. He stepped over the threshold and slowly entered the kitchen.

"Sam?" he called again, but there was no reply. He moved through to the bar area and froze. The moonlight shone through the windows, highlighting the overturned tables and chairs. Broken glass glistened on the bar. His heart pounded as his gaze darted around the room. Then he saw him. Slumped against the far wall, his head hanging forward. He moved quickly and knelt next to him.

"Sam?" He smelt the blood before he noticed he was kneeling in it, his trousers now soaking in the metallic liquid.

"Shit." His chest tightened.

He panicked. He knew he needed to call for help, but he also knew he couldn't be found here. This was what happened to his sort. This was what would happen to him.

"I'm sorry," he whispered. Standing, he fled the scene without looking back.

***

Tommy Lee slipped back into the party unseen. He hated these occasions, mixing with men who thought they were better than God and the women so desperate for attention they had their bodies on show.

The suite the sheik had hired was fit for a king, with its gold taps and granite tops. Everything was crafted down to the finest detail in this place. Unlike his room, this had a master bedroom at one end with a large en suite bathroom and a walk-in wardrobe. A lounge, overlooking London, which was large enough for the lavish parties he hosted. Money really was no object for this man.

Did he value it, though? No.

The three waitresses handed out the drinks topless, and the women guests, feeling they were being upstaged, had theirs out, too. He could understand the waitresses doing it, it was for a bigger wage, however, there was no need for the others to. They had no dignity, and in his eyes, they weren't appealing at all.

"Well, hello," a brunette slurred. She walked up to him and ran her hand across the cheeks of his arse, giving them a rough squeeze.

His stomach turned at the sheer audacity. He wanted a woman he could chase, not some desperate tart who was looking for a meal ticket.

He smiled down at her. She would still do as a distraction tonight, especially in bed.

CHAPTER 25

PJ opened the stable door, the sharp frosty air biting at his fingers. He let the horses out one at a time. It was only six-thirty a.m., but after yet another sleepless night he needed a distraction. Today he would muck out, a job he normally hated, but he needed to keep busy. It had been a week since he had found Sam. He had no way of knowing if he was okay. The pub was now closed with police tape outside because it was a crime scene.

He picked up the pitchfork and started to shovel the straw and horse shit into a barrow. He was on autopilot while his brain continued to worry. He had replayed every scenario in his head. What if the attacker had caught them both, would he have been able to fight him off or would he now be in hospital, too? Should he have stayed with him until the ambulance got there? That's what a decent human being would have done.

Don't be stupid. Everyone would find out your dirty secret.

He wiped the sweat from his brow, not knowing if it was caused by the strenuous work or his shame.

"PJ. Tea's ready," Maeve called from the mobile doorway.

For a moment he hesitated. He didn't want to be around anyone, least of all his family. Would they know, could they tell? With a sigh, he leant the pitchfork against the stable wall. He needed to get a grip. If he didn't then they would find out. He had to act normal, otherwise he could draw attention to himself.

He stepped into the mobile after slipping his boots off. It was warm and welcoming. The smell of bacon filled his nostrils; it was better than the horse shit he'd just been sniffing. He threw his coat over a chair.

"Come and take a seat, boy," Paddy told him. "I'm thinking of buying a couple of mares next year to start breeding with Blaze."

PJ nodded, his gaze resting on the local paper. He stared at the bold print. His heart stopped briefly as he read the heading. *Landlord Murdered in Pub.*

"Dunno what the world's coming to," Paddy said, following his gaze. He then picked up the paper. "I know he was a wrongun; maybe this is God's punishment."

PJ forced himself to nod, as if he agreed with him. He wondered if his father would feel the same if it was his son.

"You're awful quiet and you're looking a bit peaky," Maeve remarked. "You sure you're all right?"

"Yeah, just tired," PJ replied. "I best get on and finish mucking out." Without waiting for a reply, he grabbed his coat and rushed to the door. Slipping on his boots, he marched back to the stable. The cold air stung his lungs as he gulped it in; it was a pathetic attempt to hold himself together. Once inside, he leant against the wall for fear of his legs giving way, then crumpled into a heap with tears running down his cheeks.

***

Tommy Lee jumped out of his motor. It was now December. He had been away just over two weeks and felt ready to face PJ.

The mobile door burst open. Maeve's face appeared, then she came bounding towards him. "What you doing here?"

"Thought I'd surprise you." He grinned. "I'm staying for Christmas."

"Oh, praise be to God, I'll have all my boys with me." She beamed. "Come in, and I'll put the kettle on. Your father's sitting by the fire."

Following her in, he scanned the area for any sign of PJ. He would have that chat with him sooner rather than later. The air needed to be cleared so they could all enjoy Christmas.

PJ peeked out of the trailer window, spying silently on his brother. Whilst Tommy Lee had always been the one he could talk to, things had changed. Especially since the comment he had made when leaving last time.

Make better life choices.

PJ had kidded himself, pretending it was about something else, but no, of course it was about Sam. Would Tommy Lee have it out with him, or would it never be spoken of again? Buried, just like his lover's body. His mouth twisted into a bitter smile.

He slid down onto the bunk, lost in his thoughts until a loud knock broke the silence. He hesitated, then grudgingly stood to open the door.

"What do you want?" PJ said aggressively.

Tommy Lee pushed the door open wider. "To talk." He stepped in without waiting for an invitation, his presence dominating the room.

"Well, go on then, spit it out," PJ said, eyes full of resentment.

"Drop the fecking attitude." Tommy Lee sat on the bunk opposite and glared. "I know everything. I followed you to the pub, I saw you kiss…a man."

"And you're ashamed of me. I get it, don't you think I'm ashamed, too?" He dropped his head into his hands.

"PJ. This isn't about shame. This is about the family. Mother. I will not have that woman hurt, boy, she's been through enough in her life already. Don't you care about anyone but yourself?"

"Do you think I enjoy this…feeling this way…not being normal?" PJ stood and walked to the door. "I think you should go now."

"For your own sake, if you choose to live like this, you gotta hide it. Drive way out where no one knows you. I don't understand it, it turns my stomach, but you are my brother, and I'll keep this secret… Just remember this, if it comes out, I'll not be able to protect you, PJ, you'll be on your own."

The trailer fell silent apart from the faint creaking as it shifted in the wind.

After a few minutes he responded. "I'm on my own anyway. The one person I could talk to is dead…"

"That could be you next time." Tommy Lee left, closing the door firmly behind him.

PJ stared into space, trying to make sense of his last words.

That could be you next time.

Strange. He didn't ask who he was talking about.

"No…"

The harsh reality of Tommy Lee's words hit him. Had he killed Sam?

CHAPTER 26

Tommy Lee was relieved. Christmas had been a relatively quiet job so far. PJ had kept his head down and stayed out of trouble. No drama, no distractions. Just the way he liked it.

Now, it was time to move on. His next job was waiting in the Costa del Sol — better known these days as the Costa del Crime, thanks to the wave of British villains hiding out there, dodging the Old Bill. It was a four-week gig, babysitting an ex-con named Benny the Blade. The name alone told him everything he needed to know. This prick had a habit of slicing people up.

Normally, Tommy wouldn't go near a job like this. He had standards. But the money was too good to pass up, plus he had worked many times for this particular employer, and the money was always paid without any quibble.

"Can I have a word?" John Jo asked, while stepping up into the trailer.

"Take a seat." Tommy Lee motioned with his head. "What's it about?"

"How would you like to make a lot of money quickly?" John Jo grinned.

"How much money, and by doing what?" He wasn't daft, he could see the pound note signs in John Jo's eyes. As a general rule, if he thought it was easy money it meant there was a high chance it was illegal and carried a hefty prison sentence, if caught.

"I've found a bank—" John Jo began.

"*No,*" Tommy Lee snapped.

"You haven't heard me out."

"John Jo, your wife is expecting a baby in a few months. You really want to gamble your freedom for a bit of easy money?"

"Money's been tight lately… I promised Gypsy we'd get a mobile like Father's. Trouble is, there won't be much left after."

"You shouldn't promise things until you're in a position to carry them out," Tommy Lee warned him. "What happened to the money you earnt from guarding that woman?"

"That's stashed."

"I've got a job abroad, gotta leave in a two days. They need more men if you're interested. It's four weeks, and the pay's good." The words came out before he had a chance to think it through.

"What about Sean Paul?" John Jo asked.

"I'll get him on board, too."

"That's a long time to leave Gypsy and Shirley Ann."

Tommy Lee sighed. Did he have to sort everything out? "Pull the trailers here while you're gone. Mother will love having the children here, and they'll be safe and have company. Now I need to know if you're interested so I can make the arrangements."

"Sign us up, boy." John Jo grinned and slapped him on the back.

Tommy Lee rolled his eyes. He had a feeling he may regret this.

***

PJ sat on the edge of his bed, his body tense, his mind racing. He hadn't meant to eavesdrop, but Tommy Lee's sudden shout, 'NO!' had stopped him in his tracks. He'd then lingered while the conversation between Tommy Lee and John Jo unfolded. He was still on edge in case his brother let out his secret. But as it turned out, they were all going away to work and he would be left here.

The world was becoming increasingly hostile. He didn't fit in, not even with his own family. The fear of rejection, of being cast out by them, had become a familiar feeling. He wiped the tears that trickled down his cheeks. Music played from an old radio that sat on the table. Once upon a time it brought him comfort, but not now. He knew no one would accept him, his preference for men was a death sentence, not only in his community, but in the world at large.

He wanted it to stop, the thoughts, the desires, the loneliness. It was a pain so deep inside that he knew it would never go away unless he made it.

He could stop the hurting, the pain, he could end it. He reached for the pills. Would that be enough? Grabbing a handful, he stared down at them, his mouth slowly opening.

"What the feck do you think you're doing?" Tommy Lee roared as he entered the trailer. He smacked PJ's hand away, the pills scattering over the floor.

"Leave me alone." PJ's voice broke a little more with each word.

"I won't leave you alone... Jaysus, PJ." Tommy Lee rubbed his hand over his face. "You don't ever do that, do you hear me?" He grabbed PJ and wrapped his arms around him. "You talk to me."

"I can't, I can't talk to anyone." PJ sobbed.

"Look at me, PJ." Tommy Lee pulled back and stared into his eyes. "Nothing is worth taking your own life over."

PJ's face was filled with pain, his eyes deep pools of misery. Tommy Lee now had a dilemma. There was no way he could go to Spain. Not now.

CHAPTER 27

The four brothers stepped onto the tarmac. Tommy Lee could see they weren't impressed.

"Thought it was gonna be hotter," John Jo moaned.

"It's January, and besides, it's still warmer than home. Come on, we need to get our cases." Tommy Lee glanced at PJ.

He hadn't said much during the flight, but he looked better than he had a few days ago. Tommy Lee marched off with his three brothers in tow. He felt like their father, keeping them all in check. Maybe it was time he took a wife and settled down himself. A nice woman to keep his bed warm at night. Who was he kidding, he was not the marrying kind. No woman had ever caught his eye who he could be faithful to. He may well fancy one, but that wasn't enough. He wanted — no, he needed — a challenge. A woman who would keep him on his toes. Trouble was, they just didn't exist.

He collected his case and watched Sean Paul running around the luggage carousel.

"Jaysus, my case is going." He panted.

Tommy Lee decided not to tell him it would reappear, preferring to laugh at his expense.

Once the four of them had their belongings, they headed to the exit.

"Someone should be here to meet us," Tommy Lee said, scanning the area.

"Mr Ward?" a young Spanish man asked.

Tommy Lee nodded, then followed to an old beat-up estate. He glanced at John Jo who was still moaning.

"Travelling in style, I see."

"Keep your fecking voice down. Remember, I know these people. I've worked for them before, and they don't take kindly to loudmouths." Tommy Lee opened the door and climbed into the front before he really lost his rag.

It was only a thirty-five-minute drive from Malaga airport to the villa where they would be working. There was also guest accommodation on site, separate from the main building. They were shown to their quarters and left to unpack and unwind after the journey.

"Feck, boys, we have a bar," Sean Paul said from the lounge.

"And a swimming pool," PJ added.

"Maybe it ain't so bad after all." John Jo grinned. "Who wants a drink?"

"I need to go see the boss. Yous stay here and, for feck sake, don't get drunk." Tommy Lee walked out into the sunshine.

Although it was January, it was like a glorious spring day here, which was his favourite season. Everything came to life this time of year. He followed the path up to the main house. It was dotted with palm trees either side and giant urns full of foliage. Large buds adorned the greenery that would flower in the next few weeks.

He kept his head down as he approached the main building, his thoughts flickering to PJ on and off. He was certain the Spaniard had been eyeing up his little brother. It wouldn't have mattered so much here, but while John Jo and Sean Paul were about, PJ would have to watch himself. He didn't know what they would do if they found out his secret. Maybe mock, bully, or worse. He himself had wanted to give him a hiding, but what good would that do other than give him another reason to end his life? He shook the dark thoughts from his head, put a big smile on his face, and burst through the patio doors, ready to sort business.

***

The villa's dining room was large with a high ceiling. The floors were tiled as all the rooms were. It helped keep it cool in the summer months. It had floor-to-ceiling windows that you could view the sea from. The cook had prepared their meal, and it was laid out on a long table.

The men sat and gazed at the food. A large paella sat proud in the middle, steam drifting upwards. Fresh seafood platters were placed either side, a wooden bowl of Spanish bread at one end and a wooden bowl of fresh fruit at the other. Oil and vinegar accompanied the bread. Bottles of red and white wine, uncorked, had been placed on the sideboard.

"Fecking hell, Tommy Lee, I can see why you love this type of work," John Jo mumbled through a mouthful of bread. "Food's fecking amazing."

Tommy Lee smiled and glanced at PJ who seemed increasingly uncomfortable. The Spaniard, a tall slender man with dark hair who had an air of Frank Sinatra about him, had picked them up from the airport. He had offered earlier to take PJ into town. John Jo and Sean Paul had thought this was a great idea and egged him on to go. Tommy Lee, though, knew it was a bad idea so offered no encouragement.

"Go easy on the wine. We start work tomorrow, don't forget, we all need to be sharp," he warned them.

They were knocking the drinks back like there was no tomorrow.

"The man will be here midday. We'll go and collect him from the marina."

PJ was picking at his food. Was he worried? His eyes had lit up earlier when he had got the invite. It was like the old PJ was back. But now he had obviously had time to think it through, he also must realise it was a bad idea. He sighed. Was it, though? Wouldn't it be better for him to go out, maybe get this silly notion out of his system?

Sean Paul spoke, pulling Tommy Lee from his thoughts.

"I'm going to get my Shirley Ann to make this stuff."

"It's called paella," Tommy Lee told him. "And the bread you keep stuffing in your mouth, John Jo, you dip in the oil." He then turned to PJ. "It might do you good to get out for a couple of hours, go see how the Spanish live. The bars are quiet, not like our pubs."

He noticed the surprise in PJ's eyes, but a slow smile spread across his face.

"Just don't get into any trouble."

"Yeah, don't go getting any girls pregnant. You don't want one of those Spanish nutters after you," John Jo added.

Tommy Lee stiffened at that comment. If only that were a possibility, then he wouldn't have to worry about PJ getting caught and his head bashed in for being a queer.

"Eat up. He said he'd be cleaning the cars till nine, so you haven't long to catch him."

PJ nodded. "I'm full."

"You're a bit keen to get your cock played with." John Jo wiggled his eyebrows.

Sean Paul roared with laughter.

Tommy Lee's jaw tightened. PJ's face had gone red.

"Leave the boy alone."

"What? Just having a laugh." John Jo held his hands up in mock surrender. "To be honest, if I wasn't married, I'd be out with you."

Sean Paul nodded in agreement then turned his attention back to his plate while Tommy Lee followed PJ to the door.

"Be careful," Tommy Lee said softly, then waited for him to leave.

When he went back to the table, his brothers, in their drink-fuelled state, were reminiscing. Sean Paul was recounting the time they had fought a bunch of lads at Appleby. One boy got his jaw broken by

Tommy Lee. John Jo chipped in with the odd detail, exaggerating as usual.

Tommy Lee smiled but wasn't listening, not properly, until Sean Paul piped up again, his voice thick with nostalgia.

"Do you remember that time Father bought us that horse, what was its name…" He scratched his head. "The one we had to sell to pay off that debt?"

"He was called Deisel," Tommy Lee said.

"Yeah…and PJ cried for a week after, couldn't shut him up." John Jo laughed.

Tommy Lee's smile fell. PJ had always been different, even back then. Why hadn't he seen it? He was softer, cared more. It had made him a target on more than one occasion. Was that why he felt he had to protect him? He wasn't weak by any means, he could still throw a punch. He just didn't have that killer instinct that Tommy Lee and the others had.

"He's tougher than you think," he blurted out.

"What's that supposed to mean?" Sean Paul asked with a frown.

He shook his head. "Nothing, I'm just saying he'll be fine."

John Jo refilled the glasses and raised his. "Here's to PJ then. May he find himself a nice Spanish girl to keep him out of trouble."

Tommy Lee clinked his glass and silently prayed that PJ would come home safe and with no more thoughts of men.

CHAPTER 28

Gypsy and Shirley Ann had nipped home to collect post and check on the ground. Gypsy couldn't wait for John Jo to return, it had been the longest nearly four weeks of her life. With only another two days to go, including this one, her mood had improved. She rubbed the baby bump. The little blighter had been kicking for the last hour.

"You okay?" Shirley Ann asked as she slammed the Transit into gear.

"Feels like my insides are bruised. I can't wait for this one to pop out," Gypsy said. "I'll open the gate."

When the motor came to a halt, she opened the door and slid down to the ground. Waddling over to the post box first, she unlocked it and grabbed the letters, then opened the gate and waited for Shirely Ann to drive through.

"Everything seems okay. I'll be glad when the boys are home and we're back here. Never thought I'd miss the place as much as I have," Gypsy said distantly. Thoughts of John Jo filled her head. His cheeky grin, his sparkling eyes, and the way he made her feel loved.

"That's because it's home. What's that letter, the one that looks official?" Shirley Ann pointed.

Gypsy glanced at the front. It was addressed to her husband. Without thinking, she ripped it open and read the first paragraph. She flung her hand to her chest and gasped. "They wants us off."

"Who do?"

"The council, they say we gotta get off," she repeated. "They say they've had complaints."

"Complaints?" Shirley Ann took the letter and scanned it. "Don't worry about this, they can't just kick us off. It'll have to go to court first, and John Jo and Sean Paul will fight it," she reassured her.

Gypsy wasn't so sure, though. Her family had had dealings like this before, and they never ended well. Not for gypsies anyway.

***

In the study, Tommy Lee sat opposite his boss. The rest of the villa was done up in the usual way: porcelain tiles covered the floors, lots of Spanish ornaments adorned the place, but in here it was more sterile. There was nothing of sentimental value. It was purely a room for business. A large mahogany desk and three chairs. There were no shelves or cabinets. No pictures. Just a bad atmosphere.

This man had no morals which set him apart from most of the villains Tommy Lee had dealt with. Death meant nothing to him, he would have someone killed purely for the way they looked at him.

"You're due to fly home tomorrow?" he said in a deep gravelly voice.

Tommy Lee didn't know if he had always spoken like that or if it was his Cuban cigar habit; he was always puffing away on one of those bloody things. "Yes."

"I understand the package has caused you problems?"

By package, he meant Benny the Blade, and yes, he was right. He had been a nightmare the whole four weeks. "Yes, he's uncontrollable."

"I bet you wonder why he's here, why I've taken the time to smuggle him out of England and bring him to safety?"

"It's none of my business, you pay the wages, and I do as you say." Tommy Lee didn't like the way the conversation was going. Was he going to ask him to do something else?

The man eyed him; he looked like he was thinking. "He did a job for me, fucked it up, and I had to rescue him before he said anything detrimental to my wellbeing…unfortunately, with the way he's been acting, he is of no further use to me."

"You want him taken care of."

He nodded. "You're one of the few men I trust, and of course, I will make it worth your while."

"Okay."

"Take him up the mountains, make it look like an accident. I don't need anyone asking questions. Understand?"

"Of course."

"Your money will be here waiting, and it was nice to meet your siblings. I noticed the young one has taken a shine to Carlos."

Tommy Lee winced. If he had noticed, had John Jo and Sean Paul?

"Don't worry. He's quite safe here. Right, I'll let you get on. Oh, and sort it today." He motioned to the door.

That was the end of the conversation.

Tommy Lee traipsed back to the guest villa where Benny the Blade was also staying. The gravel path crunched with each step he took. He would have to make sure PJ stayed. Would Carlos take him out? He could hear Benny before he saw him. His loud mouth and raucous laugh jarred his senses. He found the man irritating. He stepped into the main room and glanced around for PJ.

"Everything okay?" John Jo asked.

"Everything's great," Tommy Lee lied. "Right, who's up for a trip around the mountains?"

"What, we're actually allowed out?" Sean Paul said while pouring a drink.

"It's our last full day, may as well see a bit of the place. Bring the expensive whiskey. PJ, Carlos was looking for you." Tommy Lee grabbed the car keys and strolled out to where the car was. The one they had been allowed to drive when picking up Benny. He waited for them to load in.

"I'm going out to town, I'll see you later," PJ called over.

"Make sure you're back by six p.m.," Tommy Lee told him. Not that he needed to be, he just didn't want him spending any more time away when they were flying home tomorrow morning.

It took forty minutes to get to the highest point of the mountain. Tommy wasn't too sure of the way and relied on his senses more than the map. The road was steep, rocky terrain on one side and a sheer drop the other. His mind was firmly on the job. He had his doubts; doing this in front of his siblings wasn't ideal. What would they think of him? No one knew how he earnt so well. He didn't want them to. This was his personal business, and to be honest, if he'd known this would've been part of the job, he wouldn't have brought them. Could he distract them? Maybe, he'd have to play it by ear.

He pulled up in a little lay-by, pleased that it wasn't the season for tourists. There would be no witnesses, only John Jo and Sean Paul.

"Look at the fucking view, boys," Benny called.

Tommy Lee glanced at John Jo. "Yous wait here," he whispered. He trudged over to the edge and stared down. "Feck, that's a steep drop."

He took a step back and waited for Benny to peer down. When he did, he pushed him, hard, and watched him topple over the edge. A loud, shrill cry carried on the air, almost echoing. He heard footsteps rushing towards him, and when he spun around, John Jo and Sean Paul stood, both ashen-faced and mouths gaping.

"Orders, boys, they need to be followed."

Tommy Lee strode back towards the motor, his brothers beside him. He climbed in and gripped the wheel. John Jo and Sean Paul clambered in, still silent.

Tommy Lee twisted around so he could see both.

"This stays between us."

"I never liked the annoying fecker anyway," John Jo replied. "Come on, we've one last night, then home to see my sweetheart."

CHAPTER 29

The boys had been home a couple of weeks. PJ had stayed on in Spain, much to Tommy Lee's annoyance. It seemed he was having a good time with Carlos. John Jo and Sean Paul thought he had a girl out there, but Tommy Lee knew differently. Maeve had blown her top when the three of them returned without her baby boy. But as he'd told her, he was a grown man and needed to live his life as he wanted. That hadn't gone down too well, but he had other things on his mind. Lately he had a sense of loneliness. He didn't know why, he'd always been content with his own company. Maybe it was because he was getting older, although he wouldn't class twenty-six as old.

John Jo and Sean Paul had been busy with the council, trying to sort out their application to stay. Their father, Paddy, had told them to get a couple of horses to keep on the ground, so that's what they intended to do once the stables were built.

Tommy Lee sat with his father in front of the fire. He sipped his tea while his father read the newspaper. He had been offered another job but wasn't needed for another month or so. He felt restless, like his life was running out while he was just sitting around. He could set up a fight or maybe a poker night, but that was pocket money. He was too used to earning big. He had a bank account, unlike his brothers, not that he kept much money in there. He preferred to stash his cash or invest in gold or land.

Maeve was on the phone. He couldn't hear who she was talking to, but he did catch the odd tut. When she walked back into the room, her gaze was downcast.

"What's happened, woman?" Paddy asked, throwing the paper onto the seat next to him.

"It's Patience, she's died." She held her hand to her chest. "I'll have to tell Gypsy, they're family."

"Wasn't she really old?" Tommy Lee held his breath and waited for the bollocking that was sure to follow.

"That's neither here nor there, and I'll thank you to keep your thoughts to yourself." Maeve rolled her eyes. "Honestly, don't say that at the funeral."

Paddy laughed. "Here lies Patience, it's okay, though, she was really old."

"I expected better from you." She huffed and stormed out of the room.

Tommy Lee settled back into his seat. He'd never liked funerals. He couldn't say it was because of the dead, it was more the fact of being around so many people. Half would be sobbing, and the other half would be pissed up. It was always a bad combination and often led to a fight.

He would go, though, for his mother and the family honour, just like hundreds of other Travellers and gypsies.

He stood and wandered into the kitchen. His mother sat at the table; she still looked mad.

"I'm going to go see John Jo," he said. "I'll let him know what's happened, and he can tell Gypsy."

"Don't you go upsetting that girl," Maeve ordered. "Cos if I find out—"

"Give me some credit. I'll see you later." He grabbed his jacket and left.

He loved his mum, deeply, but she was always nagging and moaning. He couldn't stay there anymore. He needed to get his own place. A flat? No. He didn't want anyone above or below him.

He concentrated on the road and drove out. His mind then returned to his problem. He had a few bits of land dotted around, but would he want to live on his own? No. He would be too isolated.

He indicated and turned into his brothers' ground. It was handy being so close to his parents. With just a ten-minute drive you could get there, with ease, if ever there was an emergency.

"And to what do we owe the pleasure?" John Jo called from the door.

"I need a word." Tommy Lee motioned for his brother to join him.

"What's wrong?"

"It's Patience, she's dead. Thought it best you telling Gypsy."

"You coming in for a cuppa? I'll tell her later, once you've gone." John Jo turned and led the way in.

After greeting Gypsy, Tommy Lee took a seat on the bunk. "I'm thinking of moving. Once PJ's home. I can't live there anymore. I've got Mother watching my every move, Father wanting me to help with the horses. I need to get away."

"Why don't you get a trailer and move here? Be like old times, us boys back together."

"It's worth a thought, but you know I'm away a lot, it'll be only when I'm in the country," Tommy Lee informed him.

"You're a grown man, you can come and go as you please."

He took the cup of tea from Gypsy and grinned. This would be perfect. "Okay." He sipped his tea quickly. Now he knew what he was doing, he could go and find a trailer.

CHAPTER 30

The day of the funeral came. The church was packed to the rafters. Gypsies and Irish Travellers had come together as one to pay their respects and say their goodbyes. The coffin stood proud at the front of the church, adorned with wild flowers. Candles flickered either side, throwing a splash of light on the proceedings.

Tommy Lee glanced up at the stained-glass windows. They had turned the sunlight into an eerie orange glow that rested on the pulpit. He hated churches. Unlike his mother, he wasn't religious. Why would he be when he had seen so much death? He listened to the quiet murmurs of the congregation. He couldn't understand why so many had come, most were scared of Patience. She was a seer, she knew things that no one else did, not all nice. Maybe that was why. They were scared she'd haunt them from the grave. That thought made him smile.

He himself was only here for his mother. It was what they did at times like this, show a united front. He looked up as the priest started speaking. It was the same old drivel. Loved, respected, blah, blah, blah. Why didn't he mention feared? It was at that point he zoned out.

"Tommy Lee," John Jo whispered. "Come on." He stood and edged out of the pew.

Tommy Lee was hot on his tail. He wasn't much of a drinker, but he could do with one now. "Where's the wake?"

"Just up the road, there's a pub with a big room at the back," Gypsy answered.

John Jo caught a young woman who tripped as she stepped in front of him. Her eyes went wide with embarrassment.

"Sorry," she mumbled.

"How are you, Millie?" Gypsy asked, tilting her head around her husband's large frame.

The woman's gaze drifted to Gypsy's swollen belly.

"I'm fine, I-I just need some fresh air." She pushed away from his grasp and practically ran to the exit.

Tommy Lee stared at the woman, her blonde hair, those big blue eyes. There was something striking about her.

"Who was that?" he wondered out loud.

"That. Is trouble, stay away," John Jo snapped. "Gypsy, where are you going?"

"I'm just going to check on her. Make sure she's okay. She was acting odd."

They made their way outside, ready to view the hundreds of floral tributes left in Patience's honour. Tommy Lee kept a look out for the woman, but he didn't see her again. Maybe she had already left.

"Wait!" Gypsy said while squeezing through the crowd. "Didn't think I'd find you amongst all these people."

"Was she okay?" Tommy Lee found himself asking.

"Yeah, I guess it's not nice when your marriage ends. Still, she's better off without him, he wasn't a nice man."

So she's single.

He turned and scanned the sea of faces in the hope of spotting her, his grin broadening. Maybe today wouldn't be so bad.

***

Tommy Lee stood at the bar. He'd caught sight of Millie. She seemed to be knocking the wine back. Did she have a drink problem? He spotted Duke who grabbed her arm and led her to the buffet. Was he telling her off? By the way she shook him off, it certainly looked like it. She shot outside, so Tommy Lee decided to follow.

"You all right there, darling?" he asked in his soft Irish tone.

Millie turned to him. "I'm fine, thanks."

"I saw you run out. I thought you were a damsel in distress." He beamed. "I'm Tommy Lee," he added while holding his hand out.

Glancing back up, she placed her hand in his and almost choked when he kissed the back of it. His smile broadened.

"I'm Millie, now if you don't mind, I need to find my family." She disappeared inside without another word.

He watched her sashay away, annoyed that he couldn't take his eyes off her.

Jaysus, what an arse.

He composed himself and stepped back into the pub. Normally, he had no trouble with women, but this one was either playing hard to get or she wasn't interested.

"Where have you been?" John Jo asked while walking towards him.

"Getting some fresh air. I'm gonna get something to eat." Tommy Lee stood at the table and surveyed the food spread across it. He'd lost his appetite the minute Millie had blown him off.

He glanced over to the other end of the table. She stood there chatting to Duke. When Duke finally walked away, he took his chance and approached her.

"Would you like a drink?"

She looked up, hair partially covering her eyes. He wanted to sweep it away so he could see her properly.

"My dad's just gone to get me one, but thanks for asking." She blushed.

Tommy Lee smiled. This woman was different; she seemed confident, but there was a shyness to her.

"Where do you come from?"

"Stepney. I'm stopping with my mum and dad until I find somewhere to live. Do you live around here?"

"Not far from here. I'm staying on John Jo's land, in Wickford. I work away a lot so haven't really got a home, as such." Why was he giving her so much information?

Because she's easy to talk to.

"Would you like to—" he began.

"Mil, here, take yours," Duke ordered. "Your mother's over there. Go and rescue her from Reuben's wife."

She peeked at Tommy Lee and smiled, raising her eyes to heaven. "Okay, but I'm not getting left with her, the woman don't stop moaning." Millie turned and vanished through the crowd of mourners.

"So how have you been?" Duke asked.

"Good, life's good. And you?"

"So-so. Bloody chavvies will be the death of me… You not settled down yet?"

Tommy Lee knew what he was doing, he didn't like him talking to Millie. Well, tough shit. He would talk to whoever he wanted, and there wasn't a man on this planet who could stop him.

"No. I work away too much, never know where I'm gonna be from one week to the next." He eyed Millie. She was dragging Connie away from a group of women and pointing at Duke. "I think you're wanted." He nodded.

"I'll see you around." Duke headed towards his wife and daughter.

"We're gonna make a move in a bit," Sean Paul informed him. "You coming?"

Noticing Millie was on her own, he shook his head. "Not yet. Can you take Mother and Father home, I've got a bit of unfinished business to take care of."

He would stay here all night if he had to, until he got what, or rather who, he wanted.

***

John Jo parked up outside his trailer. He glanced at Gypsy. She looked tired. It wouldn't be long before the baby would be here. It must take it out of a woman, carrying a life inside you.

He had recently concreted a large base for when the mobile arrived. His only hope being that the council would grant them permission to stay. Sean Paul also had one ready. He needed it more than them, he already had two children and a third on the way.

They had started building a paddock at the back with a stable. His father reckoned if they had horses they would get granted permission. It was worth a try, cover all bases. He quite liked the idea of having a couple for the children to ride. He'd had the opportunity as a child, so he'd give his own children the same.

"I'll put the kettle on," Gypsy said, dragging him from his thoughts.

He turned to her. "You okay? It must have been hard seeing Henry and Prissy today."

"I'm fine. They had their chance to make amends," she said flatly.

He walked around to her door and helped her out. "I'll get the fire started. And then we can have a quiet night in."

She nodded but didn't reply. Was she still worried about the ground? He'd told her they would be okay, that they would win. He felt helpless. It was his job to look after her, keep her safe, and bear the brunt of problems. He sighed wearily. What if they didn't succeed?

CHAPTER 31

Both mobiles had been delivered. Tommy Lee had come over to help his brothers get set up with the plumbing and electrics. His parents helped get the Cobs settled in the paddock.

"They's a lovely pair, girl," Paddy said approvingly. "Look, Maeve, they like the space."

She nodded but paid little attention. She stood with Sean Paul's littluns, trying to keep them out of mischief while her boys worked.

With the mobiles now wired up, the men turned their attention to the plumbing.

"This might take a while," John Jo called to Gypsy. "You want to stay for dinner?" he asked Tommy Lee.

He replied with a quick grunt as he attempted to push the soil pipe into place. "This is fecking tight," he moaned.

"Needs to be, don't want no leaks."

"You'll need to test everything to make sure it don't. You moving in here tonight?" he asked when finally done.

"No, Gypsy's going to the launderette, she wants everything clean before we move in."

"What's happening with the council?"

"Got to get all the paperwork in by this Friday, then we'll get a court date. Hate to think what will happen if we lose."

"If you lose, appeal and keep appealing until they grant you." Tommy Lee wiped his hands on an old towel and passed it to John Jo. " But I can't see you losing."

"But what if we do?"

"Then we find a solution. Come on, I need a cuppa."

***

Tommy Lee wiped the last mouthful of bread around the plate before shoving it into his mouth. "Thanks, Gypsy, it's nice to get a home-cooked meal."

"Get yourself a wife then, boy, best thing I ever did," John Jo said with a chuckle.

"I'm not the marrying kind, and who you calling boy? I'm two years older than you, little brother." Tommy Lee laughed. "Besides, why would I marry when I can come here and eat like a king?"

"I'm going to the launderette. Is there anything else you want before I go?" Gypsy asked, rubbing her back.

"No, darling." John Jo stood and pecked his wife on the lips. "See you later."

Tommy Lee waited for her to leave then turned to John Jo. "Remember Patience's funeral, the woman I was talking to, Millie, what do you know about her?"

"Stay away from her," John Jo said with no further information.

"What if I don't want to?"

"Jaysus, Tommy Lee, you don't half know how to pick them… Her old man's a gangster, I've done a bit of work for him. He don't mess about, he carries a gun. Why her? Of all the women who fall at your feet, why her?"

"I heard Gypsy say they're not together anymore." Tommy Lee reached for his beer and took a sip. He wasn't a big drinker, he much preferred a nice cup of tea with his meals.

"They're not, she's living with Duke Lee, but Paul Kelly is the type to think he owns her." Shaking his head, John Jo sighed. "Please stay away."

Tommy Lee smiled. He might pay Duke a visit. After all, Millie was the first woman to make an impression on him, and he was the type who always wanted what he couldn't have.

***

Gypsy took a sharp breath and held on to the dryer. Shirley stood by her side, folding the washing.

"You feeling all right?"

"This backache is getting worse." She moaned.

"I think we should get back, the baby could be coming." Shirley pulled the last few garments from the dryer and shoved them into the bag. "I'll carry this lot, you get in the Transit."

"I'll be glad when I've got me own washer, sod coming out in all weathers just to do this." Gypsy took another deep breath and doubled over.

Shirley Ann waited for the pain to ease and then loaded the car.

Gypsy waddled out and climbed up onto the seat. "I think you're right, the baby is coming."

Without another word, Shirley Ann started the engine and pulled away. It was only a seven-minute drive back to their land, but to Gypsy it felt much longer. With the growing backache and now twinges in her stomach, she found it difficult to relax. She winced as the vehicle hit a bump in the road, causing the pain to worsen.

"Sorry," Shirley Ann mumbled.

The truck pulled to a halt, then she hit the hooter and waited for John Jo to rush out.

"What's happened?" His voice was panic-laden.

"She's in labour."

"Shit."

Tommy Lee appeared next to him. "Take her straight to the hospital. I'll go and get Mother and meet you there." He turned and headed to his car.

"I'll stay with the children," Sean Paul told Shirley Ann. "You drive. John Jo, follow in your motor."

"Can we just go. Please," Gypsy shouted, her patience non-existent with the growing pains. Her nerves were shot. Despite being pregnant for nine months, she really hadn't thought about parenthood. Would she be a good mum? Would she know what to do if her baby was crying? Would she survive these growing pains?

She let out a cry. "They're getting worse."

***

Four hours later, Tommy Lee sat in the waiting room. His mother walked in.

"Another boy." She beamed.

"How's John Jo and Gypsy?" he asked.

"He's over the moon, she's tired but happy. I've come out to give them some time on their own." She paused.

Was she going to lecture him?

"Don't you think it's about time you settled down?"

"When I'm ready, I will." He had to change the subject quick. "You heard from PJ?"

"No... I did say you shouldn't have left him there, on his own in a foreign country."

"He will be fine. He made friends and he's got to live his life as he sees fit, the same as me. You can't dictate what any of us do."

"Maybe so, but I won't be happy until he's back safe." She sighed. "You'll understand, when you've children of your own."

He rolled his eyes. His mother's lectures were becoming more frequent. "I'm gonna be staying with John Jo for a while. He said I can stay in his trailer now he's got the mobile."

"It will do you good to be around your brothers and their families, might make you see what you're missing." And with that, she rose and left the room.

Tommy Lee blew out slowly. His mother always had to have the last fecking word.

***

PJ climbed into the taxi and gave the driver directions. He had been travelling most of the day, and it was now late. He wondered what his parents would think of the bruising on his face. His ribs still hurt from the kicking he had received. What excuse could he tell them? A fight over a woman? They would believe that, but Tommy Lee wouldn't. He would know the truth.

PJ had decided to go to John Jo's instead of home, hoping he could hide out there until his face had healed. John Jo had said he could go and live there. They would question him, of course, but he could pull the wool over their eyes. Not his mother's, though, she was like a human lie detector. One wrong word and she would pounce. One wrong word and then they'd all know his secret.

He held his ribs, his mind turning to Carlos. Finding him in bed with that fat prick who Tommy worked for. No wonder he hadn't minded him staying. Did he want to get his hands on him, too? He shuddered, the thought making him gag.

He should have walked away instead of confronting them. The look on Carlos' face had said it all. The shame dripped off him. As for Fatty, he'd called his men and a swift kicking had followed. The only reason they had let him live was because of Tommy Lee. His reputation, for doing whatever was needed, made him valuable. What did he mean by that?

The streetlamps hurt his eyes, so closing them, he rested his head back. He only had one option left: he would have to play the game. Marry, have kids, and have his fun without anyone knowing. As long as he was careful, he would be fine.

CHAPTER 32

Tommy Lee left the hospital after seeing his new nephew. He'd arranged with John Jo to drop their mum home. He was going to pack up his few belongings and stay with his brother until the trailer was emptied and he could move into there. He needed some time alone.

Millie.

She kept slipping into his thoughts, and it was starting to annoy him. With his mother's nagging, worrying about PJ, and needing to find himself somewhere permanently to live, did he really have time to chase a woman?

You're the one who can't stop thinking about her.

New plan. Tomorrow he would go and see her, offer to take her out to dinner, bed her, and that would be that.

He pulled onto his brothers' land and parked up near the trailer. Before he'd had a chance to get out, Sean Paul came stomping towards him.

Now what?

"PJ's back. He's been beaten black and blue." Sean Paul huffed. "Come in and talk to him, he's not saying much other than he don't want Mother to see him like this."

"Send him into John Jo's, I'll speak to him in private." Tommy Lee grabbed his bags and unlocked the trailer. It was now the early hours of the morning. All he wanted to do was get some shuteye.

Seconds later, PJ appeared.

"What happened?" Tommy Lee asked without turning around.

"I don't want to talk about it." PJ flopped onto the bunk and yelped.

"Maybe so, but something bad has happened, and it might do you good to talk about it. Now I'm not stupid, I know this has got something to do with a man… Who caught you?" He looked up, and his eyes went wide. The whole of PJ's face was bruised. "Fecking hell, boy, start talking," he demanded.

"It was your boss… Did you know he liked young men?" PJ asked accusingly.

"What?" Tommy Lee snapped. "Did he…?"

"No, he didn't touch me, I caught him in bed with Carlos, so his men gave me a good kicking." He held his ribs. "I should thank you, you're the only reason I'm still alive."

"How so?"

"You're someone he can rely on for doing whatever it takes… What does that mean, Tommy Lee, you're a thug like the men who did this?" PJ pointed to his face.

"Is that what you told Sean Paul?"

"No. Don't worry, your secret's safe with m—"

Before PJ had finished the sentence, Tommy Lee grabbed him by the collar, drawing him nearer to his face. "My fecking secret? You're the one who likes men's cocks up your arse." He pushed him back. "This is all your doing, so you deal with it."

***

Tommy Lee was up early. He had driven to Stepney, after the argument with PJ, and checked into a hotel for a few days. He would kill two birds with one stone. He had a business meeting with a prospective employer in a couple of days, so first he would go and see Millie. He showered and dressed, humming to himself. He always got a buzz from his line of work, but today it was definitely the thought of seeing her.

When he pulled up on Duke's land he started to sweat. Was he nervous? He approached the open door. He could see her sitting on the sofa.

Duke stood and greeted him. "Well, to what do we owe the pleasure of this visit?"

"Thought I'd pop in while I'm in the area on business." Holding his hand out, Tommy Lee gave a firm shake, then entered.

Before Duke answered, the sound of another motor driving through the gate rumbled. "Looks like our guests are starting to arrive. Millie, make Tommy Lee a cuppa while I sort them out." With that, he disappeared.

"Sugar?" she asked.

"No thanks." He followed her into the kitchen. "So, how have you been?"

"Okay, how have you been?" Her voice was awkward.

"I've been okay, too… I enjoyed chatting with you at Patience's wake." He smiled.

She was blushing again. "Listen, I'm married, so can you stop flirting with me?"

"I didn't realise I was." He placed his cup down and sighed. "Shall we start again?" He held his hand out. "I'm Tommy Lee, it's nice to meet you."

"Millie. Nice to meet you, too." She gripped his hand. "What brings you to Stepney?"

"Business. I'm meeting someone about a job."

"So you'll be working here?" She sounded intrigued.

"It's overseas, normally three or six months at a time." He couldn't tell her too much, despite wanting to. "If I take the job, would you like to come out and celebrate with me?"

She frowned as if thinking.

"Just a meal, no partying," he added.

"Depends when. I'm busy tonight, with my friend, Rosie."

"I'll be in the area for a few days. Give me your number and I'll let you know."

"Okay," she agreed. "It's a date."

You've still got it, boy.

She jotted down her number and handed it to him. "I'll just get the tea."

"You having a party?" he asked. "There's another trailer coming in."

"Just family coming to visit." She handed him his cup then sat at the table.

Duke reappeared and reached for his. "I won't be long."

"It's okay, I can see you're busy and I need to make tracks. I'll pop in another time." Tommy Lee swallowed the last of his tea, winked at Millie, then left.

***

"I want to know why Tommy Lee left," John Jo snapped. "It was agreed he would stay here until he had work."

"He said he wanted some time on his own," PJ said. "Maybe he's fed up looking after everyone."

"Everyone? He doesn't look after me." John Jo paced the ground outside the mobile.

"Doesn't he? He got you and Sean Paul work, and he took me, so I wasn't left alone. He does a lot for us all."

John Jo had to agree, he'd always looked out for all of them, so no wonder he couldn't wait to get away. "Well, he was helping me move the stuff into the mobile, so you'll have to do it instead."

"See what I mean." PJ shut his mouth when his brother glared at him.

"Come on. I ain't spending another night with you tossing and turning. Later I'll go and get your trailer... I'll tell Mother you phoned and said you'll be coming home next week. That should please her."

He had to get back up the hospital also, check Gypsy and Jonny boy were okay. They had agreed he would be called John Paul, but shortened to Jonny. His mother was over the moon, a grandchild named after the Pope, that would give her credence at Mass amongst the travelling women.

The sound of a motor driving in had him glancing round the side of the mobile. "Shit, Mother and Father's here, go and hide in the shed," he warned PJ.

All their lives would be made hell if she saw the state of his face.

***

PJ had spent the last three hours hiding in the shed. He was starting to get cold, and he needed a piss. Not only that, it was also now dark. What was Mother doing here for so long? Probably helping clean the mobile and moving the stuff in. If Tommy Lee had stayed and helped, PJ wouldn't have been stuck in the shed for hours.

A motor started, and he prayed his parents were leaving. There was no window so he couldn't check. Would his brother tell him when they had gone? Not if he was still in a mood.

Footsteps approached, crunching in the gravel. He held his breath.

"You can come out now," John Jo told him.

"Thank the Lord, I'm fecking freezing." PJ jumped up and followed him inside. "It's ready to live in then."

"Yep, its ready for Gypsy and Jonny boy." John Jo grabbed two beers from the fridge, handing one to PJ. "Are you going to tell me who did that to your face now?"

"I told you it was a girl's dad and brother... They caught me with her," he lied.

"You know how to fight. I find it hard to believe only two men did that to you," John Jo quizzed.

"Look, I just want to forget about it. I'll find myself a nice girl here, then maybe everyone will get off my back."

"Who's everyone? As far as you've told me, only Tommy Lee and I know?" John Jo stared in disbelief. He could obviously smell a rat.

CHAPTER 33

Tommy Lee had dressed up tonight. Black trousers, a crisp white shirt. No tie. He reserved those for funerals and weddings. The stiff fabric of his freshly starched collar rubbed against his neck, an irritation he'd have to endure for the sake of appearances. If the night went as he hoped, everything, including the shirt, would be coming off soon enough.

He sat at the table, biting his nail, the sharp tang of nerves settling in his stomach. He wasn't sure why he felt so on edge. He had ordered champagne to ease her into the evening, but now, watching the bubbles rise in the glass, he figured he needed it more than she did.

Then he saw her.

Millie appeared in the doorway, and for a moment, the air in his lungs locked tight. It was like seeing her for the first time all over again.

She moved with effortless grace, the dim lighting of the restaurant casting a golden hue over her skin. A black pencil skirt hugged her hips, stopping just above her knees, paired with a pale-blue blouse that skimmed her curves, the top buttons left undone just enough to hint at what lay beneath.

Jaysus, am I in Heaven?

Her hair was swept up, but loose strands curled around her face, framing it in a way that made her look both elegant and completely untamed.

Sexy.

Tommy Lee stood as she approached, pressing a polite kiss to her cheek. The scent of her perfume, something warm, with a trace of roses, washed over him, and he swallowed.

He pulled out her chair, the legs scraping lightly against the polished floor as she sat.

"It's lovely to see you again," he finally managed, his voice rougher than he intended.

"It's lovely to be here," she said, glancing around the candlelit restaurant. A flicker of amusement danced in her eyes. "I didn't realise you liked the finer things in life."

It was spacious, round tables with white tablecloths, fancy cutlery, and lead crystal glasses adorned the place with huge potted palms dotted around. The three chandeliers that hung from the ceiling were massive.

"Do you?" he asked.

"Do I?"

"Like the finer things in life?"

"I suppose we all do to a certain extent, although I'd rather be with loved ones, wherever that may be."

He liked that answer, she knew the true value of family. "Champagne?"

"Yes, please."

She was nervous, too, he could tell by the way she lifted the menu. Her hands shook. It was slight, but he always picked up on the tiny details.

"What would you like to eat?"

"Grilled salmon." Her eyes met his over the menu. "What do you fancy?"

Now that was a double-barrelled question. His body heated up along with his manhood. "I think we both know what I fancy."

***

The meal was rushed, and within an hour he was showing Millie into his room. He pushed the door shut behind him and grabbed her around the waist. His lips met hers, and all his problems melted away.

They fumbled with each other's buttons, their clothes dropping to the floor. He pushed Millie back onto the bed and gazed over her body.

Damn.

He rested on top of her, kissing down her neck with the odd nibble. His heart beat wildly. She groaned with pleasure as he kissed her stomach, then down farther to her thighs. He pushed her legs open wider, then slipped in his tongue. Her hips bucked in rhythm, egging him on until a piercing scream left her lips. He kissed his way back up, sucking and kneading her voluptuous breasts.

"Have you got protection?" she panted.

He reached to the drawer and grabbed a pack of three; shit, he had one left. Unwrapping it, he pulled it over his cock. The thing split.

Feck. Feck. Feck.

He glanced at Millie who stared back wide-eyed.

"Oh sod it." She dragged him back down, her mouth covering his.

He lay on top and positioned himself before slipping inside her. Pushing harder with each thrust, filling her completely. She groaned again, her movements in time with his, until he exploded. His breathing laboured, he tried to control himself.

That was quick. Too quick.

He rolled over, taking her with him. He held her tightly to his chest. "That was… fecking fantastic." He panted.

There would have to be a round two.

***

"Do you really have to go? Why not stay the night?" Tommy Lee asked while grabbing Millie's bra and holding it over his head.

She stood on tiptoe but still couldn't reach. "I've got things to do. Besides, my dad will question me, and I'm not in the mood for the third degree."

Three times he'd had her, and that still wasn't enough, he wanted more. "I'll go and tell him you were with me. I'll phone him now."

"No. My dad's worried about me, I don't want him to think I'm reckless." She sat on the end of the bed. "I've given him enough to worry about already…"

"Do you regret coming here?" He felt deflated at the thought.

"No. Tonight's been great, and I'm really glad I came."

That lifted his spirit, although he wouldn't have said great, he thought it was perfect. So perfect that he wanted more.

"Look, you're going abroad to work for months, I'm here sorting out a messy divorce, it's best we go our separate ways now."

"Can I see you again, when I'm back?"

"Maybe. You know you may meet someone wherever you're going." She smiled, but did she really think that?

He handed her back her bra. "I can guarantee you I won't meet anyone." He didn't want to, not now.

She tugged her blouse over her head and quickly buttoned it. With one last kiss, she grabbed her bag and coat then left the room.

Tommy Lee continued to stare at the door long after she'd gone. He felt empty. It was a feeling he wasn't used to.

***

Millie stood in the softly lit hotel lobby, her heart racing. She adjusted her coat, the warmth of the evening still lingering on her skin like the faint scent of Tommy Lee's cologne. The air was thick with unspoken words and fleeting glances, memories of laughter and shared secrets echoing in her mind.

She had told herself it would be a one-off, a simple escape from reality and the looming divorce. Yet, as she glanced back at the lift, a pang of reluctance tightened in her chest. The evening had unfolded like a beautiful dream, with candlelit conversation and laughter.

Don't forget the fantastic sex.

Millie shook her head, trying to dispel the thoughts that threatened to anchor her to this fleeting encounter. She left the building, her feet heavy, like they were fighting against her resolve.

"It was just one night," she whispered to herself.

Outside, the night was alive with the hum of traffic. She took a deep breath, grounding herself in the present. This was her life, one of independence and freedom, not of entanglements. Yet, the memory of Tommy Lee's laughter, his easy smile, and the way he looked at her with those piercing blue eyes made her heart flutter with something she couldn't quite name.

You are getting divorced.

She paused, her fingers brushing the cool metal of the taxi door, contemplating her next move. She could feel the pull of attachment, urging her to turn back. But she inhaled deeply, reminding herself: "No," she murmured, sliding into the cab.

With each minute passing, the farther away from the hotel she got, she felt a mix of exhilaration and sorrow. She was leaving behind a moment that had felt almost magical.

Get a fucking grip, woman.

Millie glanced back through the rear window once more, catching a glimpse of the hotel's neon sign flickering in the distance. She smiled softly, a bittersweet farewell to a night that would linger if she allowed it. She had her own path to follow, one that didn't include the temptation of getting attached again. Not after the disaster of her marriage. Paul's betrayal. Would he be angry if he found out? Was that why she'd done it? Revenge?

No.

Tommy Lee had been a temptation, and she'd wanted him, just for one night. It had given her the strength she needed to divorce Paul.

But no one must find out.

And with that thought, she continued onwards, the road stretching before her.

CHAPTER 34

Tommy Lee had spent the week plotting his next job. It wasn't for someone else like he'd told everyone. This job was personal. It was about family, more precisely PJ. The thought of two of Fatty's heavies doing that to his little brother was unforgivable, and it needed payback.

He planned on flying to Portugal and then getting a private boat around to the Costa del Sol. He needed to be in and out, under the cover of darkness, without anyone seeing him.

With his plans now sorted he could relax, and there was only one person he wanted to do that with. He picked up the phone and dialled the number.

"Millie?"

"Tommy Lee. I thought you were leaving last week?"

"It's been delayed till this Friday. I was hoping to see you again before I leave?" he asked.

"Wednesday?"

"Great, shall I pick you up?" he suggested.

"No, I'll meet you, same place at one p.m."

The line went dead.

He grinned. This was worth delaying his plans for. He could have had the job done by now, but with thoughts of her tormenting his mind, he had to see her again.

***

Gypsy returned home with the baby wrapped in a blue lace shawl. John Jo was pleased to have his wife back. It would make a pleasant change staring at her beautiful face rather than PJ's miserable one, so he'd said.

"Here, let me." He held his hands out and took the baby from her. He stared down into the tiny face. Jonny boy was sleeping.

"Have we got food in for dinner?" she asked, stepping up into the mobile. She looked around, smiling. The place was perfect. She had stepped straight up into the front room. This door, she had decided, would stay locked, and they would use the door in the hallway. She wouldn't have the carpet ruined, which was new. There was a three-seater sofa and two armchairs, plain peach, with her lace cushions propped up on them. She only had four and would need another for the other chair. The log burner was on the far wall near the door to the kitchen. Above it hung a big mirror with a gypsy wagon etched into it. That was new. In the corner stood a display cabinet with all her Crown Derby on the top two shelves and her lead crystal on the bottom two. On the windowsill, a porcelain bowl of fruit stood proud with the wedding photos of her and John Jo either side. The smaller window had a vase of fresh flowers.

"Mother's done the shopping, she cleaned this place and helped put stuff away," he told her. "But Shirley Ann said she'll cook tonight, so you go and sit down, I'll put the kettle on."

"So what's going on with PJ?" she asked, sitting slowly on the sofa.

She held her arms out, and John Jo handed her the baby.

"I haven't got a clue, he's different since he came back from Spain. For one thing he's not telling the truth… I need to see Tommy Lee, but I don't know where he is either."

"Take it easy on him. If he's been beaten black and blue, he must have got involved in something dodgy. I just hope it doesn't follow him back here," she said.

John Jo stiffened. "I don't want you worrying, cos if anyone comes here they'll get more than they bargained for."

His eyes flicked to the cupboard. Was that where he'd stashed his guns? At least she knew if any unsavoury characters showed up here, they'd wish they hadn't.

***

PJ drove past Sam's pub. He wasn't sure why. He missed it, missed belonging somewhere where he didn't have to pretend. It looked like it was open, probably new owners. Would they be like him and Sam? Doubtful.

This wasn't doing him any good, he knew that, but you can't turn off your feelings. And he felt a lot. Mostly shame for wanting men. Shame for lying to John Jo. And shame for not being normal for his family.

He sighed. This was eating him up inside. He could be a proper man, he was sure of it. Maybe it was Sam, he'd put a spell on him, turned him into a poof. He'd never touched a man before he'd met him.

But you wanted to.

"Shut up."

All he had to do was find a wife, then he would be fixed.

***

Millie lay on her bed, thinking. She had met Paul for lunch earlier because he needed to see her. She wanted to discuss the divorce. He, however, wanted to give their marriage another go. Paul was too good at this game, she knew she wasn't his equal when it came to manipulating. He had promised her the world. In his words, he'd do whatever it took. He seemed to forget the fact that he'd stuck his dick in an old woman just to get his hands on the scrapyard. He should never have forged Ronnie Taylor's will. She knew it would end in disaster. They already owned the docks, Kelly's nightclub, and the brothel. Why wasn't that enough for him? Why wasn't she enough for him?

She'd put him straight, and still he couldn't see what he'd done, asking if she was all right.

No, I'm not all right. My husband cheated on me, broke my heart, and while I was losing our baby he was on his jollies, which broke my heart again.

The grand finale had been when she'd told him she'd slept with another man. His words had stung.

'Does it make you feel good, putting it about like a slag?' he'd spat.

Well, if she was a slag, what did that make him? "A selfish bastard…a male slag…a man whore."

She'd asked for fair settlement, but now he wouldn't give her anything, in his words: *You're not having the house or the girls, you won't get a penny. Whoever this fucking bloke is, he can keep ya.*

It was clear he valued possessions above people, above her.

She sighed. There were many words she could use to describe Paul Kelly, but unfortunately, loyal wasn't one of them. She could never trust him again, and without trust, there was no marriage.

***

Gypsy watched everyone fawning over her baby. Whilst she felt proud, she also felt slightly jealous. She wanted him to herself.

"He's a handsome baby, John Jo." Shirley Ann smiled. "Typical Ward boy."

He glanced at Gypsy and grinned. She could see he was proud; she was, too.

The door opened, and PJ appeared. "Any dinner going?" he asked, not to anyone in particular. "Thought we could go pub after and wet the baby's head."

He seemed a bit erratic, not his usual calm self. She wondered if anyone else thought the same, or would they gloss over it like they normally did when one of them acted out of character? Shirley Ann handed her back the baby.

"I'll go dish you some up." She took her two littluns with her.

PJ followed.

"He seems more his old self," John Jo said to Sean Paul after they had left.

He nodded but didn't reply. Did he feel the same? Gypsy was sure she spotted doubt on his face.

"I'm going to put the baby down now, all this attention has wiped him out." She was hoping he would take the hint and leave. She needed to speak with John Jo, in private. She would voice her concerns, and if he choose to ignore her, then at least she had warned him.

CHAPTER 35

Wednesday had taken too long to come around as far as Tommy Lee was concerned. He sat drumming his fingers against the white tablecloth, impatiently. He glanced towards the entrance every few seconds, anticipation tautening his chest. Then, Millie appeared, looking better than he could have imagined. She was breathtaking. Her hair, loose this time, hung in perfect curls, cascading down her back. Her dress, light blue, was tight in all the right places, clinging to those voluptuous breasts.

Jaysus, those tits.

For a second he could do nothing but drink her in. His breath caught.

Calm down, you fecking eejit.

His eyes met hers. She smiled while making her way towards him. He stood. "You came."

"I said I would," she said nervously as he pecked her on the cheek.

He pulled out her chair, and once she was seated, he then sat and waved to the waiter to order champagne.

"I can't stay too long this time," she told him.

Was that disappointment in her voice?

"We should make the most of our time together then... Come upstairs with me... We can have food sent up if you're hungry."

She seemed to hesitate. Had he read the signals wrong?

"This seems like forbidden fruit." She laughed.

He smiled and covered her hand with his. "Then let's be sinners together."

***

The moment the door clicked shut, he drew her to him, their lips smashing together in a passionate kiss. A collision of longing and restraint unravelling in an instant. He fumbled for the zip on her dress, finally sliding it down. She stepped out of it, unbuttoning his shirt at the same time. Clothes were discarded in minutes, and they finally fell onto the bed. His hands exploring her body like it was the first time all over again. Nothing else existed, no doubts, no world beyond this, only her. He kissed down her body, spending time licking and sucking her nipples. They stood to attention to greet him. He loved the way her fingers brushed through his hair, grabbing and then yanking. He lifted his head and gazed at her flustered face. His whole body tingled.

Is this love?

He ignored that thought. She was obviously enjoying this as much as him, judging by the groans leaving her mouth. He continued slowly down her body, kissing gently. He wanted to take his time, but he also needed her now. Feeling like he was on the verge of euphoria, he slipped his tongue inside her. Within minutes she bucked her hips until she climaxed, and her body shook. He crawled back up and thrust inside her, the warmth and wetness welcoming. He couldn't control himself. Seconds later, his throbbing cock exploded, filling her completely.

They lay together in each other's arms. Tommy Lee stroked her hair; her gentle breathing tickled his chest.

"It's going to be harder leaving you this time," she eventually said, breaking the silence.

He pressed a kiss to her forehead. "Then don't."

Millie sat up, sadness flickering in her eyes. "You know I have to."

His jaw clenched. He ran his hand up and down the curve of her back. "I don't care about your soon-to-be ex-husband or your father, Duke. In fact, I don't care about anything else, Millie. I just want you."

"It's complicated," she whispered.

He held a finger to her lips. "Shh. When I get back from working away, I'll come and see you. You can give me your answer then, but for now, we still have a couple of hours." He brought her back down into his arms. Never had he been so content in his life.

Is this love?

***

PJ peered up at the small sign. Sam had told him about this place. It was a discreet bar. If you didn't know it was there, you would never find it, tucked away down a side street in Dagenham. The gay scene had been forced underground in the sixties. It wasn't until 1967 that homosexuality was decriminalised, but even so, straight people wouldn't accept it. This made PJ feel worse, like he was a leper. Along with that and knowing his family would disown him, it had left him no choice but to now start frequenting these places. He just had to make sure no one caught him.

He glanced around before moving closer. Should he risk it? He knocked, putting the thought out of his mind. The door opened, and a skinny man appeared. He studied him for a moment.

"Can I help you?" he finally asked, after giving him the once-over.

"I've come for a drink," PJ said.

The man nodded and motioned for him to follow. They walked down steps into a basement room. It was large and had a dance floor in the centre, an L-shaped bar to the left and seating to the right.

There were various doors leading off from the main room. A DJ set stood to the left as he came in. A sign for toilets next to it. He thought the place was a bit dingy, maybe in need of a coat of paint.

"Bar's over there." The man pointed. As if he hadn't seen it.

"Thanks." PJ headed to the bar. A drink was needed. He was shaking inside. Was he scared or excited? He wasn't sure.

"A pint, please, mate," he asked the barman.

"A pint? We don't get many here asking for that." He laughed. "Love your accent, where are you from?"

"My family come from Ireland, but I was born here… What do you suggest I drink?"

"How about a white Russian. After all, who would say no to a white Russian, all those rippling biceps."

"Okay." So the bartender was flirting with him. He had nice eyes. They twinkled with mischief.

"This your first time here?" he asked.

"Yeah, can't you tell?" PJ mumbled.

"I'm due a break in a minute, I'll show you around if you want."

Was that code? He felt himself getting slightly hot under the collar. "Sure." Maybe this wasn't going to be so bad.

"Daz, can you take over?" he called to another man at the other end of the bar. He nodded in return. "I'm Pete, by the way, and you are?"

"Sam." PJ wouldn't give his real name, he wasn't that stupid.

"Nice to meet you, Sam. Follow me." He lifted the bar hatch and marched to one of the doors. "These rooms are for privacy, you know, if you wanna chat or…"

He left the rest unsaid, but PJ knew what he meant. It seemed a bit seedy for his taste. Men coming here to have sex.

But you're here for exactly that.

He swallowed down the thought and entered the room behind Pete. He was here now, so where was the harm?

***

Tommy Lee watched Millie dress. Her movements seemed deliberately drawn out, like she was making their time together last longer.

"I wish you could stay." The words came out before he knew it.

She glanced at him with a sad smile. "I don't know how to stop wanting you."

His throat tightened. "Then don't."

She slipped on her shoes, then grabbed her bag. "You have business to attend, and I have my—"

"Divorce. I know." He sighed. "I'll see you when I'm back," he confirmed. Was that for her benefit or his?

She lingered at the door, her fingers resting on the handle. "Goodbye, Tommy Lee."

Then she was gone, leaving him alone in the quiet room, the scent of her still lingering in the air and the ache of her absence settling deep in his bones.

Is this love?

CHAPTER 36

Tommy Lee sat in the cabin, sipping a whiskey as the plane's engines hummed just the other side of the window. Another thirty minutes and he would be stepping onto the Portuguese tarmac. He felt the thrill of his mission already building inside him. The revenge had been simmering away all this time. PJ's faced flashed before him, the bruises that had only just started to vanish. The fat prick, who thought he was untouchable, had made a major mistake when he'd let PJ live. He would be sure to tell him before he killed him.

He necked the remainder of his drink and passed the glass to the air stewardess. She smiled, brushing her fingers against his hand. He ignored the come-on. His head was filled with business, no time for pleasure, and if he had, it would be Millie he would be having that with. He glanced out of the window and smiled. She kept popping into his head, and as much as he wanted to have nice thoughts, he needed to concentrate.

The aircraft touched down. He wasted no time grabbing his rucksack and exiting, mixing with the crowd and keeping his head down. He was due to meet a friend outside. An old army buddy. Someone he had fought side by side with, someone he trusted. He left the airport and stood by the road, waiting.

The motor screeched to a halt beside him, and he was greeted with Robbo's smiling face. Most people were scared of this man. He was a wild card, loud, without fear, and a temper that could take on the Devil. He had a jagged scar that ran from his forehead down to his chin. It was caused by a land mine going off in Northern Ireland. Robbo said it was his lucky scar, as six of the other men with him that day weren't so lucky.

He jumped out of the motor and embraced Tommy Lee. "Good to see ya, mate." He grinned. "Everything's ready and in place. Come on, jump in."

He climbed into the passenger side and held on to the seat. Robbo like to drive fast; for anyone who didn't know him, they would think he had a death wish.

"I've loaded a few beers on board, as it's gonna take a few hours to get round to the Costa del Sol," he informed him.

"It's okay, I need to do this under cover of darkness anyway," Tommy Lee said. "So there's no rush."

"You sure you don't want me to help?"

"You've done enough, picking me up, getting the boat, all I need you to do now is wait for me. Pity we couldn't have travelled by car. The way you drive we'd be there in minutes." He laughed.

"You haven't seen me skipper a boat, pal, we'll make good time." He grinned again.

"Just make sure you keep me in one piece. I've stuff to do when I get home." His thoughts turned to Millie. She would be his next mission.

***

The boat pulled into a little cove. Tommy Lee glanced at his watch. It was now three-fifteen a.m. With a quick nod to Robbo, he placed the balaclava over his head, slipped on his gloves, and began to scale the rocky embankment. This was done with ease, thanks to his army training. He was now dressed in camouflage combat trousers with matching jacket to blend into the scenery. He had a small torch poked into the breast pocket. His trusty flick-knife in his boot and a gun in his waistband. That was only for if things didn't go to plan.

The villa, which was perched just at the top of the embankment, was in total darkness. He spotted a figure guarding the building. Making his way into the bushes, he waited for him to walk past. He sneaked behind and jumped him. A tight chokehold, and the man soon went down. He dragged him behind the bushes, satisfied that the first target was taken care of. Yanking down the man's trousers, he withdrew his knife and hacked off his cock. This would be for the grand finale.

The second target Tommy Lee found sleeping soundly in his bed. He snatched the pillow and held it over the man's face. The thrashing lasted a matter of minutes, and when the body went limp, he took the pillow away. Again he pulled the man's pants down and cut off his cock.

Fatty was the last target; he knew where he would be. He crept along the hallway to the man's bedroom. It was empty.

Shit.

He slowly moved towards the main room. He could just make out the man's silhouette. He was sitting on the balcony, overlooking the sea. As he neared him, he could see he had a glass of wine in one hand, a cigar in the other. Tommy Lee yanked his balaclava off and stepped forward, into the moonlight.

"Tom—"

His name had barely left his lips before he had struck. A swift movement, a hard kick to the chest, sending Fatty teetering backwards. His arms flailed, fingers grasping at empty air. The sound of the glass smashing. Then gravity took over and Fatty plummeted to the floor. His head smashed against the porcelain tiles, blood immediately pooling. Annoyed with himself for killing the prick too soon, Tommy Lee reached for the knife and opened the man's dressing gown.

"Jaysus fecking Christ, where's your cock?" he mumbled in disgust. All he could see were layers of fat. He rolled the man onto his side and pushed one of the cocks up his arsehole. He picked up the wine bottle and rammed that up there to make sure it had gone in far enough. Then he rolled him back over and stuck the last cock into his mouth, again using the now shit-stinking bottle to ram it in farther.

When he had finished his task, he stood and stared down at the piece of crap who thought he was untouchable. "No one hurts my family. No one," he whispered.

He turned and walked to the door, pausing briefly. There would be money here. Plenty of it, too. Instead of leaving like he had intended, he entered the office. He knew it was stashed somewhere under the floor. Flicking the torch on, he shoved the desk over. He felt for a gap in the tiles, and there it was. He reached onto the desk, feeling for something to help. A metal ruler — why did Fatty have that? He held it and levered up the floor. Inside there was a bag. He dragged it out and rummaged inside. British notes. A lot of them. He grinned and made his way out of the office. Would the police think it was a robbery? He walked back through to the main room, placed two bottles of scotch under his arm, and slipped back into the night, undetected.

CHAPTER 37

Tommy Lee had returned home. He had stashed most of the cash under his clothes and in his shoes to get through airport security with a hefty wedge in his bag. That he would be able to explain, but not all of it.

He planned on burying the money on his father's piece of land, without anyone knowing. As much as he loved his family, if they knew it was there, they would undoubtedly dip into it. The temptation would be too great.

He had made his way back to the hotel and packed his stuff. He would go and see his mother before heading off to his next job. He also wanted to catch up with PJ. Let him know that justice had been served.

He was booked up for the next two months in Liverpool as a hired gun for some gangster who ran slot machines. He didn't need to go, not now he'd had his little—or should it be huge—windfall. He also didn't want to go because of Millie, but he knew he needed to give her time to sort her life out. If she hadn't done so by then, maybe he could help her.

***

PJ cursed himself. It was nearly lunch time. He'd stayed with Pete last night. The gay club had come to life after seven p.m. Men drinking, chatting, dancing and…he still couldn't believe he was there, partaking in sexual activities that blew his mind and disgusted him at the same time.

He pulled the motor to a standstill and climbed out, landing in the mud. His shoes squelched.

"Shit."

"Where the feck have you been?" Maeve asked, marching towards him.

His heart thumped harder against his ribs. He knew he looked a state—his hair was tousled, his shirt a bit creased from dancing, and there was a faint scent of cologne on him that wasn't his own.

"I was with someone," he said lamely.

His mother smiled. "Thought so, you've got that look about you."

"What look?" He frowned.

"You know." She raised her eyebrows, her smirk widening. "The look of a lad who's been with a girl."

"What?" His stomach lurched.

"Oh, don't play coy with me. Coming home after being out all night, all flustered. Bit of cologne on you. That shirt's been grabbed at, I'd say." She waggled her finger at him. "I knew you'd get yourself a romance sooner or later."

PJ forced a chuckle, heat creeping up his neck. He needed to shut this down before he got himself tangled in a lie he couldn't keep straight. "Ah, yeah, well, just a bit of fun, nothing serious."

His mum nodded knowingly, clearly pleased with herself. "Well, don't break too many hearts, boy. And be careful, all right?"

The rumble of a motor had them both turning. It was Tommy Lee. PJ could do without him right now.

He joined them, his expression unreadable. "What's happening?"

"Your brother's got himself a girl." Maeve beamed.

PJ's breath hitched. He waved a hand dismissively. "Ah, nah, Mum's just—"

His mother cut in with a teasing grin. "He won't tell me much, but I reckon she was all over him."

Tommy Lee's expression didn't shift, but his gaze lingered on PJ a second too long. "That so?"

PJ laughed, too forced, too eager to deflect. "Yeah, yeah, just a bit of fun. You know how it is."

Tommy Lee said nothing for a beat. Then, with a small nod, he said, "Right."

PJ's stomach twisted. He knew Tommy Lee wasn't buying it.

"I'll go and put the kettle on." She disappeared inside.

As soon as she was gone, PJ turned to Tommy Lee, his voice hushed. "Don't start."

Tommy Lee raised his hands innocently. "Didn't say a word."

PJ sighed, running a hand through his hair. "It's just easier this way."

Tommy Lee seemed to study him for a moment then nodded slowly. "All right. If that's what you want. I actually wanted to talk about something else."

But PJ knew the conversation wasn't over. And deep down, he wasn't sure how much longer he could keep up the act. "What is it?"

"The men who hurt you, I've dealt with them." He turned and walked away, leaving PJ standing, reliving that awful night's events.

***

Tommy Lee waited until PJ had gone out, no doubt off to see his latest man. He didn't believe for one minute that he had come to his senses and started seeing a woman. No. He was lying.

"It's late, Mother, I'll sleep in the trailer tonight and leave for work in the morning if that's all right with you."

"Of course it is, boy, you don't need to ask," Maeve said. "I'll be heading to bed in a bit. Do you want anything before I go?"

"No, you go and keep Father warm." He winked.

She tutted. "He's quite capable of that himself. Goodnight, son."

He made his way to the trailer and unpacked the bag of money. Placing a handful on the side, which he would use, he wrapped the rest securely into a watertight bag. He then sat and waited until he was sure his parents would be asleep before taking it out to bury it.

***

Millie lay in bed, unable to sleep, her thoughts drifting between Paul and Tommy Lee. Her best friend, Rosie, had questioned her when she had met her after the rendezvous. She wanted to know if she knew what she was doing, and while Millie had made out it was a one-off, she knew she was lying to herself. There was something about this man. Different, unpredictable, intense. She had been certain she had loved Paul, but was it security she really craved? A man to look after her?

No, you had security working for Finn in the Old Artichoke, and a home.

She sighed loudly. Then was it because she'd grown up in a children's home? Unloved and unwanted?

You need to stop using that as an excuse, it's getting old.

"I know," she whispered.

"Mil?" A gentle tap came from the door.

"Come in, Rosie." She flicked her bedside light on, squinting until her eyes adjusted.

"I can hear you tossing and turning, what's wrong?" Rosie asked in a hushed voice.

"My brain won't switch off. It's driving me crazy." Millie moved over in the bed and pulled the covers back.

Rosie climbed in and grinned. "This is like old times, back in the home."

"We did have some good times," Millie agreed.

"I take it this is Paul you're tinking about?" Rosie snuggled down into the bed.

"Partly. Let's face it, this whole thing is a shitshow. I want a divorce, he wants to try again. How can I after what he's done?"

"And where does this mystery man fit in all this?"

"Tommy Lee." Millie found herself smiling, she couldn't help it. "He was a distraction, but…"

"But you like him. Bloody hell, Mil, you sure know how to complicate things. Paul Kelly will not let you go, you belong to him, you know how he thinks."

"He's had another woman in my bed. If he thinks I'd ever take him back now, he is sorely mistaken."

Rosie frowned. "Then what are you going to do, cos we both know what Paul wants, Paul gets, and he doesn't care how he wins, he just does."

Millie didn't need reminding, she knew exactly what he was capable of. "I'll play him at his own game then, let's see how he likes it."

CHAPTER 38

It was a glorious May day. The sun shone, and a gentle breeze softly swayed the trees. The horses frolicked in the paddock, Jonny boy was sleeping in his pram, and Gypsy was hanging the washing out. John Jo watched her closely. She already had her figure back after having the baby. She glanced at him and smiled. His heart swelled. He loved her more and more each day. He wanted to give her the very best of everything, but to do that he needed to get the money in. He made a modest living, fighting and gambling. It was always enough when he was single, but now he was a married man with a son, and no longer dealing with Paul Kelly, he wasn't earning nearly enough. He had to do better.

"Do you want tea?" Gypsy asked while heading towards the mobile steps.

"Yes, please, my darling." He nodded.

She disappeared inside, leaving him with his thoughts on making money.

He planned on breeding the Cobs which would eventually give him and Sean Paul a steady income, but that would take a couple of years to pay off.

A fight was arranged for the following weekend, but money was running low. He'd been stupid. The wages he'd earned in the Costa del Sol, which was a tidy sum, he'd spent like it was going out of fashion. He couldn't go to Tommy Lee again and ask for work, even if he did know where he was.

The bank job kept creeping into his mind. It would be easy money. He'd already done the legwork, all he had to do was get Sean Paul back on board.

He glanced over towards his brother, who was hosing down his truck.

"No time like the present," he muttered and, standing, he headed towards him.

***

Tommy Lee was glad to see the back of Liverpool. Not technically the city, but the prick he had been working for. Were all gangsters up their own arses? Probably, he decided. They all thought they were untouchable, just like Fatty. He grinned, wondering what the police thought when they'd discovered the cocks.

Pushing the door open, he entered the pub, the smell of stale beer and fag ash hitting his nostrils. He wasn't keen on pubs for that very reason. Unfortunately, it was pubs where most of his work contacts met, and the Traveller community loved a booze-up along with a sing-song. This place was in need of a fresh lick of paint. Its once white walls had yellowed like badly stained teeth. Then again, they matched the landlord's, so at least there was a colour theme.

He had only been back a few hours. He'd met a man about a job in London and now wanted a beer before returning to Essex. He spotted Duke sitting at a table playing cards. Duke gave him a weird look.

What the feck was that about? Has Millie told him about us?

He glanced back at Duke who was grabbing his winnings and wandered towards him. "What brings you back here so soon? Thought you were working abroad."

"Nice to see you, too, Duke. Do you wanna drink?" he asked calmly. No fecker was winding him up today.

Duke shook his head. "I know about you and Millie. I want you to stay away from her."

Thought so.

Tommy Lee turned and stared him in the eye. "Doesn't she get a say in this?"

"She's a married woman."

"Separated, soon-to-be divorced."

Duke sighed. "Her old man won't take kindly to this, and I'll not have my daughter caught up in the middle."

"If Millie tells me to stay away, I will. As for her shit-cunt of a husband, I know all about him. If he wants to come for me, I'll fecking kill him with my bare hands."

"But what happens if he comes for Millie?"

Tommy Lee slammed his glass onto the bar. Just the thought of that happening riled him. "Then I'll be waiting for him."

***

PJ sat perched on a stool in the gay club. His gaze wandered around the room. He felt at ease now, after visiting a few times each week. Maeve thought he was courting, which suited him for now. It kept her off his back while he was having fun.

Men were dancing; well, he wouldn't have really called it dancing, it was more rubbing themselves against each other. Some were openly snogging before dragging each other into the side rooms. He could imagine the dirty deeds they would be doing because he had done the same. In his mind that was different, though. It was with Pete, his friend. Boyfriend? It sounded wrong, perverse even. A man having a boyfriend wasn't natural. But it was fine, he'd get a girl soon enough and marry her, then he'd be normal again.

"Hey, I've got some good news," Pete said, grabbing his attention.

"And what's that?"

"We need another bar hand. You up for it? Wages ain't that great, but you'll share a room with me, and you'll get to spend your nights in here, apart from Mondays and Wednesdays when we're closed. What do you say?"

PJ frowned. "And they want to offer me the job?"

"I put in a good word for ya... Well, Sam?"

Shit, maybe I should have told him my real name?

No, your dirty little secret would be found out.

His mind whirled, trying to work out the details. He could say he was working away for a couple of months, after all, that's what Tommy Lee did, and no one questioned him. He could visit his mother on his days off if he wanted to.

What about the horses?

Father can look after them.

What about finding a woman?

That can wait a few months.

This isn't normal.

This is my life.

Could he pull this off?

He grinned. Life, he decided, had just got a whole lot better. "Sounds good to me."

***

It was two-thirty a.m. The streets were deserted and peaceful. John Jo and Sean Paul had parked their motor up just outside of town and walked the rest of the way. They stood in the shadows, across the road from the bank.

"Are you sure about this?" Sean Paul whispered nervously.

"Yes."

"And you know the layout?"

"Yes."

"But what if—"

"Jaysus fecking Christ, Sean Paul, stop talking, we're supposed to be keeping a low profile," John Jo warned in a quiet voice. "Come on, follow me."

He ran across the road and down an alleyway adjacent to the bank. Then made his way across the gardens. Heaving himself up and over the last fence, he finally reached his destination, Sean Paul next to him. When they made it to the back door, John Jo took a crowbar from his jacket and began to jimmy.

"Do you know what you're doing?"

"Do I look like an fecking eejit... Don't answer that," John Jo snapped.

When the door gave way, he tumbled inside. His brother followed, helping him up.

"There should be a safe out the back." John Jo tiptoed towards the manager's office where he assumed it would be.

"I thought banks kept their money in a vault?" Sean Paul surmised. "They ain't going to leave it lying around, anyone could take it."

John Jo, ignoring him, pushed the office door open, but before he stepped in, the sound of distant sirens caught his ear.

"Shit. We need to run." He took off back the way he'd come, knocking over a pot plant and banging his hip into a desk.

"Feck."

The two men made it out into the fresh air. The sirens were close.

"We need to get to the car," Sean Paul told him between deep breaths.

"We need to be quick, they're nearly here. Look, we'll take that." John Jo pointed to an old bike.

He grabbed it and pushed it out into the alleyway that ran down behind the bank and shops. He threw his leg over and motioned for Sean Paul to sit on the handlebars.

"This is a terrible idea," he muttered, raising his backside onto them.

"It's the only fecking idea we've got." John Jo groaned. "Jaysus, you weigh a fecking ton."

He began peddling like he was an Olympic cyclist, his movement fast but gradually declining the farther he went.

"Can't you speed up a bit?"

"I'm going as fast as I can." John Jo puffed. "Jaysus, I can't go much farther. We'll have to swap."

Once the bike had ground to a halt, Sean Paul jumped off the bars and rubbed his arse. "That fecking hurts." He moaned.

John Jo, ignoring him again, positioned himself ready for Sean Paul to start. The bike wobbled as it propelled slowly forward, until Sean Paul, no longer able to keep it upright, ended up on the ground with John Jo and the bike on top of him.

***

It was five forty-five a.m. Gypsy sat with Shirley Ann, chewing her nails. She had gone to bed with her husband and woken this morning without him.

"Where do you think they can be?" she asked, glancing at the clock.

"You know what they're like, up to no good—"A noise from outside stopped her mid-sentence.

The door opened. John Jo and Sean Paul appeared, looking the worse for wear. Their clothes were muddy, and they both had blood on them.

Gypsy's hand flew to her chest. "What's happened?"

"We had a bit of business to take care of…nothing for yous to worry about," he assured her. "I'm going to get a couple of hours' kip, you coming?"

She nodded without answering. As she left, she overheard him whisper to Sean Paul.

"We never speak of this again."

Speak of what?

CHAPTER 39

Tommy Lee turned into the lane that led to Duke's ground. It was now June, and he had decided he'd left it long enough without seeing Millie. Would she be pleased to see him? Did she miss him like he missed her? There was only one way to find out.

He was met head-on by Duke who was driving out. The lane was only wide enough for two small motors at a time, not a Transit and a Range Rover. He wound his window down and popped out his head.

"I'm here to see Millie," he said.

"She's not here. Look, I'm in a bit of hurry, can you call back later?" Duke went to wind the window back up, but Tommy Lee stopped him.

"So you don't mind me calling in now? Why the change of heart?"

"Can you please move your motor? Like I said, I'm in a hurry," Duke spat.

"Where is she?" Tommy Lee wasn't going to be brushed off this time.

Duke sighed. "She's passed her driving test and gone out."

Tommy Lee watched him closely. His eyes were narrowed. He was worried about her.

"I'm coming with you." He reversed and left his motor at the opening. Then jumped in next to Duke. "Why are you worried about her, is her driving that bad?"

"Her driving's fine. I taught her," Duke snapped. "I've got a bad feeling. I told you about her husband, Paul Kelly. She's gone and bought herself a brand-new Range Rover with his money, he ain't gonna like that."

Tommy Lee gritted his teeth but kept his thoughts to himself. If this Kelly prick hurt Millie, he would finish him for good.

They drove the rest of the way in silence, pulling up at the back of the club. Smoke drifted out from the open door.

"Shit." Duke jumped from the motor and grabbed the hosepipe attached to the outer wall. He turned it on and sprayed into the hallway.

"Hold this and spray me," he shouted to Tommy Lee.

But he was already running into the building.

He had his T-shirt over his mouth and nose to protect him from the thickening smoke. The fire appeared to only be at one door. He tapped the handle, it was hot.

"Stand back," he roared before kicking the door in.

There on a chair Millie sat, slumped backwards. Was she dead? Without thinking, he swooped her up and ran out of the club.

***

Tommy Lee had sat in the waiting room surrounded by Millie's family. He'd been here what seemed like hours. Finally taking his chance, when everyone was busy, he sneaked out, making sure no one was looking. He headed down the hall and opened her door. Was she asleep? He couldn't tell. Slipping inside quietly, he closed it and sat next to her bed. The oxygen tube disturbed him the most, that and the rasping sound she made with each breath. She seemed peaceful, though, and at least she was still alive.

"I'm not asleep," she said, opening her eyes. "And if you've come in here for a bit of the other, you're out of luck, I'm afraid. Doctor's orders."

He laughed softly. "That would have been nice, but I'm the patient type, I can wait." He placed his hand on top of hers; it was cold. "Mil, do you know who did this?"

"Do we have to talk about that now?" She sighed. "I—"

"I know, you want to forget it, but this is serious, so tell me what you can remember."

"I can remember everything. The sound of the petrol being tipped against the door. The roar of the flames..."

He held her hand and gave it a gentle squeeze. "Who did it?"

"I don't know..." A single tear ran down her face.

He wiped it away with his thumb. "They'll not get away with this. I promise. Now you get some rest, and I'll see you in the morning."

"No. Don't leave me, I don't want to be alone. Every time I close my eyes I'm back in that office surrounded by smoke, struggling to breathe, waiting to die..."

"Okay, I'll sit here while you sleep." He leant over and kissed her forehead. Still holding her hand, he sat back.

Was this a random act or something more sinister? He wouldn't believe it was against her, more than likely it was aimed at that fecking piece of shite, Paul Kelly.

He closed his eyes, knowing he wouldn't sleep tonight.

***

John Jo stepped out of the Cross Keys Inn, Dagenham, with a drunken Sean Paul following. He'd been playing poker and had won over a hundred quid. He looked around Crown Street. It was empty apart from two lovers canoodling across the road, half hidden by bushes that protruded from Saint Peter and Saint Paul's parish churchyard. He unlocked the car and helped his brother in, then nipped around to the driver's side. As he opened the door, he glanced over to a pair of young lovers; they both emerged from the shadows.

He stopped, frozen to the spot. It was two men, fondling in the street for all to see, but that wasn't what had shocked him.

Had his eyes deceived him?

He got into the car slowly, maintaining eye contact with the men. They turned and walked along the road, appearing more as mates now, but he knew what he had seen, who he had seen. Starting the motor, he swallowed down the bile that threatened to leave his mouth, then drove off in the opposite direction. This was a family problem.

***

Tommy Lee stood next to Duke. He had quizzed him about Kelly and his enemies. Duke seemed clueless, or maybe he wasn't letting on what he knew. Suddenly Duke's expression changed. His face hardened. Tommy Lee followed his eyes and took in the man in front of them. So this was Paul Kelly.

"How is she?" Paul asked breathlessly.

Duke's glare was icy. He stepped forward, squaring up to him, his hands clenched into fists. "You've got a fucking nerve showing up here. Haven't you done enough damage?" he growled.

Tommy Lee stepped back. He knew this was Duke's fight as a father. He wouldn't appreciate anyone stepping in.

Paul stopped dead, his gaze flicking over Duke's shoulder to the open door. "I need to see her."

"You think now's the right time, after everything you've put her through? She almost died, Paul. In your fucking club," Duke snapped. "You're toxic, I want you to stay away from my girl. I'll be the one to keep her safe. Me and her family."

Paul's face twisted in frustration. "I know I've messed up, but I love her. I have to see her, see that she's okay."

Duke shook his head and took a step closer. "You love her?" he asked in disdain. "You call this love? She's in that hospital bed because of all the crap you've done."

Tommy Lee turned when Connie came rushing out of the room, her eyes wide with worry. "Stop it, the pair of you, Millie can hear. This isn't the time or place," she whispered.

Paul obviously took his chance and pushed past the pair of them. Fecking prick.

The last thing Tommy Lee heard before leaving was Paul telling her he loved her, and she seemed all right with that. Had he wasted his time on a woman who didn't know what she wanted, or was he just a bit of fun, a distraction?

Maybe it was time to cut and run.

***

John Jo had lain awake all night, scared to close his eyes for fear of seeing PJ kissing that man again. He had thrown up three times already as the vision flashed before him. Gypsy now thought he had a sick bug and was keeping the baby away from him. He couldn't tell her, not yet. He needed to speak to his brothers first. No one knew where Tommy Lee was, nothing new there, and Sean Paul he would talk to later in private. Hopefully he wouldn't have too much of a hangover.

None of this made sense to him. The boy had a baby with some house dweller and was to be married…to a woman. Okay, so it hadn't happened, but that was because of the crow, not because he liked cock.

Bile filled his mouth again. He spat it out into the bowl Gypsy had placed next to him.

He needed his brothers. They could find PJ and bring him back here. Even if they had to tie him up and stick him in a cage, they would do so. Until he came to his senses, they would have to make the decisions for him.

Gypsy appeared at the bedroom door, her face taut with worry. "How are you feeling now?"

"I'm fine, darling, I think it might be something I ate last night," he lied. "I'll get up and have a shower."

"Tommy Lee's here, he's talking to Sean Paul outside."

He pushed the covers back and swung his legs round, grounding them firmly on the floor. "Tell them I'll be out in ten minutes and they are to wait for me."

***

Tommy Lee took the cup of tea from Shirley Ann and smiled. "Thank you." He had always been polite, his mother had always told him manners cost nothing and can open doors. He'd lived by that, and as far as he was concerned, she was right.

He glanced up. John Jo marched towards them. He didn't look his usual happy self. More problems. Tommy Lee sighed.

"Morning, boys," John Jo said as he made his way closer.

"So what's happened?" Sean Paul asked.

"Girls, can you leave us." John Jo waited for Gypsy and Shirley Ann to go into the mobile before he continued. "We have a problem. There's no easy way to say this but…" His face drained of colour.

Tommy Lee stood and pointed to his chair. "You better sit down before you fall down… Now start at the beginning."

John Jo took a couple of deep breaths and then relayed the previous night's events. Sean Paul gasped almost theatrically while Tommy Lee cursed himself for not having done anything sooner.

"We keep this to ourselves," he finally mumbled. "Because if this gets out, Mother and Father will be heartbroken."

"But what about PJ, we can't let this go on?" John Jo asked.

Sean Paul nodded in agreement.

"Do you know where this mystery job is he's got?" Tommy Lee knew his brothers would act hastily if he didn't rein them in.

"No, no one does, but at least we know he's in Dagenham."

"We can't spend time looking for him, it could take weeks." Tommy Lee rubbed the back of his neck, silently cursing PJ. Didn't he have enough to contend with? Millie was still firmly wedged into his brain and making it difficult to form any coherent decision on his own life, never mind his little brother's. "How often does he see Mother?"

"He hasn't been back for three weeks," Sean Paul informed him.

"I'll stay at Mother's until my next job. If he turns up I'll call you, and when I have to leave, you'll have to spend time over there. He can't stay away forever."

"And what do we do when we get him?" John Jo asked, swatting a fly away. "Feck off, you fecking pest."

"You keep him here. I'll leave a contact number when I know where I'm going, you phone me, and I'll be straight back. You do not do anything else." Tommy Lee handed his cup to Sean Paul. "I need to go, Mother's got the bacon pudding cooking, and I'm in need of a good home-cooked meal."

"I've got to say, Tommy Lee, you're taking this very calmly," John Jo said suspiciously.

"I had an idea he was…different. But he's still our brother, and we need to protect him. Now remember, just keep him here."

"You're not telling us everything."

"For feck sake, John Jo, drop it." Tommy Lee stood and glared at his brothers before walking away.

He climbed into his motor, his head full of questions.

Had Millie been discharged from hospital?

Was she really going to forgive Kelly for all the things he'd done to her?

Just fecking forget about her.

And then there was PJ. What were they supposed to do with him? They couldn't lock him up indefinitely. No. He needed to find out where he was and neutralise the problem, just like he had with Sam.

And look what happened then, PJ tried to take his own life.

He wiped a hand down his face. This was a problem he doubted he could fix.

CHAPTER 40

Three days had passed, and there had been no sight nor sound of PJ. It was as if he had vanished off the face of the earth. Tommy Lee was ready to give up and take an urgent job, just to get away. John Jo had been round questioning him again, and it had now come to the point where Tommy Lee wanted to clobber his brother if one more accusation came out of his mouth. He cursed PJ for bringing all this shit to his door. He had his own life to live.

He sat outside watching his father, Paddy, tether a Cob to his racing cart. At least he was oblivious to PJ's antics, and Mother, too. Although she moaned most days that she hadn't seen her baby for almost a month.

"You want to come for a trot down the lane?" Paddy called over.

"Yeah, why not. It's been a tidy while since I've been on here." Tommy Lee climbed on.

"Here, you take the reins." Paddy passed them to him. "You look like you've got the weight of the world on your shoulders, boy. A ride out might help you clear your head."

His father was a dark horse, never said much, but he was acute, took in all around him, and could read a man better than anyone. Maybe it was time to tell him the truth, let him know what was going on so he could advise.

He wouldn't understand.

Neither do I, but I'm expected to deal with it.

His generation would disown PJ, then what?

"You're right, Father, I need to clear my head." He smiled weakly. Because the problem was his to carry.

They sped down the lane at a hefty pace, the breeze cooling their faces from the summer sun. The trees and bushes whizzed past in a green blur. The clip-clop of the hooves on the road, although fast, was soothing. This reminded him of his childhood, it was comforting, familiar. They made it to the end of the lane too quickly for his liking, then turned around and trotted back.

He pulled onto the ground feeling refreshed, until he spotted John Jo's truck parked up. Then did a double-take when he saw PJ standing next to him. He slowed the trap until it stopped and jumped off.

"Thanks, Father, I'll let you finish up."

"Wait, boy. Whatever's going on, remember yous share the same blood, and that's important in times of trouble." Paddy shook the reins, and off he went.

Tommy Lee marched towards his brothers. He glanced at PJ who was obviously unaware of all the shit he had caused. This riled him more.

"Thought we could take a drive over to mine," John Jo told him. "PJ hasn't seen Jonny boy for weeks."

"Good idea, I'll come, too," Tommy Lee offered. "I'll jump in with yous."

The three of them piled in to John Jo's truck, with PJ in the middle. There was no way he could escape.

"So where are you working?" Tommy Lee asked him.

"Just doing a bit of work with a mate," PJ replied.

"And whereabouts is that?" John Jo added.

Tommy Lee could tell PJ was having trouble keeping his temper in. "Maybe it's a secret." He laughed, trying to lift the declining mood.

"No. No secret, it's different places, we travel around." PJ was nervous.

The rest of the journey was done in silence, and once there, John Jo told PJ to look in the stable.

"We've got a new Cob, you'll love him, go and see." John Jo grinned.

When PJ walked through the door, a muffled scream left his lips.

"What the feck are you doing?" Tommy Lee asked in disbelief.

Sean Paul had him on the floor, binding his hands with rope. "This is the only way."

The air inside the stable was thick with the smell of hay and horse shit. Tommy Lee couldn't stand it, it was suffocating. He glanced at PJ who struggled against the rough rope holding him. John Jo grabbed a chair and placed it behind him.

"Sit," he ordered. "You've gone wrong, boy, we all know your dirty secret, but we're here to set you right."

"You think tying me up is going to change who I am?" PJ's voice was hoarse but resigned. "You think I don't know this is wrong... I can't help it."

John Jo balled his fists. "Shut your mouth and listen." He sneered. "Have you thought about Mother and Father in all this? How they'll feel knowing their son's a fecking poof?"

"You lot are scared. Scared of anything that don't fit into your tiny little world."

Sean Paul's hand twitched by his side, his fingers curling into a fist. His breath came hard and fast. "We're trying to help you, PJ. You're sick in the head, but we can fix it. You just need to be—"

"What?" PJ cut in, laughing bitterly. "Beaten straight? Huh? That the plan?"

Sean Paul raised his fist. PJ seemed to brace himself.

"Enough!" Tommy Lee shouted. His voice cracked through the stable like a whip.

He had been leaning against the doorway, watching. His face was tense, his eyes dark with something between anger and disgust. He stepped forward, shoving Sean Paul back hard enough to send him stumbling.

"We're not doing this," he growled.

Sean Paul's face twisted. "He's a fecking queer."

"And what? You think beating the shite out of him is going to make him different?" His voice was razor-sharp. "You think we can punch the gay out of him?" He looked around, his gaze cutting through each of them. "If you do, you're even stupider than I thought."

"You defending him, then?" John Jo asked.

Tommy Lee's jaw tensed. He stared at PJ, then back at them. "I'm saying you're not laying a fecking hand on him."

A tense silence settled between them.

John Jo scoffed. "Jaysus. You gone soft, have you?"

"No." Tommy Lee stepped between them and PJ, his stance solid. "But I know what's right. And this?" He gestured around the stable. "This is a load of shite."

Sean Paul exhaled sharply, running a hand through his hair. He glared at PJ, then at Tommy Lee, then back at PJ again. He shook his head. "Feck this," he muttered, storming out of the stable.

John Jo followed, though he shot PJ one last look of disgust before disappearing outside.

Tommy Lee crouched, pulling a pocketknife from his boot. The blade glinted in the sunlight as he cut through PJ's bindings.

PJ flexed his wrists, wincing, then glanced down at Tommy Lee. "Why'd you stop them?"

Tommy Lee sighed, shaking his head. "Because what they were doing was wrong."

PJ gave a weak, bitter laugh. "And what now? You gonna tell me I'm wrong, too?"

Tommy Lee met his gaze. "Nah." A pause. "I don't understand it. I won't lie to you. But I'm not gonna be the kind of bastard they are, and besides, you know it's wrong. Why else would you hide it?"

PJ swallowed hard, nodding. "I want to, but I don't know how to change."

Tommy Lee stood, offering a hand. "Come on. Let's get out of here."

PJ hesitated, then took it.

Outside, the sun had dipped behind the treetops. Tommy Lee knew he wouldn't have to fight his brothers, they knew better than to take him on, but there was no way they would let this go.

"You'll need to face them at some point, and I may not be here to stop them," he warned. "Otherwise you'll need to pack up and run, there will be no returning. Can you do that?"

"But what about Mother and Father?"

"You've a choice to make: you stay and let us help or you go. There is no in between."

Silence followed. Tommy Lee could see PJ was thinking, different emotions crossing his face, until he finally spoke.

"I want to get better, be normal. I want help." He looked into Tommy Lee's eyes, his own watering.

"We'll help." But did he believe that? No. PJ was different, he always had been, no amount of beatings or tellings-off would make him anything other than what he was. His life would now be a miserable one.

CHAPTER 41

Tommy Lee sat on a bar stool next to John Jo and Sean Paul in a little boozer in Romford. "What did you want to see me about?"

"We've got a job lined up. Pay's good. Thought you might be interested," John Jo replied.

"Doing what?"

"Security for a scrapyard," Sean Paul added.

"Now why did yous think I'd be interested in a fecking job like that?" Tommy Lee shook his head.

"Because of who it's for." John Jo grinned. "You remember Millie? Wasn't you sweet on her, despite me warning you off?"

Tommy Lee's heart rate increased. "I'm all ears."

"Turns out her old man was killed in a hit-and-run."

"What. When?" His reply was a little too eager.

"A month or so ago, I'm not sure, anyway, she's left running his kingdom. Now some arsehole is playing games with her. That's where we come in. She needs us to run the place and guard it."

"She contacted you?"

"No, a man called Tony did, that was Paul's right-hand man... So what do ya say, you in?" John Jo raised a questioning eyebrow.

Tommy Lee rubbed his chin. He still had moments where she filled his head, despite him fighting it. Her soft body and pouty lips filled his mind. This wasn't his normal line of work, though, but maybe it could be fun. "Count me in, boys. So when do we start?"

***

Tommy Lee stood leaning against the filing cabinet. "Shouldn't she have been here by now?" He glanced at his watch. He was annoyed, not because of her but because he wanted to see her. He walked over to the desk. The sound of a motor pulling up stopped him complaining more.

Millie stepped up into the Portakabin with Rosie, her best friend and now employee behind her. She appeared to freeze when she spotted him.

Tommy Lee was now perched on the edge of her desk. He smiled at her before his attention dropped to her bump.

She's pregnant.

"Sorry I'm a bit late," she told them before sitting at the desk. "I take it Tony has filled you in?" She kept her eyes on the paperwork in front of her.

"We know what we need to do," Tommy Lee replied softly, his Irish accent caressing each word.

She glanced up at him. "Good."

He had caught her totally off-guard, he could sense it. So much so she appeared vulnerable.

"Tone, can you show them around, please? Rose, perhaps you should go, too, so you know what happens here." Millie refocused on the papers and didn't lift her head until the door closed. She let out a long, slow sigh.

"Is there anything you want to tell me?" Tommy Lee hadn't left. Instead, he stood by the door, his gaze on her.

"About?"

"Don't play games, Millie, you're having a baby. Am I the father?"

"That's no concern of yours, but if you must know, it's Paul's. Now you're here to do a job, so if you don't mind…" She pointed to the door.

He lingered for a minute, unsure, but then finally left and joined the others. He didn't understand why she was so cold. Hadn't he saved her life the last time they'd been together? And sat with her so she could sleep.

"Ungrateful woman," he muttered.

"What?" John Jo asked.

"Nothing," Tommy Lee snapped. "We're here to do a job, so let's do it." He glanced at the Portakabin. Millie was staring straight at him. "Wait there, I'll only be a minute."

He marched back in. She was already seated behind her desk. He stood there with his hands in his pockets.

"We've got the measure of the job. I think it's best if you stay away. A woman in your condition shouldn't be around a place like this." His voice was now cold on purpose.

"Very well, but there will be times I'll need to be here." She grabbed her bag and brushed past him.

He felt her like an electric shock pulsing through him. Breathing in her perfume, he closed his eyes. It was like the first time they'd met, only now she didn't want anything to do with him.

She's carrying another man's child, he reminded himself.

Or was she?

***

Tommy Lee sat in the Portakabin with his feet up on the desk and his hands behind his head. He was fecking miserable. John Jo had poured them all a drink of the scotch Millie had left them. Thank God there was a kettle there, too. He could take or leave booze but not his cuppa. Gazing at the mismatch of china, he wondered what cup was hers. Probably the black one, it matched her attitude.

Millie? She had played on his mind all day. He could have sworn she was lying when she'd said the baby was Paul's. Had he been wrong about her? Was she just another tart looking for a bit of rough? Why did it bother him, though?

A loud crash had him jumping up and running out of the door before John Jo had even put his glass down. He snuck around the edge of the yard, listening for any telltale signs of intruders. He wanted to find out how they had got in.

"Anything?" John Jo whispered.

"Shh." Tommy Lee held a finger to his lips.

The squeaking of a door caught his attention. He slowly moved towards it. Yanking it open, he stared down at two eyes that caught the faintest glow of moonlight. He smiled when the fox shot off between his legs.

He marched back towards the Portakabin with his brother in tow. "That crash wasn't caused by the fox."

Sean Paul stood outside, scratching his head. "Whoever that was then, they've gone."

"I'm more interested in how they got in here. All the gates are locked. Go grab me a torch, I'm gonna check the walls," Tommy Lee ordered.

"Don't you think it would be better to check in the morning?" Sean Paul asked.

"I want to look now. They may not have had time to cover their tracks properly, and anyhow, I doubt I'll be sleeping now." Tommy Lee made his way back to the shed. He shone the torch up the wall, looking for a light switch. He flipped it, and the place lit up.

John Jo stood beside him.

"You take that side, I'll meet you the other end." It was a large shed, full of copper wire that had been stripped. There were old oil drums crammed with the stuff. He'd bet they were worth a tidy sum.

"Over here," John Jo said.

"What is it?" Tommy Lee asked, crouching next to him.

"These boards are loose." John Jo pulled one away. "You can get straight out into the street."

Tommy Lee took a closer gander. "The screws have been undone from the inside... It's got to be someone who works here." He stared around the shed. "We need to fix these back up, then put something in front of it that can't be moved."

"Where are you going now?"

"I'm going round the other side, I want to know why there's no fence." Tommy Lee opened the small gate that was inside the entrance gate. He marched along the road until he came to a gap. He studied it; the wire had been cut away. Whoever had broken in hadn't had the time to roll it back into place. There was an old cable tie hanging from the top.

He now had the how, he just had to figure out the who and why.

**

"You checked everything's in order?" Tommy Lee asked Sean Paul.

"Yep, it's all good," he said with a wave of his hand. "Have either of you checked on PJ?"

"I phoned earlier. Gypsy said he's been as good as gold, he hasn't left them once," John Jo answered. "I can't see him sneaking off, not when the girls are there on their own."

"Good idea of yours, Tommy Lee, getting him to help with the horses and look after Shirely Ann and Gypsy," Sean Paul said thoughtfully.

Tommy Lee knew it was only a matter of time before the urge took PJ and he'd need a man, but at least he wasn't able to slip away for the time being. Noise of motor pricked his ear. He glanced out of the window. Millie. She entered the Portakabin.

"You're in my chair." She frowned.

"I thought I told you not to come back here," he said through gritted teeth.

"I wanted to see if you've made any progress." She threw her bag down on the desk. "So have you?"

"It's only been twenty-four hours."

"So nothing's happened. Great." She sauntered to the window and stared out.

Tommy Lee stood and walked behind her.

"The men are all busy working, as you can see," he said pointedly. "So you can relax."

"I don't expect anyone will try anything now they know you're here."

"Someone did—" he began.

"So something has happened. Why didn't you say?" she snapped.

He sighed. "I think it's someone who works here, trying their luck."

"What do you mean, trying their luck?"

"From what I can make out, someone's been sneaking in and taking the copper wire from the shed. I found a length of it on the path outside when we disturbed them last night."

"Oh great, my own employees stealing from me." She threw her hands up in the air. "Do you think you can find out who?"

"And what do you want me to do if I find them?" he asked.

"I don't know, what would you do?"

"Find out why they are stealing from you. There may be a good reason for it."

"A good reason for it? I want my employees to respect me, not think they can get one over on me just because I'm a woman."

"That's not respect you want, Millie, you want them to fear you. Is that what you learnt from your husband?"

"Maybe." She walked to the sofa and sat. "You're being paid to do a job, not to question me."

"Well, I think it's time for you to stick your job, I'm done."

"What are you doing?" Her gaze followed him as he grabbed his belongings.

"I told you, I'm done." He pushed the door open then turned to her. His eyes narrowed. "I don't know what's happened to you, but if you want respect, sometimes leniency is better than punishment."

CHAPTER 42

Tommy Lee was now living on his brothers' piece of land. He was using John Jo's trailer, and PJ was using Sean Paul's. On the one hand it was nice all being together, on the other it was tiring watching PJ's every move. They had been to the local pub a couple of times, but he'd warned them that it might be putting temptation in their brother's way. Things seemed to change when Shirely Ann's cousin, Marina, came to visit. They sparked up a friendship quickly, and while John Jo and Sean Paul thought it was more, Tommy Lee had his reservations. After a week PJ was courting her, then he'd proposed two weeks later. The wedding had been planned for April; they had decided on a spring wedding. But something still seemed off for Tommy Lee.

He sat in the trailer with the fire roaring away. It was now fast approaching December. He had never been lonely in his own company but lately he had started to feel different. Was it his age? Did he need to find a wife? Millie popped into his mind. Had she had the baby yet?

Stop it.

He switched the TV on; he needed a distraction. A knock came from the door, and then it opened. John Jo appeared.

"You'll never guess who's just turned up here, and she's asking for you," he said. "And—"

"Millie?" Tommy Lee's heart beat a little faster.

"Yes, and she's had twins. Gypsy reckons they look like—"

Before his brother had finished, Tommy Lee leapt up and left.

He marched towards the mobile, his head bursting with questions he couldn't answer. Letting himself in, he stopped and stood in the doorway staring at the babies. He stepped closer. John Jo had said they looked like him. He couldn't see it. Babies all looked the same. "You wanted to see me."

She didn't answer, she just sat there, her face red. He could see she felt awkward.

"I haven't got all day, Millie."

"It was about the scrapyard… You told me it was one of my men nicking a bit of scrap on the side. I just came to tell you, you were wrong, but you probably already know that. How much did he pay you?"

"You're not making any sense, woman." What the feck was she talking about? "And who's he?"

"The man who's now come to take everything I own. He calls himself Sid, ring any bells?"

"I think you should start at the beginning." Tommy Lee took a seat opposite her. His gaze rested on the twins when they squirmed. "Here, give me one. What's his name?"

"Duke, after my dad. I call him baby Duke." She gazed at Tommy Lee as he stood and rocked baby Duke back to sleep. "You're a natural."

"Sean Paul has three chavvies and John Jo has one, so I've had plenty of practice." He glanced down at Millie. "So what's the other boy called?"

She paused for a moment, her mouth gaping like a fish out of water.

"Well?" He pressed.

"Tommy."

"Named after?" He wasn't letting her off this lightly.

"You," she finally admitted.

"Would you have told me, if it wasn't for coming here about that fecking scrapyard?" He glared down at her.

She remained silent.

"I thought so," he added. He placed baby Duke down onto the sofa and left.

***

PJ sat across the table from Marina and held her hand. He had never been one for fancy restaurants, but Tommy Lee had bunged him a few quid and told him to spoil her. So here he was, smiling through the pain. She was a nice girl, kind, loving, and gentle. Pretty enough, but the trouble was, he didn't fancy her. Having only been with men recently, he wasn't even sure he'd be able to get it up on his wedding night, which was why he had declined any intimate relations before the big day. While she thought he was noble, he knew he was a fraud. He wanted to do right by her, of course he did, and once they were married things would be different, better even. He would keep telling himself that in the hopes that it would be true.

He glanced at the waiter, a tall slim man, handsome with a nice bum. His cock twitched.

Shit.

Focusing back on his fiancée, he put the crude thoughts out of his head. "Would you like more wine?"

"No thank you… I was talking with my mum; she wanted to know where we'd be living after we're married. I told her probably on my dad's land."

He stiffened.

She continued, obviously not noticing his reaction. "What do you think?"

"I need to be with my brothers, we're breeding the Cobs next year. It's going to be a big job, but the money will be good," he assured her. "Maybe when I've got enough cash behind me we can move somewhere and start breeding for ourselves."

Her smile faded. He felt guilty, but there was no way he would move away.

"Let's worry about that nearer the time," he added. "I best get you home, it's getting late."

He paid the bill then dropped her home, relieved that she had gone. He looked at his watch. He wouldn't be expected home just yet. Did he have time to pay a little visit to Pete?

CHAPTER 43

The weather had been reasonably mild so far this winter, but today Tommy Lee was freezing. He blew into his cupped hands, trying to bring the feeling back into his fingers, while he stood behind the Transit.

"You need to reverse a bit more," he shouted to John Jo. "Whoa, that'll do." He then began unloading the logs.

His brother appeared at his side and picked up a couple. "It's been two weeks since Millie was here."

Tommy Lee nodded but didn't reply. Did he think he hadn't thought about her?

"Don't you wonder what those chavvies are like now?" John Jo continued.

"Listen, I know you mean well, but I'm not interested in her or the chavvies." Tommy Lee threw the logs into the shed. "She had the chance to tell me." He snatched two more. "I even asked her outright." He stopped and looked at John Jo. "She bare-face lied to me. Now just drop it."

"Okay." John Jo held his hands up in surrender. "I just don't want you regretting your decision."

Throwing the wood down, Tommy Lee marched to his trailer, cursing under his breath. He'd always prided himself on knowing everything that happened in his life. He was in control. There were no secrets in his world, at least none that could stay hidden for long. He was angry, angry at the situation and angry with himself. He'd had a nagging suspicion he was the father, but he'd taken her word for it, the word of a fecking liar.

When he stepped inside the trailer, he slumped down onto the bunk. He'd had many a sleepless night, thinking about the twins. Thinking about her. How could she? And then there was this Sid she'd accused him of working with. The woman was mentally unstable and a fecking liability. But what worried him the most was what if the children weren't safe with her? What if she wasn't safe?

He picked up his keys and left.

It was six-thirty when he pulled up at Millie's house. He knocked on the door then stood back. The door opened. It was Connie, Millie's mother.

"Can I see Millie?" he asked, now feeling nervous.

"She's not back from work yet. Come in and see your boys."

He stepped inside. This was the first time he'd been here. He thought it was a bit showy, nothing like Millie, or was it?

He stood between the two cribs. Both boys were snuggled in their blankets. "They look bigger."

"They grow up too quickly," she agreed. "Here, take a seat with this one."

She handed Tommy boy to him, and he sat in the armchair.

"What's going on?" Duke snapped, entering the room.

Tommy Lee turned to face him. "Good question. Does she leave my boys every day, cos if she ain't capable of looking after them, they should come and live with me."

"These babies ain't going nowhere with you. They belong with their mother," Duke said.

"Then where is she?" He stood and passed Tommy boy to Connie, readying himself to square up to Duke. "Maybe we should take this outside."

"No one's taking anything outside," Millie said as she stormed into the room. "What are you doing here?" she barked at Tommy Lee.

"I've come to see my sons, or are you going to stop me from seeing them?"

"I think you should leave," Duke intervened.

"If I leave, I'll be taking my sons with me."

"Enough!" Millie screamed. "No one will ever take my children away from me, no one." She picked baby Duke up as the shouting had woken both babies. "Mum, thank you for watching them for me. Pass Tommy boy to his father. Dad, take Mum home."

"I'm not leaving you alone with him." Duke stabbed a finger at Tommy Lee.

"I'll be fine, now please, I'll phone you later." Millie walked to the kitchen with her parents.

"If he hurts you in any way," Duke warned.

"Dad, he won't hurt me." Millie closed the door and joined Tommy Lee on the sofa. "Why did you really come here?"

"To talk."

"About?" she asked.

Why was she surprised? They were as much his sons as they were hers. Shouldn't he be responsible for them, too?

"Firstly, why didn't you tell me about the twins... I asked you if I was the father."

"I wasn't sure they were yours, I didn't want to mislead you... I only realised a few weeks ago when I looked into their eyes and saw you staring back." Millie stood and laid Duke back into his crib. She then took Tommy boy and laid him down. "I didn't mean to hurt you. I'm sorry."

He gave a nod, unsure how to answer.

"You can see them whenever you want, I would never stop you," she added. "But they live here with me… What else did you want to know?"

"The scrapyard, whatever's going on there I don't want you involved." He sighed.

"You are aware that I own it… Christ, you sound like my dad. He hasn't put you up to this, has he?" she asked.

Tommy Lee shook his head. "No, but if that's what he thinks, I agree. Have you even thought about the twins in all this? What happens if this Sid bloke decides to come after them?"

"I asked you for help, you weren't interested," she reminded him.

"Surely Duke will help you."

"Nope, he wants me to sell up or take on a partner." Avoiding his stare, she walked to the fridge and poured a glass of wine.

He watched her closely. There was a sadness about her he'd never noticed before.

"Can I get you a drink?" she asked.

"Tea, please."

"I have beer."

"I'm not a big drinker, tea will be just fine." He turned and headed back to the lounge. "They're handsome boys."

Millie laughed. "Is that because they're like you?"

"I can see you in them as well, they both have your lips… I want you to keep away from that man."

Millie passed him his tea. "I'm not letting him swoop in and take everything, this is my livelihood, and the twins' inheritance."

"They need their mother, Millie, not some dead gangster's legacy."

"It's all under control. Drink your tea while it's hot." She smiled.

He knew she was lying, her eyes betrayed her.

CHAPTER 44

"I'll raise you fifty." John Jo threw the notes in.

Tommy Lee sat holding his cards close to his chest, while his mind was elsewhere.

"Your go," Sean Paul nudged.

"What?" Tommy Lee glanced around the table.

Everyone was staring back at him. He grabbed some notes and threw them on top of the kitty.

"There's a tidy sum in there, boys, reckon it's got my name on it." John Jo laughed.

Tommy Lee himself wasn't expecting to win, he was only playing as a distraction. He needed distracting from the guilt he felt. Had he put Millie in danger by not doing the job she'd paid him for and then losing his temper? He'd never lost his temper with a woman, least of all a woman who was paying him. This was different, though, she'd got under his skin. He could kick himself because he'd allowed himself to break his own number one rule. Never mix business with pleasure. Now, here he sat, wondering if she and the children were safe.

"Tommy Lee," John Jo shouted. "Are you in or not?"

He threw in his cards. "I've got a bit of business to take care of. I'll see you in the morning."

He left the pub, thankful that the raucous noise of the Travellers faded as the door closed. Walking to the motor, he wondered what she would be doing now. Would the twins be in bed?

He unlocked the Range Rover then climbed in. Was he doing the right thing?

***

PJ lay on his back while Pete pleasured him with his mouth. He was now at the point of no return and grabbed his head, pushing himself deeper between his lips, sliding against his tongue. He let out a groan and shuddered. Pete rolled over, wiping the remnants of PJ's sperm from his chin.

"You never answered me earlier. Are you coming back to work at the bar?" Pete asked.

"I can't, I've got family stuff going on."

"They don't know, do they?"

"Know what?" PJ asked innocently.

"Oh, come on, Sam, if that's even your real name. You disappeared without trace. I'm not stupid."

"My family are different to most people. If they found out about you, you'd be dead. I didn't come back because I was protecting you," PJ assured him.

"So what, you come here when you can for a quick blow job... I want more from life, I want someone who wants me."

"I do want you, and one day we'll be together, you've just got to give me time to sort everything out." PJ grabbed him and pulled him into an embrace. "I promise, you just need to trust me."

He had amazed himself at how easy it was to lie to Pete just for sex, and Marina to make him appear normal. But the biggest lie was to himself. He couldn't live like this for much longer. At this rate he would need to go to confession. On second thoughts, with all the sins he had committed, the bloody priest would spontaneously combust.

***

Tommy Lee knocked on the door then stood back. Rosie appeared.

"Hello," he greeted. "Millie home?"

"You'd better come in." She stood back so he could enter. "Look who's here, Mil."

"Hello. What brings you here so late?" She frowned.

"We need to talk… In private," he said firmly.

"I'll be in my bedroom." Rosie stood and stared at him for a few seconds. "If I hear screaming I'll be straight back down."

"I'm not gonna hurt the mother of my chavvies," he snapped.

"Not her screams, yours. She's the one likely to inflict pain these days. Maybe you can have a word with her, make her see sense." Rosie brushed past him and ran up the stairs.

"Is she always like that?" he asked, sitting next to Millie.

"She's protective. Anyway, you wanted to talk, so talk." She turned towards him.

His body heated up under her gaze. He glanced around the room while finding the right words until his gaze rested back on her. "I know you well enough to know you're not gonna back down from this man, so I've got a solution." He could see he had her interested. That was a good sign.

"And that is?" she asked eagerly.

"I take over the fight. I'll watch the scrapyard and deal with him. In return, you look after our boys."

"You're banning me from my businesses?" She laughed.

"No. When you need to go there, either I take you or Duke does, but your first priority is the twins… I'll leave you to think it over."

He stood, having laid his cards out for her. He wasn't sure what he would do if she said no. Take the chavvies to keep them safe? He looked down at her, a little flutter building deep inside him. No woman had made him feel like this before.

"You've got until tomorrow night to give me your answer."

***

When Tommy Lee returned home he was met by John Jo and Sean Paul. They motioned him into the trailer.

"Now what, and why all the secrecy?"

John Jo closed the door and peeked out of the window. "I think PJ's sleeping as his trailer's in total darkness." He sat opposite Tommy Lee. "I think we might have a problem."

"Go on." Tommy Lee nodded.

"PJ said he was going out with Marina," John Jo began.

"We didn't think nothing of it." Sean Paul shrugged.

"Do you want to tell him or shall I?" John Jo said. "Like I was saying, he said he was taking Marina out, only she phoned to speak with him. Turns out she didn't see him tonight, and when he came home I asked where he'd been, and he reckoned he took her to the pictures. So not only is he a fecking poof, he's also a liar."

"You can't be sure he was with a man," Tommy Lee said. "He could have been anywhere."

"You don't believe that and neither do we… What we going to do?" John Jo asked with a sigh.

"I'll be away working for the next few months, yous will have to follow him, find out where he's going, and once we know, we can plan our next move." Tommy Lee ran his hand over his face. He needed this like a hole in the head. "And don't hurt him, or I'll hurt the two of you."

"Where are you going?" Sean Paul asked.

"I'll be running the scrapyard for a bit, with Duke."

"I hope she's paying you well, taking you away from your family when we need you most," John Jo said bravely.

"Those babies are my family, first and foremost." Tommy Lee growled.

The twins, his twins, would come first from now on. His brothers could sort their own shite out for a change.

PJ knelt on the bunk, peering out through a gap in the curtains. With his trailer in total darkness, his brothers wouldn't have spotted him while he spied on them. He could see them through the mobile window. It looked serious. Were they talking about him? His senses said yes. John Jo and Sean Paul had been questioning him since he had returned from seeing Pete. Stupid questions, like what film did he see, what happened in it. Had he slipped up? He spun around and flopped back on the bunk. This double life was killing him. He hated lying, but now it was becoming second nature. Each day was harder to navigate in case he said the wrong thing.

Marina deserved better. Her gentle mannerisms and sweet smile filled him with guilt. She seemed so in love with him, and he was using her. Thank God she was oblivious, because he really didn't want to hurt her. Then there was Pete, who wasn't, he knew he was being used. The look of hurt on his face tonight had said it all.

Standing, PJ walked to the bedroom at the end of the trailer. Kicking his boots off, he lay back on the bed and stared into the darkness.

He missed the days where all he thought about were the Cobs. Looking after them, riding them, showing them off to other Travellers and gypsies. He'd had none of these wrong thoughts about men then.

You also didn't think about girls.

He rolled over, pulled the covers up to his chin, and put the thought out of his head. Tomorrow would be a new day. He could try and be normal again.

CHAPTER 45

It was Christmas Eve morning. A sharp frost covered the landscape. PJ and Sean Paul drank the last of their tea before venturing out into the cold. The Cobs needed cleaning out today, that way they could take it easy tomorrow and enjoy the day with family.

Maeve and Paddy would be over, spoiling the grandchildren with gifts and hugs. Sean Paul loved Christmas. It was Christmas Eve he had met Shirley Ann, five years ago today. Now he was married to her with three children, the youngest only two months old.

He stared around the paddock while heading towards the stable. "Reckon we could get some more mares." He unhitched the gate and waited for PJ to walk through. "What do you think?" He refastened it and stomped towards the stable. "We could build another stable, then start breeding springtime."

He glanced at PJ who seemed to be in a world of his own, his hands shoved deep into his pockets and face stony.

"What's up, boy?"

No answer.

"PJ!" Sean Paul roared, his temper getting the better of him.

"Huh?" PJ appeared stunned.

"I'm talking to you, and you're ignoring me, so what's on your mind?" Sean Paul opened the first stable door and watched as Cornelius trotted out, then picked up the wheelbarrow and manoeuvred it into the stall.

"Marina wants to move onto her father's land when we're married," PJ moaned. "I told her I want to stay here cos of the horses."

"You're the man, you live where you say. You can still go and stop there a bit from time to time." Sean Paul decided a change of subject was needed. "Are you coming to the fight tonight? Tommy Lee will be there."

"I can't believe John Jo's fighting Gypsy's uncle Henry after all this time. Would've thought the man had enough the last time he got put on his arse."

Sean Paul laughed loudly. "Some men are simple, besides, feuds can last a lifetime, especially when it involves family."

PJ nodded in agreement.

"So are you coming?"

"I can't, Marina wants me to go there as I won't be seeing her tomorrow."

"You'll be missing a good night, but I'm glad you've got your priorities straight." Sean Paul passed him the pitchfork. "You make a start here, I'll do next door."

With the mood lighter, he headed to the next stable. Had PJ now come to his senses, or was this a ploy? Sean Paul was undecided. While he wanted to believe his brother was now seeing things as a man should, there was a little niggling feeling he couldn't shake.

***

The gym was packed when Tommy Lee arrived. He made his way through to the back and spotted Sean Paul.

"Where's PJ?" he asked, scanning the area.

"He's had to go see Marina. Poor lad's already under the thumb and they ain't even married yet."

Tommy Lee hoped that was where he really was, he couldn't put up with any more problems. It was bad enough Millie not talking to him after their bust-up, and now he'd bought half the scrapyard, he expected it to only get worse when she found out he was the mystery buyer.

He'd been to the solicitors today and signed on the dotted line, paid the money — Fatty's money to be more precise — and become her partner. It thrilled and scared him in equal measure. He wasn't sure what she expected from him. He had responsibilities to her and the twins. Keeping her safe was a full-time problem in itself. He'd pick the right moment to tell her, maybe doing it with witnesses so she couldn't kick off. He glanced over towards the door.

"Duke, over here." He waved his hand in the air.

"Who's taking the bets, lads?" Duke asked.

"See that man over there, with the grey cap on? Him," John Jo said, joining them.

"I'll walk over with you." Tommy Lee pushed through the waiting crowd. "How's Millie?"

"She's okay." Duke pulled out a roll of ten-pound notes. "You still coming tomorrow?" he asked while counting them.

"Don't know if that's such a good idea."

"It's your chavvies' first Christmas. Personally, I wouldn't miss that for the world."

Tommy Lee stood with his hands in his pockets and shrugged. "I don't want to make it awkward for anyone, besides, me mother will want me at hers for dinner."

"Suit yourself, but just remember, you're gonna have to face her sooner or later."

He wanted it to be sooner, but the thought of what she might say worried him. Why? He had never given a feck about what anyone thought or said.

She's not just anyone.

He sighed. No, she wasn't, she was the mother of his children, and no matter how they had been conceived, he still had a responsibility to all three of them. The funny thing was, he wanted that, he wanted her. As hard as he fought against the notion, the more he realised this was what he needed. Her and the twins.

"Fight's about to start." Sean Paul nudged him.

They made their way to the corner of the ring where John Jo sat, the air thick with tension. The mixed cries of jeering, taunting, and cheering came from the rowdy crowd. The Irish Travellers and gypsies goaded one another.

The bell sounded, and both men jumped to their feet. Tommy Lee stood between Duke and Sean Paul, his attention glued to John Jo. He'd placed a hefty wedge on his brother winning, he wasn't in doubt of the outcome.

John Jo was tough, and he was in good shape. Tommy Lee almost felt sorry for Henry. The man was already breathing heavily.

Henry threw the first punch, a brutal right hook aimed at John Jo's ribs. He twisted his body just in time, the glove grazing his side but not landing cleanly. John Jo countered with a swift jab to Henry's jaw, snapping his opponent's head back. Henry staggered but quickly regained his stance, responding with a furious combination—left jab, right hook, uppercut. John Jo absorbed most of it, his guard holding, but the uppercut clipped his chin, and he stumbled back a step.

He feinted left, then threw a devastating right cross that landed flush on Henry's cheek. The impact sent a shockwave through the room as his head flicked to the side.

He reeled, blinking rapidly, his balance wavering. John Jo surged forward, unleashing a rapid-fire barrage, left, right, left, right, each punch striking home. The crowd's roar reached a fever pitch. Henry's knees buckled. He staggered back, barely managing to keep his feet.

John Jo didn't let up. He launched one final, thunderous right hook straight to Henry's jaw. The punch landed with a sickening crack, and Henry's body went limp. He crumpled to the canvas, and the entire room fell silent.

"Jaysus, has he killed him?" Sean Paul whispered.

"Shh," Tommy Lee warned.

The referee stepped in and began the count.

"One! Two! Three!"

Henry twitched, trying to push himself up.

"He's moving." Duke said.

"Four! Five! Six!"

The crowd chanted John Jo's name, the sound reverberating through the building.

"Seven! Eight! Nine!"

Henry groaned, his arms shaking as he tried to rise. But it was no use.

"Ten! Out!"

The referee waved his hands. "It's over!"

The Irish Travellers exploded, their cheers deafening. John Jo raised his arms in triumph and grinned at his brothers.

The ref standing next to him bellowed to be heard. "Your winner, John Jo Ward!"

"I'm going to get me winnings, you fancy coming for a pint?" Duke asked.

Tommy Lee nodded. He needed to unwind. Maybe a good drink would help him do that. Then he'd sleep without her in his head.

***

Both men drove back to Stepney in their own motors and parked up outside the Old Artichoke public house. John Jo and Sean Paul had declined to join them, instead choosing to go home and celebrate with their wives. Tommy Lee felt a pang of jealousy when Millie popped into his mind.

He and Duke entered the pub. The landlord, Finn, greeted Duke like family. He was a six-foot Irishman with a broad Southern Irish accent and easy smile.

"What can I get yous two fellas?" he asked, giving Tommy Lee the once-over.

"Two whiskeys, please, Finn, and one for yourself," Duke said. "So what's bothering you?" He turned to Tommy Lee.

"Who said anything was bothering me?" he asked.

"There you go, two whiskeys." Finn placed them on the bar. "I'll leave the bottle. I know a man with woman troubles when I see one." He then walked back to an old man he had been chatting to.

"Cheers." Tommy Lee knocked his back in one.

"Woman problems, well, I know he wasn't talking about me," Duke said after taking a sip. "And judging by the way you knocked that back, I'd say you've got it bad."

"I just want to forget about her." Tommy Lee reached for the bottle. "She's in my head all the fecking time."

"Sounds rough, lad. Who's the lucky girl?"

"Millie." He sighed.

Duke leant in and whispered, "Millie, my Millie?"

"Your Millie," Tommy Lee agreed.

They both took enormous gulps of their drinks.

"I thought it was just about the twins." Duke took another sip. "But it makes sense, buying the scrapyard, trying to protect her."

"Well, it doesn't matter, whatever I do is wrong." Tommy Lee reached for the bottle and refilled both glasses. "When she finds out I'm the one who bought half the scrapyard, she'll probably never speak to me again."

"I wouldn't be too sure of that… She asks about you every night."

"She does?" Tommy Lee smiled. Maybe there was a chance after all.

CHAPTER 46

PJ woke and rubbed his eyes before stretching his arms above his head. He scanned the room with blurry eyes. This wasn't his trailer. He glanced next to him when movement caught his eye. A man squirmed, then rolled over with his back to him.

Shit!

He slid out of the bed, quietly wincing. His head throbbed, and his arse hurt, the pain increasing as he reached for his clothes. Something was wrong, his movements slow and clumsy, as if he were under water, and that searing pain seemed to be deep inside him. He stared at where he had been lying. Blood. Had this man raped him?

Panic set in. How the feck was he going to explain this to his brothers when he didn't know how to explain it to himself? He could remember going to the bar after leaving Marina, he even remembered having a couple of drinks, but not enough to get pissed and lose his memory. He needed water—his mouth was dry with a funny taste. He walked towards the door, each step using the little energy he had. The floor creaked beneath him. He pulled on the handle. It was locked.

Shit.

"Not thinking of leaving, are you?" a deep voice came from behind him.

***

Sean Paul opened the stable doors and let the two Cobs out. He had expected PJ to do it, but as he was on the missing list, he had to do it himself.

"Where do you think he is?" John Jo asked while walking towards him.

"He could be at Marina's," Sean Paul said, despite not believing that for one second.

"I'll go and phone her." John Jo turned to walk away.

"No." Sean Paul grabbed his arm and pulled him back. "What if he ain't there? She's going to want to know where he is, and if it comes out what he's been up to, the wedding will be off, and that's the only chance we have of making him normal."

"Fecking eejit, I'll kill him with me own two bare hands." John Jo spat. "You think he's been with a man?"

Sean Paul shook his head. "I don't know for sure, and keep your voice down, we don't want Mother and Father getting suspicious."

***

"I need to get home, before my brothers come looking for me," PJ warned while rubbing his head. The pain seemed to be getting worse.

"Oh, I don't think they'll find you here." The man grinned. "Besides, the party is only just getting started."

A loud knock came from the door. The man stood, naked, his torso flabby and hairy, his cock tiny and limp. He strode towards it, pushing PJ back towards the bed. PJ had no energy to fight.

He looked up. Two men entered the room. He felt a film of sweat cover his body. The two men handed over money then began to take their clothes off.

PJ sank back against the headboard. If he ever got out of this alive, he would never look at a man again.

**

Tommy Lee cursed as he climbed into his Range Rover. That fecking woman was the most unreasonable person he had ever met, and talk about stubborn. He started the motor and slammed it into gear. He would go and see his family and rescue the remaining hours of Christmas that were left.

He cursed Duke for putting him in that situation. Everything had been going well. The meal, the company. They had even talked like normal people. It all started with Connie. He played it over and over again in his mind.

"I've got something to tell you, Duke," Connie announced.

"Oh God." Millie put her head in her hands. Did she know what was coming?

"What is it, spit it out?" Duke said.

"I'm having a baby," she exclaimed.

Silence followed. It was the longest silence Tommy Lee had ever experienced. So he broke it. "Congratulations, Duke." But now he wished he hadn't.

"Haven't you got something to tell Millie?" Duke grinned.

Tommy Lee rubbed the back of his neck, the smile dropping from his face quicker than a ton of bricks. Was he nervous? Yes.

Millie frowned at him. "Well, I'm sure you're not pregnant, too, so what is it?"

He picked up his glass and necked the remaining whiskey. "I'm the one who bought half the scrapyard. We're partners."

Then it had all gone tits up. While Duke sat there shellshocked from Connie's revelation that she was pregnant, Tommy Lee had the fallout from Millie. It was also the look on her face, like she had been betrayed. As if he would ever do that to her. Well, whatever happened now, they were partners and parents to the twins, so she was stuck with him. She would have to like it or lump it.

He pulled onto his brothers' piece of land. It was now starting to get dark. He stopped and jumped out, putting a smile on his face for everyone else's benefit. He marched towards John Jo's mobile, because that was where all the noise was coming from.

Before he reached the door, Sean Paul and John Jo came out, their faces speaking louder than any words.

"What's happened?"

"PJ's missing. He went out yesterday to see Marina and he hasn't come home," Sean Paul explained.

"We thought he'd gone to, you know, but it's unlike him to miss Christmas with Mother. You know how she gets," John Jo added.

This was just what Tommy Lee needed after today's catastrophe with Millie. "Have you phoned Marina to see if he's there, or when she last saw him?"

"No, we thought she might find out about him..." Sean Paul sighed. "What the feck are we going to do?"

"Go and phone her, then if she hasn't seen him we'll take a trip to Dagenham." Tommy Lee rubbed the back of his neck. A headache was starting to build.

"Dagenham's a big place, it'll be impossible to find him." John Jo opened his mouth to say something else but obviously saw Tommy Lee's expression.

He wasn't in the mood to put up with anyone's negative comments. "I'll go see Mother and calm her down."

CHAPTER 47

Tommy Lee had calmed his mother the best he could. Marina hadn't seen PJ since six p.m. Christmas Eve, but he never told her that. Instead, he now had to go searching.

Merry fecking Christmas.

After the last time PJ had gone away, working, Tommy Lee had made it his business to find out where. There were two dives in Dagenham where it could have been, and he had narrowed it down to one.

"Something bad's happened, I can feel it," Sean Paul said.

Ignoring him, Tommy Lee stared at the alleyway. "It's down there, hard to spot and the doors reinforced. Get the crowbar, it's in the back, and the torch, we'll jimmy the fecking thing off."

The three of them climbed out. John Jo grabbed the crowbar and followed Tommy Lee to a drab door. The place was in total darkness apart from a faint light coming from an upstairs window.

"Shouldn't we try knocking first?" Sean Paul asked.

Ignoring him, Tommy Lee got to work. "This ain't budging," he moaned. "Might have to climb up and smash the window to get in." He glanced at the drainpipe running up the wall and gave it a shake. "Seems sturdy enough. Once I'm in I'll open the door. Be ready."

Sliding the crowbar into his jacket, he began to climb, cursing silently when he scraped his knuckles against the brickwork.

"Hurry up," John Jo whispered. "Before you're spotted."

Fighting the urge to tell his brother to feck off, Tommy Lee glanced into the window. The curtain had a tiny gap where the occupier hadn't drawn them properly. He couldn't see any movement. The bed was empty; a little lamp illuminated the corner of the room. Whilst, by his standards, it appeared grotty, it was tidy. He reached for the crowbar, pulling it from his coat, then tapped it firmly against the glass. It shattered, sending splinters into the room. He grabbed the handle and yanked it open, then pushed himself onto the ledge and dived in headfirst. He stood, the glass crunching beneath his boots. He did a full three-sixty, taking in every detail. No one was there.

Good.

He headed towards the door, pausing when a photo caught his eye. It was a man standing, with his arm around PJ, and both were laughing. It reminded him of the old PJ, carefree and happy. He hadn't smiled like that for a while now.

Because he's living a lie.

Tommy Lee sighed and then made his way out onto the landing. The place was bigger inside than it had appeared from the alleyway. He passed a few doors then descended the stairs. There were four doors at the bottom. The back door, which was down a narrow hallway, had two thick bolts attached that were firmly fixed so no one could break in. He pushed the next open to find a tiny kitchen. His torch dimmed, so he banged it on his hand; that seemed to spark it back to life. The next room had a shower and toilet in it, and then the last door led into a room that was obviously where the partying happened. It had an L-shaped bar, not particularly big, but held an array of bottles and glasses. He shone the torch around to what seemed to be a DJ set in one corner, and a few doors leading off on the other side. He shone the torch to what he believed to be the front of the building and spotted the main door. It had a couple of sturdy bolts locking it securely. He pulled them back, then opened it with ease. He ascended stairs to another door; this one was more secure. It had several bolts attached, which he slid open. It also had a lock, with no key in it. He shook the handle, but it didn't budge.

"Tommy Lee, is that you?" John Jo's voice drifted through the door.

"Yes...I need to find the key." He turned and re-entered the main room. A light switch was just inside the entrance, so he flicked it on, squinting until his eyes adjusted to the brightness. He marched towards the bar. Would it be here somewhere? Pulling the contents of the shelves onto the floor, he felt around in haste.

Nothing.

Damn.

Glancing up at the door, he spotted a hook, and on it a key. Why hadn't he noticed that before?

He strode over and grabbed it, ran up the stairs, and once he'd unlocked the door, he yanked it open and stood back while his brothers entered. "Somebody's here, we need to find them."

"How do you know that?" Sean Paul asked.

"Because the door's bolted from the inside, and so is the back door. They wouldn't be able to get back in, so they must be hiding. Search everywhere, and when you find them, don't hurt them. This person may be the only one to help find PJ."

He relocked the door and placed the key in his pocket. He wouldn't have whoever was here escaping. The three of them started with the rooms leading from the bar area.

Tommy Lee pushed the first door open and flicked on the light. It was a small room with nothing more than a bed. He knew what happened in here, the smell gave tell to that. He covered his nose and glanced at the crumpled covers while fighting the urge to be sick.

There were semen stains everywhere. He knelt and checked underneath. Nothing. Then he left the room, closing the door behind him. John Jo and Sean Paul appeared, their faces letting on they had just had the same experience.

"Come on, this way." He motioned, leading them to the hallway. "Check those rooms, I'll head upstairs."

He took the stairs three at a time and landed in front of the room he had broken into. Stepping in, he stood silently listening for any telltale signs of life. A faint creak came from the wardrobe. He moved slowly towards it, then yanked the door open. There, huddled at the bottom, a man sat hugging his knees. The same man who'd hugged his brother in the photograph.

"Please don't hurt me," he begged. His body shook. Clearly, he was terrified.

"I'm not going to hurt you, but I need your help. What's your name?"

"P-Pete," he stuttered.

"Where's PJ?" Tommy Lee asked softly.

"I don't know any PJ." He whimpered.

"Don't fecking lie, you've got a photo of him on your bedside table."

John Jo came rushing in and stopped dead. "Where's my fecking brother?"

"Stop." Tommy Lee placed his hand against his brother's chest. "I'll handle this."

They were joined by Sean Paul who glared down at the frightened man.

"As I was saying, you've got a photo of PJ, so where is he?"

"You mean Sam?" Pete looked more confused than frightened now.

Tommy Lee wiped his hand over his face. Of course PJ would use his dead lover's name. He cursed himself for not handling that situation better, but what could he have done differently? He put the thought out of his head and continued.

"Look, Pete, our brother has been missing since yesterday evening. There's no way he would miss Christmas with his family, now you need to tell me where he is."

"I haven't seen him since yesterday about nine o'clock. He came in, had a couple of drinks, and then left with one of the newbies. He was drunk, and I assumed he was being helped home."

"This newbie, what's his name?" John Jo spat.

"He said it was Charles, but that doesn't mean it's real, after all, Sam was a lie…" Pete's gaze drifted to the photo of him and PJ.

Tommy Lee almost felt sorry for him. "We need to find him, he could be in danger."

"There's a place on the outskirts of town, it looks derelict, but I heard they hold parties—"

"What sort of parties?" Sean Paul asked.

"The sort you shouldn't attend. I've heard bad things about the place."

"Can you take us there, please, for PJ's sake?" Tommy Lee stared down harder. "I'll give you money so you can get out of this dump, make a new life somewhere else."

That seemed to pique his interest. He nodded then climbed out of the wardrobe. "I'll pack my—"

"No, we go now, before it's too late." Grabbing Pete's arm, Tommy Lee marched him down the stairs and out into the cold winter night.

***

PJ lay on the dirty mattress with only a sheet covering his shaking body, the pain from his arse now unbearable. The bleeding had stopped, but each time he moved, his whole body burned. The acts the three men had done to him were vile; his head couldn't make sense of it. He was pinned down while each took their turn fucking his arse. It felt like it had lasted hours, but he had overheard them say they had to get home for dinner. Their wives would be suspicious. How could they have wives and do this?

Wasn't that what you planned, marry Marina and see Pete? Maybe this is your punishment.

"Stop it," he murmured to the little voice in his head.

The fat man had taken his clothes, telling him he couldn't escape. He was theirs now until they decided otherwise. He knew they would never let him go. He was stuck here for their pleasure, and once they were done with him, he would be disposed of. Just like the last one. They'd let that bit of information slip while they were congratulating each other.

One of them had left a cup of water on the floor. He was thirsty but knew it would have something in it to keep him drowsy. He needed his full strength if he stood any chance of getting out of this. Would his brothers search for him? Of course they would, but he doubted they would find him, not here.

CHAPTER 48

Tommy Lee pulled up outside the gates to an abandoned warehouse, his headlights slicing through the suffocating darkness. The structure loomed ahead, its skeletal frame barely holding together, rusted metal groaning against the wind. It looked as if it might fall down any minute.

"Are you sure this is it?" he asked, his voice tight, wary.

"Yep, it's defiantly here." Pete's answer came out in a hushed whisper.

Tommy Lee exhaled sharply. "It's certainly out of the way. Right, boys, get tooled up, we don't know who or how many might be in there." He swung open the door, boots crunching on the gravel as he marched around to the passenger side. Opening the door, he yanked Pete out.

"You're not expecting me to go in there, are you?" His eyes widened in terror.

"You'll be safer with us than on your own."

John Jo appeared from the darkness, gripping a crowbar, his knuckles white. Sean Paul held a large screwdriver, shifting his weight uneasily. Tommy Lee reached into the glove compartment, pulling out a flick-knife which he slipped inside his boot, then a gun. He checked it was fully loaded, clicking it shut once satisfied.

"Right, keep the noise down, we need to find a way in, and don't leave fingerprints," he warned.

They moved along the warehouse's crumbling exterior, shadows stretching and shifting as the torch illuminated their way around the side, searching for an entrance. The place had an eerie stillness of somewhere long abandoned, yet something about it felt wrong.

"Look, a broken window, can we get in there?" Sean Paul pointed ahead.

John Jo used the crowbar to clear the rest of the jagged glass and then took off his coat and laid it over the window ledge. He jumped up, pulling himself into the building, then landed with a thud inside. Tommy Lee shoved Pete in next, despite his cries of objection, then he and Sean Paul followed suit.

Tommy Lee placed both feet firmly on the floor then grabbed the torch, shining it around the building. The air was cold, his breath turning white as he exhaled, the room dingy and stagnant. Dust particles caught in the beam, flickering around like a snowstorm. The place was empty, all but a small partition towards the front. He motioned for them all to follow while he crept forward. His mood, which was already thunderous, took a darker turn. The thought of PJ being in a place like this was more than he could bear.

John Jo opened a rickety door that almost fell off its hinges. He grabbed it to keep it upright, then leant it against the equally dilapidated wall. The whole place was run-down to the point of demolition. Tommy Lee shone the torch in. An out-of-place unit stood in the middle of the room. Approaching it, he shone the light over the top. Fingerprints. Someone had been here.

There was nothing else, no other telltale signs of visitors to this place. He opened the doors. It was empty. Had this just been dumped here? No.

"Someone give me a hand," he said, putting his shoulder to the unit. He pushed with John Jo's help.

"Look. A trapdoor." Sean Paul leapt forward and yanked it open. "There's stairs."

The men made their way down in silence until they reached the bottom. It was damp with a smell of death. Tommy Lee's gut twisted tighter.

"See if you can find a light switch," he told them.

The sound of a click illuminated the place, showing a long corridor with doors all on the left-hand side.

"Feck sake, you could've warned us," John Jo moaned, blinking away the brightness.

"Come on." Tommy Lee strode along the corridor. He grabbed the handle to the first and pushed it open. The bed wasn't the first thing he noticed, it was the blood. The sheets were claret-stained, not just a bit, a lot. His insides contracted. Were they too late?

"Nobody's in here, try the next room," he finally managed.

He turned to see Pete, his face twisted in terror. John Jo and Sean Paul didn't look much better, their bodies frozen to the spot, expressions carved from stone.

"I said check the next room!" Tommy Lee barked, shoving past them.

The door creaked open. A body lay on a mattress, shrouded by a filthy blanket. The moment the cover was peeled back, the smell of death thickened. Skin, grey and waxen, stretched over bone. This one had been here for weeks.

His stomach turned, but he pushed forward, dread curling tighter around his ribs.

He breathed a shaky sigh of relief, then headed to the next room. This door was locked. "Hand me the crowbar." He snatched it, and with a sharp jolt, the lock splintered, and he kicked it open.

Again another mattress on the floor with a body covered by a sheet. Tommy Lee hesitated for a fraction of a second before pulling it back.

"PJ."

He lay facedown, his body bruised. What had this monster done to him? He studied his lower half. He had dried blood crusted around his arse. The bruising was worse there.

He turned to John Jo who was glued to the spot, Sean Paul next to him; he seemed unable to move either. Pete sobbed behind them.

"I need you to get him back to the motor." Tommy Lee slid his jacket off and wrapped it around PJ.

"Tommy Lee?" he whispered.

"It's me. We're going to get you out of here." He lifted him gently and handed him to John Jo. "Go."

"What are you going to do?" Sean Paul asked.

"I'll check the other rooms." Tommy Lee disappeared without another word.

There were two more rooms after his brother's. Both in the same state, but thankfully no more bodies.

Where did he dispose of them? Somewhere on this ground?

Not my problem, he told himself, but he couldn't shake it. What if he hadn't made it in time to save his brother?

There will be more if you don't stop him.

Oh, I'm going to stop him, and anyone else who was involved, he assured himself.

When he got back to the Range Rover, PJ was lying across the back seats. Pete was in the front but kneeling so he could watch PJ, and John Jo and Sean Paul stood next to the driver's door. They spotted him as Tommy Lee walked towards them.

"What do we do now?" Sean Paul asked.

"We burn the fecking place to the ground. The fire service will discover the rooms underneath and then the gavers will search the ground. The owner will be named, then we find him, grab him, and give him the same treatment."

"The same treatment?" John Jo repeated. "I'm not—"

"I don't mean in that way. Leave it to me. Yous two will have to look after PJ, he's going to need medical attention."

"How can we take him to hospital, they'll know what he is?" Sean Paul exclaimed.

"Would you rather him die?" He was met with silence. "I'll sort that myself as well then, shall I?" He narrowed his eyes. Sometimes his brothers were fecking useless. Climbing in, he started the ignition to warm the motor up for PJ, then climbed out and headed to the boot. He grabbed a can of petrol, a box of matches, and then motioned to his brothers while pointing to the boot.

"Yous two will have to get in here."

He stomped back towards the warehouse. This wouldn't take long to burn, and he doubted it would be noticed until it was well and truly underway. He splashed the petrol over the cabinet and back towards the door. The remainder he threw up the walls, then chucked the can in. Sparking the match, he stood back and flicked it in. The flames erupted, heat searing his face. The fire spread in seconds.

Content, he walked away.

Tommy Lee dropped Pete back at the gay bar. He handed him two hundred quid along with a warning to get out of town. He then headed back to his brothers' piece of ground. The place was in darkness when they arrived. Thankfully, Father's truck was gone.

Tommy Lee carried PJ into the trailer, laying him on the bed. He motioned to Sean Paul to get the fire started, while John Jo brought fresh water. PJ gulped at it.

"We need to have a private chat, yous two leave us," Tommy Lee told his brothers.

They didn't argue, they knew better.

"Not now, Tommy Lee, I don't feel strong enough," PJ moaned.

"Yes, now. Do you know what you've put us all through today, what you've put Mother through? That woman's been distraught, she thought you were dead in a ditch somewhere." He took a deep breath before continuing. "Tell me what happened, and leave nothing out."

"I went for a drink. I had one and chatted to my friend, Pete, then ordered another. I used the loo, and when I came back this man was standing next to where I had been. He tried to talk, but I wasn't interested, so I drunk my drink… I think. Then I woke up in that place. I don't remember anything else."

"What did they do to you?" Tommy Lee pressed.

PJ rolled over, pulling the blankets over his head. The trailer filled with sounds of his sobbing. It broke Tommy Lee's heart to witness.

"Get some sleep, we'll get you cleaned up in the morning." He walked through to the fire and stood in front of it, holding his hands out to warm them. He hadn't realised how cold he was before. Now his adrenaline had dropped, he not only felt cold but also tired. He slumped down onto the bunk, propping a cushion under his head. He'd have to stay here tonight, maybe do a rota between his brothers and himself. If they would be willing to leave the warmth of their wives.

Millie.

He allowed himself to think about her for the first time all night. How he wished he were tucked up with her right now. Holding her. Making love to her. Would that ever happen again?

No.

A loud bang followed by a scream came from the other end of the trailer. He leapt up and ran towards PJ. He was thrashing about in the bed and whimpering. Was he reliving the last few hours in that room? Tommy Lee grabbed him and pulled him in close.

"Shh, you're safe now," he soothed.

PJ opened his eyes and whispered, "I'll never be safe."

CHAPTER 49

It had been two days since they had rescued PJ. Tommy Lee grabbed the local paper. A picture of the warehouse was featured on the front. It had a quote from the owner along with his photo. Councillor Wilson from Lime Tree Walk quoted, 'I haven't been there for a few years, I had planned to sell the land as the building was unstable.'

Lying cunt.

Tommy Lee took it in to PJ who was propped up in bed. He had soaked in the bath that morning getting all the vile shit off him. His arse was still sore, and he was still losing blood; he would need to get the doctor out tomorrow. Their mother and father were due to visit. He'd fed them a story about him being set upon by a group of thugs. He could hardly tell them the truth. This was best for all concerned.

"Is that the man?" Tommy Lee asked while thrusting the paper under his nose.

PJ flinched; it was something Tommy Lee had never seen him do before.

"Well, is it?" he pressed, fighting the guilt.

PJ nodded slowly. "There were three of them," he admitted. "He was the ringleader, though, the other two paid him money."

Tommy Lee's anger built. Three dirty, hairy-arsed shit-cunts had done this to his little brother. They would pay.

He knew he had to act quickly. Before the gavers got involved, he wanted to dish out the punishment, so it was fitting. Not just a quick prison sentence, where the rich prick would get privileges. He knew he would be sweating over the forthcoming discovery, but he also knew it was possible he may talk his way out of it. If you were rich enough, you could get away with anything.

He grabbed his keys, he need to get to the scrapyard. Duke hadn't been happy with his absence as he was still in Kent. He told him he had flu, another lie, but he couldn't tell him the real reason.

Sean Paul appeared at the door. "Do you have to go?"

"I do. Make sure someone's with him at all times, and don't leave Mother on her own with him." He left.

***

The scrapyard hummed away with activity. Tommy Lee sat in the Portakabin thinking about Millie. Had she calmed down yet? He didn't like the thought of her being on her own, but then she shouldn't be so stubborn.

She's not on her own, she has her friend, Rosie.

The phone rang. "Hello."

"I can't get hold of Millie, I'm worried about her, can you check on her?" Duke said.

"Okay." Tommy Lee slammed the phone down. Did he have to look after everyone?

He picked up his keys and left. The drive was reasonably speedy. He had decided once he was done with her, he'd go and check out the councillor's place.

Tommy Lee stood in front of her door, hands in his pockets and an annoyed look on his face.

Millie answered. "What do you want?"

"I'm here because your father phoned me. Why aren't you answering your phone?" He pushed past her and marched to the lounge.

"Do you mind, this is my home, you can't just—"

"Oh, I can, Millie. I know me and your dad hurt you, but it wasn't done for that reason," he snapped.

"What reason was it done for then?" she asked.

"It was done to keep you safe, it was done to give you the freedom to look after our babies, without having to worry about the scrapyard, and it was done so you wouldn't have to wonder if you were getting fleeced."

"If that's true, why didn't either of you tell me?"

"Truthfully? Because we're both scared of you," he admitted.

"What?" She laughed. "You two are scared of me?"

"You've got a bit of a temper on you…" He sighed. "Look, I want to spend time with them." He pointed to the twins. "And you. Can we please put this behind us? I've got enough problems to deal with right now and I could really do with a friend."

Her face seemed to soften. That was a good start.

"Okay, I'll put the kettle on."

He followed her into the kitchen and watched her, her movements, the way her jeans hugged her hips.

Stop that.

"Here." She placed the tea in front of him. "So what's happened?"

He hesitated, unsure how to answer.

"You don't have to tell me."

"Something bad happened to my younger brother, now I need to sort it."

"Do you need help?" she offered.

"No, but I might need the smelter." He glanced at her.

She was smiling. "It's half yours, you don't need permission, just make sure the men have gone home. I don't trust them, not after the whole takeover business."

He nodded. "I best get going."

"I hope your brother's gonna to be okay."

He stood and walked to the door then turned. "Have dinner with me tomorrow night."

"What, like a date?"

"Yes… I'll pick you up at six-thirty," he confirmed.

"Does this include a hotel room?" Was she nervous?

"Do you want it to?"

"Why don't you come here, I'll cook?"

Yes, she was nervous. "Okay, that'll be nice, we can go out next time."

***

Tommy Lee sat across the road from councillor Wilson's house. He'd been here three hours and there'd been little movement. He appeared to be home alone. Once the fat prick had retired for the night, he would make his move. All he needed were the names of the other two and their addresses. The light in the upstairs room went out, the house now in darkness. He checked his watch, eleven-thirty p.m. Pushing his hands into his gloves, he reached for the roll of plastic he had brought, for getting rid of the evidence, and the gun which he placed in his waistband. He exited the motor and ran across the road, slipping through to the back garden.

The houses here were affluent, most likely owned by judges, solicitors, and politicians. Did they know what Wilson was? Were they like him? He cleared his head, choosing to concentrate on the job in hand.

The back door was locked, as expected, so he took out the crowbar and began ramming it between the door and the frame. Three mighty tugs, and the door splintered. He pushed it open and listened.

Silence.

Treading lightly, he made his way to the bottom of the stairs, then tiptoed up. He stood at the top.

Silence.

He had a choice of four doors to choose from. The first he decided would be the bathroom. The next, he turned the handle down slowly and edged it open.

Empty.

He walked towards the front of the house. He assumed this would be the main bedroom. Opening the door, he stuck his head in. He could just about make out a large lump in the bed.

Bingo.

He sneaked to the side of the bed and stared down into the man's sleeping face. He felt sick knowing what this piece of shit had done. Tommy Lee withdrew string from his pocket, ready to tie his victim up. He placed the gun under the man's chin.

"Wh…what's going on?" He gasped.

"I've got a little problem, and you're gonna help me with it." Tommy Lee grinned. "Get up."

Shoving a pair of old socks into the man's mouth, he then tied his hands behind his back. Councillor Wilson's moans were now muted.

"Downstairs." Tommy Lee flicked the gun towards the door. Then grabbed Wilson's arm and manoeuvred him out of the room, down the stairs, and into the dining room. Moving out a chair, he pushed him down.

"Now we're both comfortable, I'll begin. You took my brother and did bad things to him, that's you and your two friends. Now I can either do bad things and kill you or you can give me their names and addresses."

He smiled. The man's eyes were wide with terror.

Good.

"Now what is it to be, your life or theirs?"

The man's head wobbled frantically as he tried to speak. Tommy Lee yanked the socks from his mouth.

"The Reverend Graham Macalister." He gasped. "And Alexander Audley-Charles."

"You mean to tell me a fecking vicar did that to my brother, and who's the other nonce?"

"Just someone with the same interests—"

"Raping a man is not an interest, an interest is gardening or fecking cooking." Tommy Lee wiped his eyes, the sting of tears threatening. "Where do they live?"

"I'll write it down for you. There's a pad and pen in the top drawer of the dresser."

Tommy Lee retrieved them then cut the man's ties. "Don't try anything, we wouldn't want anything nasty to happen to you, would we."

He grabbed the paper and read it. Shoving it into his pocket, he motioned to the pad. "Now I want you to write an apology to my brother, naming you and your friends."

"But—"

"No buts, this is the only way to make amends, and state what you did to him." Tommy Lee cocked the gun and aimed it at the man's face.

When he had finished, Tommy Lee replaced the gag and led him back upstairs. He rolled out the plastic, so it was protecting the bed.

"Get on." He watched the man fumble with his pyjama bottoms. "Now roll over."

Wilson did as he was told, his head buried into the plastic draped over the pillow.

"You still need to be taught a lesson."

Grabbing the crowbar, Tommy Lee tugged Wilson's pyjama bottoms down and rammed it up his arse, over and over again. The blood seeped onto the plastic, a smell of metallic and shit mixed together. When finished, Tommy Lee pushed his face down harder. Wilson's hands flailed about until he eventually he went limp. Now all Tommy Lee had to do was clean up the mess and dispose of the body. The letter he would post to the local newspaper.

One down, two to go.

***

It was just after four forty-five a.m. when Tommy Lee drove back to the scrapyard. He had all three bodies rolled in plastic, two tucked into his boot, the other on the back seat. He opened the gates and drove through to where the smelter was. It took a while to fire up, making sure the temperature was correct. He took the roll of plastic and laid it on the floor, ready to dismember the bodies. He then unloaded the reverend. That was a joke in itself. A holy man doing that shit. It was of little consolation that he now wouldn't be able to abuse anyone else. His brother was damaged, and Tommy Lee wasn't sure he would ever recover. He dumped him on the plastic, then returned for the other two. Content when all three were unwrapped, lying facing him, he held the chainsaw. After thirty minutes he was left with a pile of arms and legs, their heads, and torsos. He glanced at the plastic that was spattered in blood. He needed to burn that, too.

He put on the thick fireproof gloves and face shield. Then opened up the door. He could feel the heat even with the protective clothing. He picked up the body parts and began to throw them in, closing the door while the bodies burned. He repeated the process two more times, lastly throwing in the plastic, then stripped off and burnt his own clothes. He had spare work clothes in the Portakabin. All he had left to do was clean out his motor and hose down the shed. Then he would get a couple of hours' sleep. He had a spare change of clothes in the motor ready to go to Millie's later that day. He reminded himself to phone John Jo and check on PJ. Maybe that should wait until after he saw her, he didn't need any more problems, not just yet.

CHAPTER 50

The meal was going down a treat, however, Tommy Lee was a little disappointed when he saw Scott and Rosie there. He wanted to spend time with Millie, just the two of them.

"Has there been any more news on that fella's disappearance?" Scott said while stuffing a large roast potato into his mouth.

"No. I think we should consider our stakeout," Rosie replied. "I've been following the news, and there's been no more said."

"I can't stay out all night now I have the twins," Millie added.

"Can someone please enlighten me?" Tommy Lee asked, trying to hide the irritation from his voice. He stared straight at Millie.

"Okay, this is the shortened version," Rosie explained. "I went nutty and got put into a private psychiatric hospital. People were going missing in the dead of night. The private doctor told Millie I suffered from psychosis, but Millie knew there was something wrong with the place so she blackmailed the doctor to get me released, and Millie's dodgy doctor reckons they could be selling body parts."

Tommy Lee had kept his gaze on Millie the whole time. "Blackmail and a dodgy doctor, really, Mil?"

"Firstly, she's not my dodgy doctor, thank you, Rosie, and secondly, the psychiatric doctor in that place was crooked. Why else were they worried about me going to the authorities?"

"No wonder Duke's going grey." He sighed.

"He is not. I mean, it's only a few hairs," Millie said indignantly.

"I don't want you involved in this, Millie, understand?" Tommy Lee ordered.

"But I—"

"I said, *understand*?" he spat.

"Fine." She reached for her glass and drank the lot down. "Give me a refill, please, Rose."

"I'll help, I've got a few ex-army mates who will, too. They'll need paying, though."

"Money's not a problem, as long as it's dealt with quickly," Millie added.

"I'll make a couple of phone calls after dinner. Now can we enjoy the rest of the meal in peace?"

***

Scott had gone home, and Rosie had retired to her bedroom. Tommy Lee sat next to Millie on the sofa.

"This is nice," he told her. "Just the two of us, for a change."

"It is. You went a bit distant at the dinner table, is there something wrong?" she asked.

"The dodgy doctor, does she do things discreetly? Like, can you trust her?" He was taking a chance, he knew that, but his brother's health was more important.

"She's done a lot for me, off the books. I trust her... Are you going to tell me what's going on?"

He took a deep breath. "My brother, PJ, he got drugged and raped by three men."

She gasped and placed her hand on his arm. "I'm so sorry, shit… You haven't taken him to the hospital?"

"No. He won't go, he's scared it will come…"

"Out," she finished. "He's gay?"

"I've been trying to deny it. John Jo and Sean Paul think they can make him normal—"

"Normal?" She placed her hand on his cheek and pulled him round to look at her. "I don't understand men fancying men or women fancying women, but it doesn't make them freaks… He's your brother, it shouldn't matter what he does or doesn't like."

He sighed. "I know. It's just hard. You've seen how these people are treated. Beaten up and left for dead. It's worse in the Traveller community, it's not accepted. I don't want him being shunned all his life."

"Can you bring him here tomorrow?"

He studied her. What was she thinking? "I guess. Does that mean the doctor will see him?"

"Yes, I'll phone her in a little while. He may need to visit a few times. What's his injuries like?" she asked. "I need to let the doctor know in case she needs to bring anything special."

"He's bleeding from his…bum." He glanced at her.

She looked concerned. "You shouldn't have to deal with things like this on your own," she said softly.

"And you shouldn't be dealing with stakeouts," he said a little too quickly.

"Fair enough…so we tell each other everything in future?"

He leaned into her, his lips inches from hers. "Yes," he whispered before seizing his chance and kissing her.

***

John Jo stoked the fire then sat on the bunk. He could hear PJ moving, but every time he went in to him he was asleep, or pretending to be. He'd changed the sheets earlier. They were bloodstained but not as bad as the first lot, so he assumed he was on the mend.

The sound of a motor had him peeking through the curtains. It was Tommy Lee.

"Thank the Lord," he muttered.

Tommy Lee could stay tonight and watch him. John Jo needed to get some sleep in his own bed.

"How is he?" Tommy Lee asked, stepping up into the trailer.

"He's been sleeping most of the day. The bleeding's slowing down to… Where have you been?"

"I'll talk with you tomorrow, go get some sleep," Tommy Lee said, obviously avoiding the question.

John Jo didn't need telling twice. He grabbed his jacket and left.

Tommy Lee poked his head into the bedroom. PJ's eyes were closed.

"I know you're not asleep." He sat on the edge of the bed.

"I don't want to talk," PJ murmured.

"Okay, then I will. Those men have been dealt with, they'll never do that again to anyone, and I'm taking you to Millie's in the morning, she's got a doctor who will tend to you."

"What did you do to them?"

"Punished them, caused them pain, and then obliterated them off the face of the planet. Now get some sleep." Tommy Lee stood, ready to get some shuteye himself.

"Wait, this doctor—"

"Won't say a word, so stop worrying. No one is going to know."

"Does she?" PJ asked, peering from under the covers.

"Yes, but she's on your side. She's trustworthy and she's the only help we've got right now." Tommy Lee sat back on the bed. "Is something else bothering you?"

"Marina wants to come over. John Jo told her I'm laid up in bed with flu."

"Well, that's half true, you are laid up. The sooner you see this doctor, the sooner you'll be on the mend." Tommy Lee stood again. "You really need to get some sleep, we'll be leaving early."

CHAPTER 51

The motor drew up outside Millie's. It was seven-fifteen a.m. She stood on the doorstep. Had she heard them pulling in? Tommy Lee's heart missed a beat just looking at her.

"There she is, already waiting for us." He beamed.

He climbed out and walked around to the passenger door. Opening it, he helped PJ and, placing his arm over his shoulder, he guided him in, half carrying, half dragging.

"Hello," Millie said cheerfully.

"Morning." Tommy Lee pecked her on the cheek. "This is PJ."

"Hello, come through to the study, the doctor's waiting." She led them in.

Tommy Lee was surprised to see a couch like you got in a surgery. An array of dressings and instruments were laid out ready. The doctor was a Chinese woman, which surprised him further. Not the woman bit but the Chinese part. Would she know what to do?

"This is Doctor Sinman," Millie said, introducing them.

Tommy Lee gave a simple nod.

The doctor pointed to the couch. "Can you pop the patient up there, please, and remove the trousers and underwear. I'll just go and wash my hands." She disappeared from the room.

"I've sent Rosie out, told her not to come back until teatime. I'll be with the twins, so if you need me, shout." Millie also disappeared.

"She seems nice." PJ whimpered while being helped onto the couch. "She has...ow, steady."

"She has what?" Tommy Lee lifted his brother's legs up.

"Kind eyes, I can see why you like her."

The doctor re-emerged. "Right, gentlemen, shall we begin?"

***

John Jo and Sean Paul drove into the scrapyard. They had been frantically searching for Tommy Lee and PJ. This was the last place to check.

"Can I help you, fellas?" a middle-aged man asked.

"Where's Tommy Lee?" John Jo asked aggressively.

"Millie said he'll be in later." He stepped away.

"And where is she?" Sean Paul butted in. "We've got a family emergency and need to get hold of her."

"We need her address. Now."

"I can't give out her address, she'll kill me," the man replied, wide-eyed.

"And if you don't give it to us, *we'll* kill you." John Jo grabbed him by the collar. "So what's it to be?"

***

Millie was sitting by the window when Tommy Lee came into the lounge.

"We're done," he told her. "What's the matter?"

"John Jo threatened Bob at the scrapyard for my address, so he phoned and warned me. Your brothers are on their way, and judging by what he said, they're not happy."

His hackles rose.

"Anyway, enough of them, how's PJ?" she asked, turning towards him.

"He had three—" He stopped at the sound of a motor screeching to a halt.

"They're here."

He stormed out to the door and pulled it open just in time to see his brothers about to knock. "Who the feck do you think yous are, demanding Millie's address and threatening my staff?"

Before they could answer, he continued. "You ever try something like that again, I'll kill the both of you. Now feck off."

A hand rested on his arm, and he turned to see Millie.

"I expect they're worried, too. Let them in, I'll put the kettle on." She vanished into the kitchen.

"Get one thing straight," Tommy Lee warned. "You're only coming in because she allowed it. Personally, I'd feck you both off."

He led them into the lounge and pointed to the sofa. "Sit." He took a few deep breaths to contain his temper.

She appeared a few minutes later with a tray filled with cups. "Help yourselves to sugar."

"Millie, can I have a word?" Doctor Sinman said from the doorway.

"You're safe to speak in here, these are his brothers." Millie flicked her head towards the sofa.

"Very well." The doctor gave them the once-over before resting her gaze back on Millie. "So he had three tears in the rectum that I've managed to stitch, farther up looks intact. There is a lot of bruising, but that will get better with time. I'll see him in two weeks. If anything changes, call me, and I'll see him sooner." She reached out and handed her a two boxes of pills. "These are antibiotics, four a day, to fight any infection. There's a two-week course. These ones are painkillers, three times a day maximum. They are strong, so there's only four days' worth."

"Thanks, Doc, here." Millie handed her an envelope. "Same time in two weeks then," she confirmed. "I'll see you out."

Tommy Lee glared at his brothers.

"Don't look at us like that, you should've told us what you had planned," John Jo reasoned. "When you were both missing, we thought something bad had happened."

"Something bad has happened, our little brother's been raped." Tommy Lee glanced towards the window. Millie was outside, deep in conversation with the doctor. Why?

"So what are we going to do about the bastards who did this?" Sean Paul asked. "Because they can't get away with it."

"They've already been dealt with." The click of the front door had Tommy Lee turning to see Millie walk in.

"Dr Sinman has given me some sleeping pills, reckons it will aid his recovery. One a night, an hour before bed." She passed them to Tommy Lee. "Also… She said his body will heal but his mental state will take longer, if ever, to totally recover. She suggested doing the things he's most familiar with, the horses maybe?"

"We're gonna start breeding the Cobs in the spring, he enjoyed that before and it'll keep him busy," John Jo agreed.

"What about Marina and the wedding?" Tommy Lee added. "That may be too much pressure for him."

"That's for him to decide. You lot need to support him in whatever decisions he makes. Don't pressure him with your opinions…yous are family, remember that next time when things go bad," Millie warned. "I'll go and sit with him until he wakes up." She glanced at Tommy Lee. "Can you watch the twins?"

He nodded then waited for her to leave. "I need to get to work after, can yous take PJ home when he wakes?"

Sean Paul's body stiffened. "We ain't no doctors, he needs someone who knows what they're doing."

"He's got a point, after all, PJ's just had surgery. Why can't he stay here?" John Jo agreed.

Tommy Lee rubbed the back of his neck, closing his eyes and breathing deep. "You moaned earlier because I brought him here, involving Millie instead of yous, and now you know what's happening you don't want to help. She ain't a fecking doctor either." He glanced at the pair of them. "Go…go on, feck off."

He walked over to the cribs. The twins were soundly sleeping.

"Who was that?" Millie asked. "Oh, your brothers have left. He's starting to wake up."

He followed her through to the study.

PJ was lying on the sofa, all signs of the doctor's presence gone.

He groaned then opened his eyes a little. "Where…" he managed.

"Shh, it's okay. The doctor's patched you up. You'll feel drowsy for a while."

"It might take a couple of hours before he's awake properly," Millie said. "Why don't you leave the scrapyard, take him home, and I'll go there later and check on things," she offered.

"No. I told you your job is to look after our boys, I'll deal with the scrapyard." He sighed.

If his brothers had done what he'd asked, it wouldn't have been a problem.

"Why don't you go now then and show your face, he'll be okay with me," she suggested.

"Are you sure?"

"Yes," she agreed. "I'll make us dinner for six p.m., so don't be late."

***

PJ rubbed his head. The drowsiness was wearing off. He glanced up at the large clock above where he was lying. Four-fifteen p.m. Had he been out all day? He moved to sit up, regretting the decision immediately. "Shite."

"Hey, how are you feeling?" Millie asked, entering the study. "I've just brought some fresh water, or would you prefer a cup of tea?"

"Water will do." His voice sounded hoarse. "It still hurts when I move."

"You've had stitches, but the doc gave me painkillers." She glanced over to the desk. "Here they are." Placing two into her hand, she held them out to him. "These will help."

He took them, popped both into his mouth, then gulped them down with the water.

"Are you hungry? I'm making dinner for later but can make something for you now."

"No...thank you." He flopped his head down. "So what did the doctor say?"

"I think you should discuss that with your brother, it's—"

"I'm asking you, please," he begged. "Tommy Lee can sometimes brush over things, I need the truth."

"Okay. You had three tears in your rectum, along with bruising. The doc stitched them up. You have antibiotics, painkillers, and sleeping tablets. She said you'd make a full recovery."

"What else?"

"Why would you think there's anything else?" she asked.

"Because there's always something else." He groaned.

"She was more worried about your mental state, it can be harder to get over trauma than an actual injury... People are sympathetic when they see a broken leg or arm, but trauma to the mind is invisible, so you don't get the same help. It's an invisible injury." Her eyes glassed over, like she was a million miles away. Was she going to cry?

She shrugged, obviously bringing herself back to the present. "You'll overcome it, though, you're a tough Irish Traveller."

"How do you know so much, about this?" he asked.

"I've experienced it, and to be honest, it's so hard to drag yourself back from, but here I am. Two beautiful boys, nice house, businesses. No more beatings, no more abuse, no more being made to..."

He leaned up onto his elbow. "To what?"

"Some things need to stay buried. I'll go and put the kettle on." She walked towards the door then stopped. "This stays between us. I'll keep your secret, you keep mine," she said over her shoulder.

CHAPTER 52

It was now the sixth of January. The year so far had been complete shite. Tommy Lee adjusted his tie in the Portakabin mirror and sighed. Tonight he was going to tell Millie how he felt. They had been going around in circles the last few weeks, and it irked him. One minute they would kiss, the next be at loggerheads. He grabbed his keys from the desk, locked up, and left.

The drive over gave him time to think. What would his life be like with her?

Hard work?

That was still better than the alternative; watching her from a distance was a form of torture. And then there were the twins, seeing them grow up... As it was they seemed to change every time he saw them. He was missing out.

He pulled up on the drive and checked himself in the rearview mirror. Content, he headed towards the front door.

***

The waitress removed the dirty plates.

"Thank you," Millie said politely.

"Would you like dessert?" he asked.

"No, I'm stuffed." She fiddled with her dress. "God, I've definitely eaten too much, I feel like my dress is going to burst off."

He laughed, topping up her drink. "Sounds interesting, but keep it on for a bit longer." He winked.

Her face flushed hot; she knew she was turning red. He kept his gaze on her purposely while she fanned herself with the menu.

"So when are we gonna start this surveillance?" She was changing the subject.

"There's no we, Millie, I will handle it, you worry about our children."

She leant forward. "Look, you need to start treating me as an equal and stop freezing me out. This has been my life for a while now, and I'm more than capable of dealing with it."

He sighed. "And you need to get used to having a man take care of you and our boys... When I get it all arranged, I will tell you. When anything happens, I will tell you, but until that time, why can't you sit back and enjoy your life...with me?"

"With you, as in...?"

"As in being together. Let me court you, the old-fashioned way." There, he had laid his cards out on the table for all to see. Would she agree and put a smile on his face, or disagree and crush him?

"You think we stand a chance?" She nervously fiddled with the strap on her clutch bag.

"I do," he asserted.

"And if I agree?"

"Then I get to snog you in the motor when I drop you home."

She laughed. "That wasn't what I meant."

"I know, but I'm still going to snog you in the motor—"

"When you drop me home." She giggled. "I'll think about it. Shall we go?"

***

Millie unlocked the front door. Tommy Lee followed her in. He was more than a little disgruntled that he never got to kiss her in the motor. Just how long did she need to decide?

"Hey, Mil, your dad called round a little while ago," Rosie said from the kitchen.

"So they're back," Millie mumbled.

"That's a good thing, isn't it?" he asked. "You said you missed them."

"I did, do, oh God, it's this thing with my mum, she hasn't spoken to me for two weeks now. It's unlike her."

"You can't control how other people act towards you. Carry on as normal, I'm sure it will be okay."

They walked through to the kitchen.

Rosie was washing up the babies' bottles. "I've just put them up, they're fed and changed."

"Thanks, Rosie," Millie said, opening the fridge. She pulled out an open bottle of white wine. "You gonna join us?"

"No, I'm off to bed, early start in the morning." Rosie stretched her arms above her head and gave a mock yawn.

Tommy Lee silently praised the Lord. They would be alone at last.

"What would you like to drink?" Millie asked him.

"I'm driving, so I can only have one, a whiskey, thanks." He wandered into the lounge and sat on the sofa. Hopefully, she would join him.

A loud knock came from the front door, and he cursed under his breath. It was like Piccadilly fecking Circus here tonight.

He heard Millie's voice. "Dad, what are you doing here this late, is Mum all right?"

Followed by Duke's. Great.

"She's fine. I just wanted to make sure you got home safe after your meal."

"You'd better come inside out of the cold. Where's your coat?" she asked.

"I'm okay. I'll come in for five minutes."

He appeared in the lounge.

"Evening." Duke nodded.

"Duke. Did you have good time in Kent?" Tommy Lee tried to hide his disappointment.

"Dad, do you want a nightcap?" Millie held up a bottle of scotch.

"Yeah, why not." Duke smiled. "How's work been?" He sat on the armchair. "Bet it's nicer working knowing you own the place."

"Half the place," Millie said from the dining room.

She always had to get that in, and it agitated Tommy Lee.

"So you two?" Duke continued.

"Are business partners," Tommy Lee finished, saving her the trouble.

"Here, Dad." She handed him his drink. "Why didn't Mum come round?"

"She's putting all the stuff away and cleaning. You know what she's like."

"Yeah, I do, she's still got the hump with me. I thought it was just her hormones, but I must've done something really bad to upset her for this long. Can you tell her I said I'm sorry?"

"I'm sure she'll be over tomorrow, you can tell her yourself then." Duke necked his drink then stood. "I'd best get back. I'll go out the back door."

Tommy Lee sighed. "I should get going, it's later than I thought." He stared down at her. Could she see he was disappointed? "I'd like to see the chavvies tomorrow, if that's okay?"

She shook her head. "I've got a better idea. Why don't you stay tonight?"

"What?" He frowned. Had he read this wrong?

"I'm saying yes," she said, "I think we should give it ago, but as we already have two sons, I don't think it's unreasonable to ask you to stay."

CHAPTER 53

PJ lay on the bunk. The stitches were itching. He was staring at the TV but wasn't watching it. Fed up and lonely, he wished he were back at Millie's. She understood him. She knew what it was like. He needed a way to get there as he couldn't drive yet.

He glanced at John Jo. "I need to see the doctor for more painkillers."

"We can't just demand more. You're seeing the doctor next week. I'll go see if Gypsy has something you can take for now... You're definitely on the mend, you're walking better."

"It still hurts. When I had a shit yesterday it felt like the stitches burst," PJ replied.

"I really didn't need to know that." John Jo rolled his eyes then left the trailer.

PJ could phone Millie and ask, she would say yes, of that he was certain.

John Jo stomped back in. "Here, take two of those." He threw the box at him then plonked down onto the bunk. "You need to start doing more for yourself."

"I will when I'm better," PJ snapped.

"So how did it go with Marina this morning? Shirley Ann said she was here for a couple of hours."

"It was okay," PJ lied.

It wasn't okay, it was horrendous. Every time she'd leant towards him, he'd flinched. It wasn't her, it was him. He didn't want anyone getting close. He did the same when Maeve visited.

"That reminds me, I said I'd call her."

"You know where the phone is." John Jo grunted. "Or do you need help with that, too?"

***

Tommy Lee tiptoed up the stairs and stood at the door watching Millie. She was slipping on a clean T-shirt after Tommy boy had puked down her. He wolf whistled, and she spun around.

"You pervert." She laughed, picking up a pillow and throwing it at his head.

"You're only a pervert if you get caught." He winked. "You'll be pleased to know the stakeout's on for this week. I've got two mates coming with me. We'll take an old Escort van down. There's a place we can park out of the way, so they won't see us."

"How do you know that?" she asked suspiciously.

"Because, beautiful, I drove down there today and had a look around." He grabbed her around the waist and pulled her tight to his body. Before she could protest, his lips smashed into hers. He backed up to the door and pushed it shut with his foot.

"Tommy Lee, stop, Rosie's downstairs," she whispered.

"She's watching the chavvies for me, I told her I needed a private word with you. Now are you gonna take that T-shirt off or shall I?"

She whipped it over her head, and in seconds he was on her, unclipping her bra then kneading her left breast while his mouth licked and sucked at the other.

Sliding down his jogging bottoms and pants, he frantically kicked them off, readying himself to enter her. Her legs parted as he pushed inside her. Warmth and moistness enveloped his cock.

"Oh feck," he murmured against her neck.

He picked up the pace, thrusting harder. The headboard banged in rhythm with his movements, like a round of applause egging him on to the finish line. With her groans encouraging him, he leant up on his hands, staring down, watching her. Then he exploded in a moment of ecstasy. His body trembled. His heart beat wildly. He flopped down, all his energy spent.

He pulled her on top of him, her head nestling in the pit of his arm. Her breath tickling his chest. Life didn't get any better than this.

"You gonna be gone all night?" Millie asked.

"You said the patients go missing at night, no good doing it in the daytime," he replied. "I better get dressed and make tracks."

"Millie!" Rosie shouted from downstairs.

"Now what?" he huffed and jumped up.

"Someone's on the phone for you."

"Who is it, Rosie?" She peeked her head out of the bedroom door.

"PJ."

Tommy Lee drew his bottoms on then almost jumped down the stairs and grabbed the phone. "What's wrong?"

He listened intently, throwing in the odd *hmm* and then a definitive NO. He slammed it down.

"Is he okay?" she asked, running down the stairs while pulling down her top.

"He wants to come and stay here for a bit." He sighed.

"And what did you say?"

"I said no, of course. He's my brother, my problem." He pushed his hand through his hair. Would he have to go and stay back there with him and leave her? Just when things were going well. Life could be so fecking unfair.

"You best call the stakeout off then, as that's my problem and not yours," she told him.

"Don't be silly," he snapped. "That's different."

"How is it? Rosie is my friend, my problem." She turned and stormed away.

"Okay. " He followed her in to the kitchen. "What should I have said?"

"You should have told him yes. Your problem is my problem, or are we going to separate them into his and hers?"

He stomped back towards the phone. "Fine, I'll ring back and tell him to come, but only for a week or so."

***

PJ lay on the sofa watching TV. Millie had shown him his bedroom and then ran around after him like she was his mother. Tommy Lee was seething, but to keep the peace, and more importantly her happy, he kept his gob shut.

"I've got to leave now," Tommy Lee told her.

"You will be careful," she pleaded. "I want you back in the morning in one piece."

He smiled down at her. "Promise." He grabbed his bag and threw it over his shoulder. "Don't keep running around after him, he's trying it on."

He then kissed her, before she had any comeback, and left.

"Can I have another glass of water, please?" PJ asked when Millie entered the lounge.

"You know where the kitchen is, help yourself."

Tommy Lee was right, mothering him wasn't going to help him get better.

"I would, but it hurts to get up." He whimpered.

"What hurts?"

"My bum." At least he had the decency to blush.

"Hang on, I've got something that might help." She ran up the stairs and minutes later returned with a rubber ring. "Sit on this, it'll help. I had to use it after giving birth to the twins."

She helped him up and slid the ring beneath him. "There, how's that?"

"Better," he said.

"Why did you want to stay here?" she asked. "Is it because Tommy Lee's here?"

"It's because you're here. You understand, they don't."

"Understand what?"

"What it's like to be a victim."

Millie shook her head slowly. "I ain't no victim, PJ, I dealt with my demons long ago. If you want to be a victim that's on you, not those men." She knelt in front of him. "It's how we deal with it that defines us."

"What happened to you was a long time ago, mine's recent," he reasoned.

"Things like this are always recent in our minds. We have to replace those horrible memories with good and happy ones. Don't let them win." She stood.

Maybe Tommy Lee was right, he shouldn't have come here.

CHAPTER 54

John Jo stood outside the court. Sean Paul leant against the streetlight next to him. Today was the appeal for them to stay on their land. His nerves were starting to get the better of him. He glanced up to see the solicitor approaching.

"Good morning, Mr Ward, I have all the relevant paperwork with me. Shall we go inside, we should be called in soon. They are very prompt with these matters."

"What are the chances of us being evicted?" John Jo asked.

"There's always a chance, however, you have been there a while now, and there has been no harm nor nuisance caused. That and the fact you have stables and horses, I feel you stand a good chance of winning your appeal."

John Jo gave the man a curt nod then followed him in. He hated these places. The high ceilings, intricate panelled walls, and sweeping staircase made a mockery of the justice system. Every inch reeked of money, and yet most of the people brought into these court buildings had none. The solicitor alone had cost a tidy sum. It was nothing more than rich men making money from the poor man's misery.

"Are we ready?" the solicitor asked.

Again John Jo gave a nod, glanced at Sean Paul, and then followed him into the room. He ran a finger around his shirt collar in an attempt to loosen it.

Why did he feel guilty when he'd done no more than buy a place for his family to live?

Fecking house dwellers, complaining. Didn't Travellers and gypsies deserve somewhere to call home? They moaned when you parked up in a field or on the side of the road. They moaned when you got yourself a bit of land.

They moan at our very existence.

It was unfair. He wasn't poncing off anyone or asking for handouts, he just wanted to be left alone to live in peace.

He sat silently, with Sean Paul, and left his future to the man he had paid handsomely for the privilege.

***

PJ sat in the lounge, chewing his nails. Doctor Sinman was setting up the couch in the study. Today he was having the stitches taken out. He glanced up at Millie when she entered the room carrying baby Duke.

Her smile quickly turned to a frown. "Are you okay? You look pale?"

He gave her a weak smile in return. "I'm fine."

Liar.

How could he tell her how he really felt? How he was scared to have his arse touched again. That fear seeped into his very core. A reminder of the nightmare he so desperately tried to escape.

"Everything's ready," the doctor said from the doorway.

"Can you sedate him before you start?" Millie asked.

Did she know?

"If that's what the patient wants, the procedure itself will only take about thirty minutes and be relatively painless."

PJ stood. "I want to be put out," he confirmed, then followed the doctor out of the room. He paused when he reached Millie. "Thanks."

She replied with a simple smile.

"Take this, it will relax you." The doctor handed him a tablet which he swallowed down.

"Can you take off your clothing as before and pop up onto the couch facedown." She pulled on a pair of surgical gloves then turned her back.

PJ did as she'd asked, and minutes later he was asleep.

***

The twins lay on a blanket on the floor of the lounge, their little legs kicking freely. Millie held a blue rabbit up and dangled it over them, their eyes following it.

"All done," Doctor Sinman called over. "The stitches are out, the tears have healed better than I had hoped, and the bruising has all but vanished. He should be able to recommence with all his normal day-to-day activities now."

Millie stood. "That's good, thanks, Doc. How long before he's awake?"

"Any minute now. I only gave him a mild sedative."

Millie grabbed an envelope off the mantel and handed it to her. "Final payment."

"How has his mood been since I was last here?" Doctor Sinman asked.

"Quiet. A little withdrawn. He seems to talk to me more than Tommy Lee."

"I took the liberty of getting some of these." The doctor handed Millie a packet. "If he feels anxious he is to take one in the morning. They can become addictive, so I won't prescribe any more. Hopefully, they will get him through the next couple of weeks."

"You sure he's going to need them?"

"I'll leave that to your discretion. Right, I'll grab my things and get out of your way." Sinman disappeared from sight.

Millie glanced at the box. This wasn't her call, she'd leave it up to Tommy Lee.

Speak of the devil. His motor stopped outside on the drive. PJ's problems were suddenly replaced with the stakeout. Had he seen anything?

"Morning." He strode towards her. He smacked his lips into hers before she could answer.

Easing back, she smiled. "Morning. So what happened?"

"What happened?" He rolled his eyes. "I spent the night in a van with two mates, one of which was farting every thirty seconds, so we had to keep winding the window down. It was fecking freezing... Is that the doctor's motor outside?"

"Yes, she's just finished. PJ's injuries have healed nicely. He should be able to resume his normal lifestyle."

"Good, we'll take him back later. John Jo was in court today for the appeal; hopefully, that's good news, too."

"We?"

"Yes, we. Mother and Father will be there, it's about time they met the twins."

A film of sweat covered her body. Shit, what if they didn't like her? As it was, John Jo seemed to have a problem with her.

"I know that look; what are you worried about?" Tommy Lee tugged her back towards him in a tight hug.

PJ stumbled into the lounge just at the right time. He slumped down onto the sofa and yawned. "Am I interrupting?" he mumbled.

Tommy Lee snapped a sharp *yes* and Millie a soft *no* both at the same time.

"You can pack your things up, we'll be leaving at one p.m. sharp," Tommy Lee told him.

***

Tommy Lee veered into the driveway leading to the mobiles. His father's truck was already there. He ground the motor to a halt, then spun around to face PJ. "Remember, you've been staying with me because you've been helping at the scrapyard."

He then glanced at Millie. She looked pale.

"I told you there's nothing to worry about. They'll love you and they'll love the twins."

He jumped out, knowing his mother would moan about not meeting his sons sooner, but he'd deal with that. He took Tommy boy out of his car seat and handed him to Millie. PJ climbed out next, then Tommy Lee walked round to get baby Duke. When he turned, John Jo was striding towards him.

"How did it go?" Tommy Lee asked, praying for some good news.

His brother's face was set like stone. Not a good start.

John Jo stood silently for a minute, then his face broke into a smile. "We won, we get to stay here for good." He beamed. "Come on, get those babies inside, looks like it might rain."

Tommy Lee grabbed the other twin from Millie and held both in his arms. They followed John Jo to the mobile. The door burst open before they reached it.

Maeve almost leapt out, her arms open wide. "Oh my goodness, just look at those babies," she exclaimed, her eyes misty with joy. "They're the spit of you, boy," she told Tommy Lee whilst grabbing them from him.

Paddy followed behind at a more measured pace. His usual stoic demeanour softened when he spotted his son and the new additions to the family. "Took you long enough," he teased, hauling him into a firm handshake before clapping him on the back. "Didn't think you had it in you, and there you go, proving me doubly wrong."

"There's someone else you need to meet," he said, stepping to one side.

"Millie," his mother said. "Welcome to the family, girl, and well done at taming this one. Didn't think it would ever happen."

"Shall we get inside, it's starting to rain," John Jo said from the door.

Tommy Lee took Millie's hand and led her in. "I told you there was nothing to worry about," he whispered.

Gypsy greeted them, then went to make fresh tea with the help of Shirley Ann. John Jo placed a crate of beers on the table because he and Sean Paul were celebrating.

"So, Millie, I understand you're a businesswoman. How are you finding that and looking after the little ones?" Maeve asked.

Here we fecking go.

"She's staying home, the twins come before any businesses," Tommy Lee said, quickly shutting his mother down.

"That's why I was staying," PJ added. "To help out with the scrapyard."

"I still do the accounts," Millie interjected. "And deal with any problems."

"We'll get someone else to do that." Tommy Lee glared at her in warning, then turned his attention to his brothers. "So what happened in court?"

"You know the women in our family always worked. Them house dwellers think we sit home bleaching the trailers all day while our men go working, but it's never been like that," Maeve continued. "My mother, God rest her soul, used to go out selling flowers and collecting rags to feed us children while me father was away tinkering. He might be away for weeks earning money to feed us kids, and while he was, it was left up to Mother to look after all twelve of us."

"That must have been a hard way of life," Millie said.

"Mother, we don't need a history lesson." Tommy Lee pointed to the beers. "I'll have one."

"It's not a history lesson, boy, it was the good old days, when marriage was a partnership."

"She been on the beer?" Tommy Lee whispered to Sean Paul.

"Not that I've noticed. Brace yourself, you know what's coming next," he whispered back.

"So are you two planning to get married?" Maeve continued. "You've gone about it in the wrong order, but now these little darlings are here, you should consider doing it sooner rather than later."

"Right, think I'll go have a look at the horses. You coming, Sean Paul?" Tommy Lee stood, needing to get out of the room. He felt suffocated by his mother's question. Had he thought about marriage? Briefly. Did he want to marry Millie? He couldn't answer that. He knew he wanted to be with her forever, so what was holding him back?

CHAPTER 55

Things had been going well for Tommy Lee. He was settled now with Millie, the scrapyard was busy, and the family were all getting along. And then it happened, another bombshell.

He'd found out about Millie growing up in a children's home earlier, and suddenly everything made sense. The tough exterior she portrayed to everyone, a complete lie. Underneath that rock-hard surface, she'd always be that scared and broken little girl in the children's home. When he'd first met her, she'd told him everyone who'd come into her life ended up hurting her. So she made people work for her trust, her love, and her loyalty, but they still ended up letting her down. And now Duke and Connie had done the same.

They were moving to Kent, and Millie had broken down. Connie still wasn't making any effort with her, so Duke thought it was a good idea to move. Tommy Lee knew he was only doing what he thought was right for her, but Millie didn't see it that way. Instead, she saw it as rejection.

He shifted his position in the seat and kept his eye on the road. Hopefully, after tonight he wouldn't need to leave her again.

Headlights appeared in the distance.

"This is it," he announced to his mates. "Get ready."

He drove the motor out, blocking the road. The ambulance screeched to a halt.

"Radio Davey to call the gavers." Tommy Lee waited a second for confirmation.

"What the fuck do you think you're doing, you prick?" a large man called while jumping out of the ambulance.

The three of them exited the Escort and ran towards him. The two men with him grabbed the ambulance man and forced him to the ground while Tommy Lee grabbed the keys.

"Police are on their way." He smirked.

He then walked to the back of the ambulance and opened the doors. Inside, a woman in a white doctor's coat sat next to a young man. He was strapped down to a bed, unconscious. A drip was attached to his arm.

"Going somewhere?" Tommy Lee asked.

"We are heading to the hospital, this patient is very ill, now if you don't mind…"

Tommy Lee closed the door without listening to the rest of the bullshit. The sound of sirens grew louder in the distance. He would wrap this up, then go home. He had a surprise for Millie.

**

John Jo held the last post in place while Sean Paul hammered it in. The bigger paddock, that they were building, housed another double stable block.

"Think we should go Appleby this year, see if there's any deals to be had." Sean Paul huffed between strikes.

"Don't know about that, money's running low again," John Jo answered. "Need to get some more readies in." He let go of the post. "We've got to go and pick the chickens up later, too."

"I was thinking about the cash flow. Do you reckon Tommy Lee would lend us a bit? We could pay him back when we're up and running."

"Not sure that's a good idea." John Jo scanned the fence, then gave the post a shake.

"Why not?"

"Because he likes to be in control. If we borrow money, he'll want to see what we're earning." John Jo started walking back to the mobile.

"What about Millie, she's loaded, all of them businesses," Sean Paul said thoughtfully.

"Jaysus, and what do you think he'd say to that?" John Jo stopped dead. "He'd fecking kill us... You concentrate on the horses, I'll worry about the money."

He continued on to the mobile, passing PJ who was grooming one of the Cobs. He nodded as he passed. He never spoke much since he'd returned from Millie's, always looked miserable, and John Jo was sure he woke in the night, thinking he heard screams. Was it PJ, or was he hallucinating?

"I've made you a sandwich," Gypsy told him. "Tea's on the table."

He slipped his arms around her expanding waist. Another child growing in her belly. He kissed her neck. "I'd be lost without you," he mumbled into the soft flesh.

She spun around to face him. "And I you." She smiled.

A cry came from the bedroom. Jonny boy was awake.

"I'll get him."

Sitting on the sofa, he watched the child crawling on the floor, playing with his toys. His thoughts turned to making money. Last night up the pub he had spoken to his cousin, Billy. He had a little business going stealing cars. Could he do that? His dad had a large barn, he could hide them there. All he needed to do was change the plates and grind out the chassis number. And if they didn't sell, he could strip them down in there and sell the parts. He finished the last mouthful of his sandwich and guzzled his tea. He would have a word with Sean Paul, after all, it would need two of them.

***

Tommy Lee called Millie and Rosie into the lounge. "Sit down, the news is about to start."

"I don't like the news," Millie huffed.

"Shh, you're gonna like this." He focused on the television. "Here it is."

"That's the psychiatric hospital," Rosie said anxiously.

Millie glanced at Tommy Lee; he was smiling. "You did it, you caught them."

The newsreader stated that there was an ongoing investigation into missing patients. The coverage showed police officers standing guarding the front entrance.

"Rosie, they're going to get what they deserve." Millie laughed. "This is the best news." She grabbed Tommy Lee's hand. "Why didn't you tell us?"

"Because I wanted you to see it with your own eyes," he said.

"Thank you," Rosie managed, her emotions clearly a little all over the place. "I'm going to phone Scott."

"That was a good surprise." Millie smiled.

"I've got another one." He grinned.

She eyed him suspiciously.

Dragging her into the garden, he stopped just outside. "The twins love you, and so do I. I know we didn't get together in the normal way, but I'm glad we did. I don't know what I'd do without you in my life." He knelt in front of her and held up a diamond ring. "Millie, will you marry me?"

She stared down at him, her smile broadening. "Yes, of course I'll marry you."

***

John Jo and Sean Paul had driven around earlier looking for a target. They had spotted a newish Ford Cortina Mark 4. This would be easy to sell, it had won the European Car of the Year award. Everyone was buying them. This one was a looker. Bodywork white with a black roof. They circled the block, knowing not to stop without checking who was about.

John Jo adjusted his jacket, lifting the hood to cover him from any unwelcome witnesses. "Okay, drop me off over there and then drive up to the corner."

He jumped out, remaining calm. The Cortina was right where they'd seen it earlier, nestled between a clapped-out Vauxhall Viva and an old Escort. John Jo reached into his pocket, taking out a slim jim and a screwdriver. A quick shimmy of the tool and the door popped open with a satisfying click. He slid inside, shutting the door behind him, heart steady.

It took less than thirty seconds to take the steering column cover off. The wires lay exposed, a simple twist of two, a spark, then another. The Escort spluttered, then roared to life.

He grinned, throwing the car into gear. He didn't need to tell Sean Paul what to do next. He drove away smoothly, keeping to the speed limit, acting as if he had every right to be there. No headlights until he was clear of the estate, just the glow of the dashboard lighting up his face.

His brother followed at a distance, to make sure there were no blue lights or nosy neighbours suddenly taking an interest.

Fifteen minutes later, they reached their father's yard. He stopped behind the barn and killed the engine.

Sean Paul stepped out of his motor, nodding in approval. "Nice work."

"Go and see Mother and Father, they'll wonder what we're doing here. Tell them you're picking up some hay for the horses. We'll replace it tomorrow when we get some more."

He grabbed the tools from the boot, already thinking ahead. The plates came off first, quick and easy. Then the chassis number. He fired up the grinder, sparks flying as he erased any trace of the Cortina's past.

Sean Paul came back thirty minutes later. "Father was suspicious, but I think I managed to convince him… I can't believe how easy that was. How much do you think we'll make?"

They were disturbed by the stomp of footsteps.

Paddy stood shaking his head. "I want that gone. Now."

"I was going to put it in your barn, just for tonight," John Jo replied.

"No, boy. You take your stolen goods and get them off my land, and while you're at it, imagine what it would be like to be banged up for ten years, only seeing your children once a week if you were lucky." He turned to walk away then stopped. "You've just won the right to stay on your ground and you're still not satisfied. Just remember, if you get caught, you'll lose everything."

CHAPTER 56

It was now the beginning of April. Millie sat between Tommy Lee and PJ on the sofa. The windows were all open, and a gentle breeze cooled the overcrowded room. Gypsy had made tea, and they sat sipping it while chatting.

"That's a lovely sovereign, Gypsy, is it new?" Millie asked.

There seemed to be a lot of new things here lately. From what Tommy Lee had mentioned, he was worried his brothers were up to no good.

"John Jo got it for me. The date on it is the 1500s." Gypsy beamed. "He also got me those." She pointed to a pair of Crown Derby vases.

"They're beautiful," Millie lied. She'd never liked the Crown Derby, instead preferring the Royal Worcester china with the fruit hand-painted on. That filled her display units along with the Waterford Crystal she had collected.

Tommy Lee coughed. That was her cue to take PJ outside and see how he was getting on.

"Can I go see the horses?" she asked John Jo.

"Didn't think you liked them." He grunted.

"PJ, go and show Millie the Cobs," Tommy Lee snapped.

They both stood and left the mobile. The sun shone above the treetops, casting long shadows over the paddock.

"There was a bit of an atmosphere in there." She stomped towards the stables, her attention caught by one of the horses.

It lifted its tail, spread its hind legs slightly, then a strong stream of pee gushed from its nether region. It sounded like Niagara Falls, as loud and as rapid. Just when she thought it couldn't get any worse, a giant horse mounted it, and they began shagging. She could feel her face heating up. Luckily, PJ didn't seem to notice.

"John Jo's changed," PJ said. "And not in a good way."

"How?" She stood at the fence, averting her eyes from the horse porn. "He hasn't been picking on you, has he?"

"No. Not really... He's become flashy, always got wads of money, Sean Paul, too. They've both put deposits down on new motors, and yet it was only a month ago they were talking about finding work to fund this business." He pointed to the stables.

She remained silent. Thinking.

The two horses, who had now finished their sexual activity, walked towards them. PJ stood on the fence and held out his hand to pat the first. He looked better than he had in the last few months. Relaxed. Was that the effect these animals had on him?

"And what about you, how have you been?"

"Same old. I'm getting married in a few weeks and I'm dreading it," he replied.

"Then don't." She stepped back when another horse trotted towards her.

Thank fuck there's a fence.

"I have to...I need to make things right with the family, and besides, Marina's nice, I could do a lot worse."

She took in what he said, noting there was no mention of love. And what of Marina, didn't she deserve better than marrying a lie?

But she would keep her opinion to herself. It never paid to interfere in things that didn't concern you.

"What's over there?" She nodded in the direction of a large shed. "That wasn't there last time."

"They keep their stuff in there, told me to keep out."

"And you haven't had a snoop?" She laughed. "Because if Tommy Lee said that to me, I'd have to look."

"I did look through a crack at the back. Looks like garage stuff, car batteries, tools and whatnot in there. Nothing exciting."

Car batteries?

"Is there anything you'd like to talk about?" she asked.

"I'm still having the nightmares, but they don't seem as bad." He faced her. "How did you do it?"

"Do what?"

"Get over what happened to you."

"I had Rosie, Scott, and Finn. They kept me going… You've got your parents and brothers who will do the same, and soon you'll have a wife." She wanted to ask if he would prefer a man, but again, it wasn't her place.

She turned to see Gypsy coming towards them, Jonny boy nestled in her arms.

"What do you think of them?" Gypsy flicked her chin towards the Cobs.

"They're beautiful, especially the big one."

The randy bastard.

Millie really didn't have a clue about horses and couldn't say much else.

"That's Goliath. He's already started the breeding process. We're hoping to have all three mares pregnant this year," Gypsy told her.

"We've started late," PJ added. "We only got him a couple of weeks ago. Breeding normally starts end of February and stops by the end of June."

"Fingers crossed then," Millie mumbled lamely.

"Gypsy." John Jo marched towards them. "Make more tea." He stopped next to Millie.

She obediently left with PJ, leaving them both standing in an uncomfortable silence.

"I best get back inside, the twins will want feeding soon," Millie said.

"Wait." John Jo grunted. "I wanted to ask you something."

She wrapped her arms around herself. He scared her, she didn't know why. They began strolling back towards the mobile, the air tense around them.

"Your engagement to my brother. You've got a big house, money, businesses." He paused. Was he searching for the right words? "He loves you, but is he enough?"

"He is," she answered, holding her head high. She stopped outside the door and faced him. "The house and money are all very nice, but I'd give it all up and live in a tent with Tommy Lee if it meant I'd be with him for the rest of my life."

John Jo smiled. "Then I think he's lucky to have you."

"We're lucky to have each other," she confirmed before stepping inside.

***

Tommy Lee drove at a steady pace. The twins were sleeping in their car seat. He loved it when it was just the four of them. No PJ interrupting and no Rosie, although to be fair, she kept out of the way most of the time.

He glanced at Millie. She was gazing out of the window.

"I heard what you said to John Jo."

"What bit?" she asked, glancing at him.

"The bit about giving it all up to be with me… Did you mean it?"

"Yep, every single word. You and the boys are my life. I do miss running things at times, but you make up for that."

"Is it the great sex?" He grinned.

She laughed. "I'd be lying if I said it wasn't part of it, but it's you, all of you. That cheeky smile, those blue eyes, and that extremely sexy Irish accent." She returned her view to the window. "I bet you've talked thousands of girls into bed with that."

"There's only one girl I'm interested in," he said quickly. "I want us to sell up and move farther out of London, nearer to Mother and Father."

"I see."

He waited for her to continue, but she didn't. "It will be handy having them nearer. The boys would see more of them, and Mother would be there to babysit."

"You're not just talking about the house, are you?" she eventually said.

"I want us to sell the scrapyard and buy a business nearer to where we'll be living."

"Okay."

"What does that mean?" he queried. Normally when she said okay, it was anything but.

"Okay, yes. We'll sell and buy somewhere, but we both have to agree on the house and location."

"You're willing to give up the scrapyard, just like that?" He pulled the motor to a stop. "After the struggle you had to keep it."

"It was never about the scrapyard, it was about me. Me being capable of running the empire." She sighed. "I was a mess back then, two babies, businesses, and widowed. I was trying to prove something to myself. That I was good enough."

"So what changed?"

"I fell in love with a man who loves me—you. You make me feel good enough every day. It was true what I said to John Jo, I would give up everything just to be with you."

His breath caught. "Do you know I love you more every day." He peeked at the twins, who were still sleeping soundly. "Pull your seat back and lay it flat."

"What!" She glanced around the secluded lane. "You want to have sex in the motor?"

"No want about it," he said, struggling to move over to her. He slid an arm around her and manoeuvred her on top of him. "We are."

***

John Jo and Sean Paul studied the outbuilding. It was on a piece of land, owned by a farmer. It was perfect for their needs. It couldn't be spotted from the road, thanks to the trees that wrapped around it. The entrance was no more than a dirt track, and it had a cow grid just after the entrance gate. The building itself was large enough for six motors, at a push. They could set up a ramp and pully to expand their business from stolen motors into cut-and-shuts. Life was fecking perfect.

"We'll take it," John Jo told the farmer, who didn't ask any questions, not even his name. He gave a firm handshake to seal the deal then paid the first month's money.

"Get the padlock from the motor, we'll secure the place first," John Jo told Sean Paul while checking out the doors. It was sturdy enough, they just needed to add further security, just in case.

In the back of the truck they had the grinder, tools, and a welder. The rest of the stuff they would obtain as and when they needed it.

"I've got a good feeling about this place," he said, gazing around the area. "We're going to make a lot of money."

CHAPTER 57

The day of the wedding arrived. Maeve was in full panic mode, running around, checking on PJ, and muttering about the last wedding.

"It was a total disaster," she told Tommy Lee. "That crow —"

"I know, I've heard." He grabbed her by the shoulders and sat her down. "You need to calm yourself, Mother, that was then and this is now. Everything will be fine," he assured her, although he wasn't sure himself.

PJ seemed to be in automatic mode, going through the motions without any real feeling. Not even doubt. Had he resigned himself to a life he had no control over?

"I'm gonna go. Twins are in the car," Millie said from the doorway. She was driving as Tommy Lee was going there with his brothers. He would then drive back to the reception with her and the twins.

"Gypsy's coming in with me," she added, glancing at John Jo, then smiled back at him.

He strolled over and pecked her on the mouth. She then turned and headed off. This was the first time he had been best man. He didn't want to do it, however, the look on PJ's face when he had asked gave him no other option. Did he need him for support or solidarity? Both probably.

He still had that niggle at the back of his mind. It told him PJ wasn't normal, whatever normal was. Would he be able to live a full and happy life with Marina? Tommy Lee could only hope.

"Right, we best get going," he informed everyone. "It's okay for the bride to be late, but not a good sign if the groom is."

They all piled into John Jo's new Range Rover, he and Sean Paul in the front, Tommy Lee and PJ in the back.

"How are you feeling?" Tommy Lee asked his little brother, whose face was devoid of emotion.

He sighed. "It's all good."

"Can I make a suggestion? When we get to the church, you smile," he whispered.

***

Maeve took her seat next to Millie and the twins. "Here, give me Tommy boy," she said while taking him at the same time. The twins were now seven months old and becoming a handful.

Gypsy and her son sat in the row behind with Shirley Ann and her three children.

Maeve scanned the packed congregation. The wooden pews creaked under the weight of the crowd. Sunlight streamed through stained-glass windows, illuminating the church. The scent of freshly cut white roses, at the ends of the seating, filled the air.

"Everything's going to be okay," Maeve reminded herself.

She spotted her four sons striding down the aisle. John Jo and Sean Paul slipped in behind her. Tommy Lee sat next to Millie with PJ the other side of him. He snatched baby Duke and spoke softly to him. The child smiled back. It warmed her heart that he had found happiness, and she could see his boys loved him just as much as he loved them.

The organ started up, and they all stood, Tommy Lee standing at PJ's side. Maeve glanced at the giant cross above the priest's head. She could almost hear the guffaw of the crow. She crossed herself then mumbled, "In the name of the Father, and of the Son, and of the Holy Spirit. Amen," praying that all would be well.

***

The reception was in full swing. All had gone to plan, with the exception of Tommy Lee misplacing the rings. He had left them in the motor and sent John Jo to get them. It was a minor hiccup, all things considered, especially if you took into account the last wedding.

"Mother's letting her hair down," Sean Paul whispered to Tommy Lee.

"Are you surprised after last time? She's probably relieved that another son's been offloaded." He laughed.

"Just one more to go. So when's your big day?" John Jo asked.

Tommy Lee glanced at Millie who was deep in conversation with his mother, Shirley Ann, and Gypsy. She looked up and smiled. His stomach did a little somersault. Did she know how much she meant to him?

"We haven't set a date yet." He had asked, more than once, but she always seemed to brush him off. Maybe she didn't want to get married after all. Maybe she didn't want him.

"They're cutting the cake," Sean Paul informed them. "I'll get the drinks in."

PJ held his hand over Marina's, the knife resting on the cake, waiting for the photographer to give them the go-ahead. Whilst the day had been reasonably pain-free, he still felt restless. One of the waiters, he was sure, had given him the eye. It had aroused a feeling in him he hadn't had since Pete. To be fair, he never thought he would feel the urge to go with a man again, not after what had happened. But in that instance he wasn't so sure.

"Smile," the man said.

The knife glided through the cake with swift ease. Job done. "I'm going to see my brothers," he told Marina, pecked her on the cheek, then strolled over to them.

"So what's it like to be a married man?" Sean Paul asked.

"Give him a chance. The ink ain't dry on the marriage certificate yet," Tommy Lee answered.

"That don't matter to women, they assert their authority right from the start."

"Yep, and then it's a life of don't do this, don't do that. Don't walk your muddy boots across my clean floor," John Jo mockingly warned.

"The worst one is when they use sex as a weapon. You can have it if you do this, you can't have it because you didn't do that," Sean Paul explained.

"Let's get you a drink." Tommy Lee pulled PJ away.

His other brothers could be as thick as shite at times. The gag about sex had drained the colour completely from PJ's face. What were they thinking?

"You okay?" he asked when they reached the farthest end of the bar.

"Yeah, I think I need some fresh air."

"I'll come with you," Tommy Lee offered.

"No. I need a minute on my own." PJ let himself out of the side door.

Tommy Lee sighed. Something was wrong, and it wasn't just down to that chat he'd had with their brothers. He made his way over to Millie. She was strapping the twins into the pushchair.

"I'm gonna take them outside, see if I can get them to sleep. These little darlings are starting to get ratty," she said through gritted teeth.

Tucking a blanket over them, she stood and kissed him on the lips. "Maybe if they have a sleep we can have—"

"Sex," he finished.

"What!" She glanced around. "No, we are in the middle of a party. I don't intend on being the entertainment."

"You can be my entertainment anytime." He winked.

She grinned. "Maybe later. I was gonna say a dance."

Millie manoeuvred the double pushchair out through the heavy double doors, the hinges groaning when she pulled them shut behind her. Outside, darkness had settled in with the only light coming from the windows and the full moon overhead. It was colder now, and she cursed herself for not bringing a coat. She started to walk towards the back of the building, the gravel making the pushchair hard to steer.

Giving up when she was nearly at the end of the building, she bent down to check on the twins. They were both fast asleep.

"That was quick, boys," she whispered, pleased that she could get back into the warm.

She stood still when a noise caught her ear. A low, muffled growl drifted through the air, coming from behind the end wall. She left the pushchair and tiptoed towards the sound.

You do know they say curiosity killed the cat?

"Yeah, and satisfaction brought him back," she murmured.

When she rounded the corner, she covered her mouth, concealing the gasp that was threatening to escape. There in front of her stood PJ, his back pressed against the wall, his head tipped back, mouth open, and kneeling in front of him another man who had his hands gripping his hips while sucking his cock. PJ's eyes were closed, his moans getting louder.

Shit.

She turned and bolted, heart hammering as she grabbed the pushchair and all but shoved it back through the doors. Inside, the air was thick with warmth and the scent of whiskey and perfume.

Laughter and music throbbed in the background, the wedding reception a stark contrast to what she'd just witnessed.

Tommy Lee was next to her in an instant. "Are you all right, you're as white as a sheet?" he asked worriedly. "What's happened, was someone out there?"

Shit.

She swallowed, her throat dry. "I need a drink," she managed, voice trembling.

"Fine, but then you tell me what's wrong."

She rubbed the back of her neck; all her muscles had tensed. She glanced at the twins. They were still sleeping soundly, unaware of the shitstorm that lay ahead.

"Here." Tommy Lee handed her a glass of wine.

She took a couple of big gulps. Staring him in the eyes, she took a deep breath, opened her mouth, and then a racket from the other end of the room stopped her.

Six police officers crashed through the doors.

"We're looking for a Mr John Jo Ward and a Mr Sean Paul Ward," one of them said.

"That's us." John Jo stepped towards them, Sean Paul at his side.

"We need you to come down to the station to help us with our enquiries in an ongoing investigation into stolen motor vehicles."

"You come here, to my brother's wedding reception for help with your fecking enquiries. No. We'll come down tomorrow," John Jo barked.

"You don't understand, sir, you can either come of your own accord or we can arrest you," the police officer stated.

Tommy Lee marched over. "Don't make a scene. Go with them."

"But we haven't done anything wrong," Sean Paul assured him.

"Then you'll be released before you know it." Tommy Lee nodded to the door. "Go quietly, we don't need Marina's family kicking off, that'll be a fine start to a marriage."

Millie joined him. She glanced around the room. Everyone was watching, with the exception of PJ who was sneaking in from behind the bar. He caught her eye, and for a moment they stared at each other before he joined them.

"Where the feck were you?" Tommy Lee snapped

"Needed a piss, if that's allowed." PJ sighed, glancing at Millie.

She glared back. She wanted him to know that he had been found out. He had a choice, Marina didn't. She deserved better.

The police left with their two rowdy suspects. Maeve was beside herself with Paddy attempting to comfort her. Tommy Lee placed his arm around Millie's waist and guided her back to the table.

"I'll kill those two one of these days." He necked his whiskey. "So what happened outside?"

She caught sight of PJ over his shoulder. He was shaking his head, pleading.

"You've enough to deal with for now. It's not important."

She wouldn't be the reason for another bust-up. As it was, no doubt Tommy Lee would have to go to the station to pick his brothers up. If they were released. No, she would have this out with PJ.

"Oh, by the way, are you busy on the second of September?" she added quickly.

"That's four months away, why?" he asked, frowning.

"Because that's the day we are getting married."

"What?" He laughed. "Really?"

"I spoke to the priest before PJ's wedding. He has the afternoon available, so I said we'd see him tomorrow to finalise it... Is that okay?"

"Okay? It's more than okay, it's fecking perfect. I'll go get the drinks in, then we tell Mother, she needs cheering up."

She waited for him to leave and then motioned for to PJ to follow her. She slipped outside, unseen. He joined her seconds later, his face wary.

"I saw you," she told him, her voice low.

"I don't know what you think you saw but—"

"Don't treat me like a fucking idiot, you know I saw you, your face said it all when you sneaked back in." She sighed. "You've put me in a difficult position."

"It was a one-off, I promise it won't happen again," PJ replied, but his face betrayed him.

"I don't give a shit who you choose to sleep with, men or women, but you've just married a sweet girl who is utterly in love with you, and she deserves better." She turned to walk away until he grabbed her arm roughly.

"I'll do better, I promise." His voice sounded thick with desperation.

She looked into his eyes and glared. "There's a little thing in life called loyalty, PJ." She shook loose his grip. "If I find out you've not been loyal to Marina, I'll tell your family everything."

EPILOGUE

As the reception wound down, Maeve leaned back in her chair, her gaze settling on PJ. He was sitting with Marina, but something was off. His posture was rigid, his face set in stone. Had they argued already? Well, they'd have fun making up, after all, it was their wedding night. PJ was different from the others, softer, more caring. He would make a good husband. And soon, hopefully, a father.

Her eyes flicked to Shirley Ann and Gypsy, both wearing the same anxious expression. Worrying over their husbands, pair of fecking eejits, never satisfied. Always chasing after more without putting in the hard graft. Paddy had told her about the stolen motor, they had no secrets from one another. Gypsy met her gaze and smiled, no doubt putting on a brave face. Poor woman.

John Jo and Sean Paul had everything, a place to call their own, strong wives, beautiful children. They had fought for their land and won. Bred Cobs to bring in a steady wage, and yet, they had risked it all for a quick pound note. Now look, arrested like common criminals. And in front of Marina's family, no less.

Paddy placed her drink in front of her. It was one for the road, he had said. She smiled; it was always one for the road with him, wherever they went.

Her gaze drifted to her eldest, the one who had caused her more sleepless nights than the other three combined. Tommy Lee sat with his arm draped over Millie's chair, his fingers absentmindedly stroking her shoulder, a quiet, simple show of love. Funny how he was the one she worried about least now. He had grown into a fine man, father, and soon, she was certain, husband.

Despite everything, Maeve loved them all fiercely, even with the heartache they brought her. She tried to savour this moment, to push away the worry for her boys which gnawed at her. But it lingered, a whisper at the back of her mind. All four of her sons had found love, it was what she had always prayed for. And yet now they were settled, she couldn't shake the feeling that something bad was coming.

The End

ABOUT THE AUTHOR

Carol Hellier was born in Oldchurch Hospital, Essex, in the mid-sixties. When she was in her mid-twenties, she discovered her parents were in fact her grandparents, and her eldest sister was her mum.

She married a gypsy and started her married life off living in a caravan/trailer. This has given her a useful insight into the Romany world which shows in her writing.

She has lived in many different counties but now resides back in Essex. She spends her time working for the NHS, writing, and with her large family.

Book One – *The Ward Brothers, Meet the Travellers*
Book Two – Title to be announced – Coming Late Summer 2025

Previous books:
Book One - *The Stepney Feud*
Book Two – *The Stepney Alliance*
Book Three – *The Stepney Takeover*

Previous books:
Dolly King, The Gangster's Daughter
The Orion Prophecy, in the Shadows - under the author name Carol McDonald

You can follow the author on:

Instagram: author_cahellier

Facebook: https://www.facebook.com/carolhellier

TikTok: carolmc441_author

Printed in Dunstable, United Kingdom